I carried a picture of Doyle in my back p̲o̲ ̲ ̲ ̲ ̲ ̲.made a copy and tucked it in my pocket the day I accepted the case. Maybe it was silly, but I wanted to remember what I was risking my life for. A kid.

A nervous, scared kid who wasn't even sure he could survive the change from human to were.

He had blond hair, sleepy-looking eyes and the promise of what would be a killer smile. So much promise. And what was more…he had kind eyes. The kindness in his eyes hadn't been lost on me.

The cat shifters needed more kindness in their ranks…not less.

I knew his face now. He was mine. I'd do everything I could to find him and if I couldn't find him, it would be because there was nothing left to be found.

On the way down to the cold lower level of Banner HQ, I slid my hand into my pocket and tugged out the picture of Doyle, rubbing it with my thumb. I didn't look at it. There was no need. I knew his face well enough now that I could draw his picture. More than once, I'd found myself doing just that.

He didn't look like his aunt.

A hand came up and closed over my neck as the elevator doors opened. The people trickled out, but before we could follow them, Damon hit the button to shut the doors and then he just held it. "Are you trying to push yourself into a panic attack?" he asked, dipping his head and growling right into my ear.

I drove my elbow into his stomach. I might as well have been hitting steel for all the good it did. I did it again anyway.

He swore and spun around, shoving my back against the elevator doors.

My hand itched—*bad, bad, bad.*

"Listen, little girl," he snarled.

He reached for me.

BLADE SONG

BLADE SONG

By

J.C. Daniels

Shiloh Walker, Inc
Po Box 976
Jeffersonville, IN
47131

Dedication

Dedicated… as always with love to my husband and kids. Love you…
Thank God for you…

Thanks to Tori and Sara. Tori, for all the feedback and how much you believed in this book, and Sara for all the help you gave me.

aneira [a-nir-a] derived from *Antianeirai*, found in the *Illiad*, warrior women, meaning 'those who war like men'. Also known as Amazons.

Chapter One

My sword arm is mighty.
I will not falter.
I will not fail.
My aim is true.
My heart is strong.
I'm the descendant of some legendary badasses and I'll damn well make myself wake up—

"You are so lovely..."

The silken voice whispered to me in the depth of my dreams, wrapping around me and pulling me under. It was a seductive thing, full of promise. Full of warmth and wonder and lies.

Jude. The bastard had never been able to keep to himself.

It had been six years since I'd met him and in those six years, he'd done his damnedest to infiltrate my life. I'd trusted him, sort of. Once. But in the years since I'd made his acquaintance, I'd learned to place my trust elsewhere...and keep my distance.

So far, we were at a stalemate, but when it came to dreams, he usually had the upper hand. I'd always had surreal, vivid dreams anyway, and here, he reigned supreme.

Lost in the dark, velvety grasp of sleep, I wasn't able to do much more than grumble and groan when he first appeared. It always took me a few minutes to get my bearings when he shoved his way into my dreams. Jude, the bastard, took great advantage of it.

He stretched out beside me on the bed and I could even feel it giving way under his weight, under that long, lean, powerful body. His hand rested on my belly and I could feel the way my muscles reacted, the way I reacted.

"Are you going to come to me, little aneira?" he whispered, dipping his head and nuzzling my neck.

I found my voice at the brush of his teeth on my neck.

Figures it would take that.

Yeah, having a vampire pressing his teeth to your throat, even in dreams, is enough to get the adrenaline going.

Full-fledged vampires aren't the hot and sexy things of books. They are deadly. Cold. Soulless, powerful and yes, they can be sexy as hell—Jude is proof of that, but I suspected it might safer to share my bed with a pit viper.

Summoning that image to mind gave me the strength I needed to move.

1

My sword arm is mighty.
I will not falter…

Rolling out of bed and away from him, I grabbed the T-shirt from the foot of the bed and jerked it on. "Jude, seriously. How often are you going to do this?" I asked.

"You had to get dressed, didn't you?"

I shot him a dirty look and immediately wished I hadn't. Moonlight gilded him with its pale light, turning his blond hair to silver, casting that carved face into angelic lines as his eyes glowed.

They were green. When he was angry, they glowed red with blood hunger, but right now, they were alight with an emerald luminescence that raked over my skin like a caress.

It had been too long since I'd gotten laid. The last boyfriend I'd had ended up leaving town after he'd been offered a very lucrative job. He was around off and on now, but it was more off than on and we'd drifted apart. Still, there were times when I missed him. A lot. And not just because of the sex.

But if I'd gotten laid anytime in the past couple of years, Jude wouldn't seem so damned appealing right now. That look in his eyes was enough to drive me mad, but I wasn't going to let him get to me.

Not any more than I already had.

"What do you want, Jude?"

He laughed. It stroked over my skin, begged me to laugh with him. Nope. Not doing that. Definitely not. "You know what I want, little warrior. When are you going to stop avoiding me? I haven't seen you in months. You're not taking my calls and you won't take the work I send your way…foolish, that. Your silly little business is hurting for work and we both know it."

Silly.

Running my tongue along my teeth, I returned to my bed.

I could let the anger I felt at the insult get to me. Or I could use it.

I'd rather use it.

From the corner of my eye, I saw Jude's eyes widen as I drew closer. His hand snaked toward as I reached out with my own.

But I wasn't reaching for him.

I was reaching for the sword I kept under my pillow.

No, I couldn't wield it in dreams…but I could use the strength I found in it.

The hilt settled in my hand, like an extension of my arm. Just touching it made me feel like I'd…come home.

Touching a sword. Yes. I'm more than a little messed up.

Smiling at him, I said, "I'm waking up now."

My sword arm is mighty.
I will not falter.
I will not fail.
My aim is true.

2

My heart is strong.

The mantra of the aneira—the people I'd descended from. My mother had been full-blooded. My father had been human. Still, that had been drilled into my head and I'd shouted it out on the practice fields of Aneris Hall, the hell where I'd lived for the first fifteen years of my life.

The entire thing would take several minutes to recite, but the first few lines were enough to get me through the worst things. Sometimes, I had to say it several times a day.

My name is Kit Colbana.

In a world filled with shapeshifters, vampires and witches who can turn your insides into your outsides, I'm next to nothing; a peon.

I've got a knack for killing and tracking things down. I'm a talented thief, although I try to avoid that line of work, if I can. Luck tends to swing in my favor, although sometimes it's in a very odd manner. I can land on my feet when I ought to be landing in a grave or worse. And I have the ability to fade out…I can go invisible. A handy skill for an assassin, I guess.

But that's it. That's pretty much all I can do.

The magic in my blood is weak. I'm a half-breed, and while that term might bother some people, it's just a fact of life.

My human father? I don't know anything about him, other than he was human. I don't know why my mom decided to shack up with him, and I don't know why he was never in our lives.

He's just a non-entity.

My mother was aneira…think of Amazons, and imagine something more. Something magical. We were once a well-known race, assassins sent out to do the jobs no other could. Sometimes we were thieves, sent out to track down priceless treasures. We'd even been bounty hunters, if legend tells it right.

A proud, noble race.

Now we're not much more than a memory and only a few hundred of us remain. My mother had died when I was young, leaving me in the care of my not-so-loving family.

The aneira didn't smile on the half-bloods and I was worse than most, because I was half human. They'd rather kill me than care for me. Sometimes, I think the only reason they didn't is because they figured they'd have more fun tormenting me for years. If they killed me, it would be over too soon.

So they kept me, raised me. And they made sure I never forgot that although I had aneira blood, I wasn't one of them. I was just a mongrel. A useless waste.

My mother's fucked-up mistake…that's what they liked to tell me.

That was the heritage they decided to share with me. Her mistake.

But I had a few scattered memories of her…I could remember her singing. The faint echo of her voice.

Maybe I was her mistake, but I shared her heritage. I had the memory of her singing to me.

And her sword.

Alone in my gym, I practiced. Strike. Block. Downward cut.

I practiced alone. But in my mind, I saw Jude. The bastard.

Sneaking into my dreams again.

Bleed him out. If I did anything at close range, that was what I'd have to do. Nick the arteries. I was fast. He'd be faster. But vampires needed blood just as much as we did. If I injured him enough, maybe I could slow him enough to really hurt him.

It was a fun fantasy, anyway.

Not that I'd really have a chance.

Six years ago, I'd made the mistake of calling him when I tried to help a friend. I hadn't known him, he hadn't really known me, but he'd offered help just the same.

The daughter of a friend had gotten mixed up with a bad group. The worst kind —wererats. A werecreature, in and of itself, wasn't a bad thing, but the rats in East Orlando had been notoriously bad. Criminally bad, even. I found out a few weeks after my little adventure the rats had been slated for extermination by the council, anyway.

And said friend's daughter had gotten involved with one of them. She was sick, diagnosed with leukemia, and she'd gotten in her head that the bite would cure her. In all likelihood, it would just hasten her death. A were's bite is a hard, brutal thing and less than twenty percent survive it, anyway. If you're not healthy, you don't stand a chance. She hadn't been healthy.

If living was her only goal, she'd have been better off going to the vampires. Not that they were likely to have touched a sick, underage girl. Vamps were careful about that, for the most part.

In the end, it hadn't mattered. She died less than a year after I brought her back to her mom.

She died hating me, too.

It was a weight I'd carry the rest of my life.

But I couldn't let the rats keep her. They wouldn't have saved her life and they wouldn't have been kind about how they tried to mark her, either.

Too bad she had been too young to understand that.

Sometimes I felt like it was all for nothing.

All for nothing, and I still had an albatross by the name of Jude around my neck.

Bleed him. Dozens of nicks across that very fine body, preferably when he hadn't fed for a while. That would be best. And then—

I whirled, bringing my sword across right where the level of his neck would be if he had actually been standing in the room with me.

Vamps couldn't die of blood loss. It would slow him. Weaken him. But it wouldn't kill him. The older ones could even handle a bit of sun. But if I took his damned head, he was dead.

And if he didn't quit trying to snake his way into my business, into my dreams, into my life, I just might try.

Although he was right about one thing. I really, really did need to get some business, and soon. I'd rather start flipping burgers, though, or hacking trees down with my sword than accept a job from him.

Anything would be better than taking work from Jude Whittier.

Chapter Two

My sword arm is mighty.
I will not falter.
I will not fail.
Yeah, I really do have to go through those few lines sometimes, just to level out. It keeps me focused.
I will not falter.
I will not fail.
Nor will I show any sign of fear to the guy standing in my office. I don't know who he is. He hasn't given me a name and I didn't plan on asking for it until I know if I'm doing business with him. I'm thinking I'd rather *not* do business with him, truth be told. I had a bad feeling about this already and we hadn't even started talking about the job yet.

How do I get myself into these messes? Oh, right. I'd been praying, hoping—pretty much anything except standing out on the street corner holding up signs that read: *I need work*! I should be more careful about what I wish for. That streak of luck that was part of my heritage was probably what had landed him here. I'd needed work. Now I had work. I also had a lesson in *be careful what you wish for*, I suspected.

I'd been doing this a few years and I'd learned to recognize the shit jobs from the good ones. This could be very profitable.

Profit is *good*. I like profit. I like money. I don't get to see enough of it.

But I was kind of concerned about the warning in my gut.

Profitable, yes. This guy was bad, bad news, though. And every last instinct me inside was screaming, *bad, bad, bad…get away from him, get away now now now now*!

All the more reason I had to stay calm. All the more reason not to show that I was afraid. No showing any sign of fear—things like a racing heartbeat, increased respiration, sweaty palms, fidgeting. No. Forget the fidgeting. Plenty of people were the squirming sort and it had nothing to do with fear.

I fidgeted all the time, even when I wasn't afraid.

I'm not afraid—damn it, I am aneira. I've got fricking noble blood and this shifter can stand there sneering at me all he wants. What do I care?

"You know, we had a bet." Mr. Badass sat in the chair across from my battered desk, slumped in a boneless sprawl not many humans over the age of three could manage.

I didn't think he was a wolf. Wolves were very…rigid. Anally so.

If he was a wolf, he'd be in a three piece suit, pressed within an inch of its suitly life, and he'd probably have a duo of backup lawyers to witness everything. And he wouldn't have sat in my chair with that boneless sprawl, either. Hard to do with a

6

stick up the ass, really. The members of the wolf pack *always* had a stick up their collective asses.

I had no problem working with the local wolf pack. Don't get me wrong. Most of them are big on courtesy, and all about order and rules, and as long as I didn't cross them, they left me alone. The problem was when the job involved some of their assholes; their assholes tried to rip off body parts and eat innards and it got messy sometimes.

But they paid well. I could use a nice-paying job.

We had two main were factions down here. Cat and wolf. But he didn't have to be local, and I didn't like to assume.

I'd figure it out in a minute. If I had the nose of a shapeshifter, I'd have him pegged already, but I'd get there. I was good at it, unusually so. I could see the energy hovering about them and I could usually see some echo of their animal hovering about them, a skill I knew I could trace back to my aneira roots.

We were good assassins because we could understand our marks, learn them, know them and figure out the best way to kill them.

Still, anybody who knew what to look for could peg a shifter from a mile away and this guy was no different. Most of them didn't bother to batten down the hatches and they let all that raw power hang out there for the entire world to see.

They were all caged energy and strength and they emanated…something. Just… something. You meet a shapeshifter and find out what he is, and you realize what the something is once you've seen it.

He had the something. I could sense it hovering above him, power coiled and lying in wait. There was *a lot* of it, too. But he kept it chained in too tightly for me to read it as easily I'd like.

His jeans had rips at the knees. His T-shirt was clean, but faded and wrinkled and over it, he wore a flannel button down. I don't think any of the wolves I knew even had an inkling what flannel was.

"Don't you want to know what the bet was?" he asked, watching me with an odd little smile on his face.

"Bet?" I said, echoing his words.

"Yeah."

Unable to stay still, I took a pen from my desk and twirled it around on my fingers, watching him, waiting for him to elaborate. The silence stretched out for over a minute. It wasn't wasted time. He watched me. I watched him. A wide grin curled his lips, his teeth flashing white against the darkness of his skin. I started thinking about the Cheshire cat.

Bingo. Not a wolf. A cat. Even as I thought it, I could almost see that lazy energy around him flex its claws and stretch, giving me a feline smile. There were a handful of creatures to pick from in the were pool and it varied from country to country. Here in the States, the dominant creatures were cat, wolf and rat, with a few bears thrown in for fun.

7

Narrowing my eyes, I asked softly, "Is this a local job?"

"Local?" He studied me curiously.

"Local. As in are *you* local?"

A faint smiled curled his lips. "Yeah. I'm local."

Shit. This was wonderful. Just wonderful. I had some sort of cat shifter in my office. And you can't outwait a cat. Even I knew that. Since he was here on business, and since I was running a business—sort of—I figured I needed to get this over with, because I needed him out of my office. I wasn't working for a damn cat, not if he was from the Orlando clan. This wasn't courier work—I could already tell. If it was, he would have already dumped whatever and left. So that meant it was something bigger, and I wasn't interested.

I preferred to keep my investigative work to something a little steadier than the local cat pack.

They were *insane*.

I'd do busy work for non-humans and I didn't mind working for the wolves. I didn't mind courier work between any of the local factions, really. That was actually ideal, because it was quick, it was easy and it paid pretty damn well. But if I had my way, I'd never work for the cats. They were dangerous.

Unlike the wolves, they weren't quite so keen on following rules and since my office was incorporated in East Orlando—an area that had recently been recognized as ANH territory, if I accepted a job from the cat pack, it was pretty much CYA: *cover your ass*.

Bring your own back-up, make up your will, just in case, and be ready to die if you don't have sufficient back-up. I don't.

The damn cats were likely to try to rip my arms off if I screwed up. Or just to avoid paying me. Yes. Attempts had been made. It's a good thing I'm handy with all sorts of sharp, shiny objects.

"What sort of bet?" I continued to watch him, searching now for some kind of sign on just what type of cat he was. His physical features weren't much help. Oh, he was a treat to look at, definitely; probably several inches over six feet, muscled enough to make it clear he actually worked at it, and his dark hair was cropped close to his skull. I couldn't quite make out his ancestry. Multiracial, I suspected. Maybe Polynesian and black? Or Native American and black? Something else entirely? Whatever he was? Didn't matter, because he was practically a visual orgasm. And his eyes were amazing.

Deep, dark gray. Like thunderheads piling up on the sky right at sunset.

Amusement danced in those eyes, but it didn't make them any less formidable. "When you opened this joint, most of us figured you wouldn't make it a year."

"A year, huh? That's all you gave me?" I made myself smile and rested my chin in my palm. I'd bought the practice from a guy I knew—a private investigator who'd decided he wanted to get out of the business while he could. And while property in Orlando was still worth something. Things had gone downhill around the same time I'd been coming through the mess with the rats and I'd used the money I received for my part in the 'clean-up' to buy this place.

The parks were still a big tourist draw, but Orlando no longer held the attraction it once had. Even the snowbirds had given up. The tourist traps still did okay, but they had the money to spell their properties and that made mortals feel safer.

It wasn't that the place was a cesspool of danger, death and decay, but people perceived it as such and perception was everything. The parks got by because of the thrill aspect. Orlando was a thrill a minute…you had the amusement parks for the kiddies, and then if you really wanted to walk on the wild side, you could go out to East Orlando…and see shapeshifters in the raw.

Well, not really. But that was the rumor. People came here thinking you'd see them rip loose and find their beast right in front of you. It was crap. Shapeshifters didn't lose control around humans. It led to ugly things like modern day versions of witch hunts, but with shifters as the quarry, and bloodier, nastier, more widespread results.

Besides, they didn't see the point in losing control in front of humans. Humans weren't worth it to them. They were like annoying fleas. A nuisance, but just a part of life. And sadly, a flea collar didn't help.

Me? Now I can honestly say I have seen them lose their skin. I've been known to provoke people. But if I ended up hurt or dead, nobody was going to issue a quarantine or kill order, especially if it was on the job.

I wasn't human enough to matter, really.

All in all, East Orlando was safer than mortals thought, but mortals didn't like living here anymore. Not in the old part of town where the parks were or in East Orlando where all of us freaks had set up camp.

Sadly, it meant my job pickings were getting slim. The first few years, I'd had things like cheating spouses and background checks and stuff to keep me busy, but lately, not so much.

Focusing on the matter at hand, I said, "So, I made it through the year. Yay, me, right?"

"You made it through the year and then some. Surprised us." He continued to study me, still smiling. That cagey grin had me thinking about a cat watching a mouse right before it pounced. And I suspected that was exactly what he wanted me to think.

Sighing, I tipped back in my chair and put my boots up on the desk. I hate this shit. Why do they have to act like this? Territorial. Pushy. *You'll be terrified and show it.*

"Well, seeing as how I lasted six years…and counting, I guess some of you had egg on your face." I laced my hands over my belly and held his gaze. *I'll be damned if I act like the mouse, you overgrown tomcat.*

His smile widened.

I started thinking about where else I could live. Someplace with a bigger human population so I didn't have to keep tolerating the posturing bullshit.

Shapeshifters and vamps were everywhere, but there were only a few hotspots. East Orlando was one of them. Outer Indianapolis, Honolulu, Upper Denver, Anchorage, North Toronto, Buffalo…those were some of the others.

I wondered how Boise would suit me. I could live in Boise. Humans outnumbered the non-humans fifteen to one there, from what I heard. Humans still outnumbered non-humans here, but it was more like five to one in Orlando and with those odds, they considered the paranormal population the stronger one.

They called us non-humans. Made up a bunch of nice little acronyms and laws and shit. As long as we 'belonged' to the ANH and followed the laws laid out by them, we could exist peacefully. ANH—the Assembly of Non-Humans.

The Assembly was our governing council, headed by people we elected, with a couple of human emissaries so everybody could pretend we played nice with each other.

Pretend. Shit.

"Hmm. We'll keep the bets running. When you took on the Gruer job, some of us were pretty sure you'd either lose your shirt or your life." His eyes dropped. "Might have been nice to see you lose your shirt, but I still thought you'd run out of luck at some point."

Gruer had been one of the human emissaries. He was in jail now for taking bribes. They'd only charged him with the human crimes and he'd be out in a year. Somehow I didn't think he'd be alive long after that. His other crimes had included crimes against NH children. There were rumors of the prices people had put on his head. Yeah, we weren't supposed to screw with humans, but sometimes, they met with unhappy accidents, and if the bodies disappeared...?

Well.

As long as they couldn't prove anything...that was the big thing, I guessed. Gruer would get his own.

"Gruer was a stupid-ass, cruel bastard. You seriously thought he would chase me out? Thought *he* could kill me?" Not damn likely. I curled my lip at him. Seriously, they were betting on me? What the hell? "Don't the shifters have better things to do with their money?"

"Well," he said. "We always like to find amusing ways to kill time."

"Hard to believe there's nothing more amusing out there than me."

"Oh, you've been very amusing, Colbana." He leaned forward and light glinted off his eyes in the most unusual way—cat's eyes... Shit, he better not be getting ready to shift on me. I was so screwed if he did.

But even as I thought it, I realized that wasn't it. There was just something... eerie about his eyes. Hypnotic. Scary. "Want to hear how I bet?"

"Sure. Tell me, which side were you on?"

He laughed. "The side that loses, usually. After all, you're still alive..." Then his laugh faded away into a smile. "Nobody's bitten you and made you change your skin, either. And you're still here."

"Oh, I've been bitten." I smiled. "I'm immune."

Black brows rose a fraction. "That's not likely."

I shrugged. Likely didn't mean *impossible*. The were virus was pretty damn invasive. Either it killed you or it changed you—and it was far more likely to *kill* you. The virus would kill seventy to seventy-five percent of the people it infected.

10

Twenty to twenty-five percent became were. The numbers fluctuated, but they guessed only five percent of humans were truly immune.

But I wasn't human.

"Trust me. I've been bit. More than once. Doesn't take."

"Bite's not the only thing that will do it." The smile on his face went sly and damn if I didn't feel my heart kick up a little.

"Please. I've read up on shapeshifter biology. I know all about how it works. I'm less likely to catch it from the bite, more likely to catch it from sex." Swinging my boots off the desk, I shrugged. For a few very short months, I'd had a werewolf boyfriend. It had been a fluke—a guy I'd worked with and the guy he'd hired me to help track down had bitten me. Those wolves, all nice and courteous. The guy had been convinced I'd shift. I hadn't. We'd had a few weeks of fun once I convinced him of that fact. "That doesn't work, either."

"Huh." His eyes narrowed as he studied me. "I don't smell that much magic on you."

"Yeah, well." I figured he'd assume that. Witches were immune to the were virus. The magic in their blood nullified it. I figured there was enough of my own magic to do the same. Who knows? Wasn't like I could call home to ask and it didn't matter anyway. "What can you do?"

"I guess that explains why you don't change your skin," he mused. He reached down and when I saw the flash of silver in his hand, I moved.

The only sign of emotion on his face was the faint flicker of his eyelashes. Then he dropped his gaze to the sword in my hand. "You really are as fast as I've heard."

"Yeah, I bet you say that to all the ladies." I rose and lifted the blade. The swirls and runes on it danced in the dim light. There was enough silver in the blade, enough magic in her to hurt him. He knew it…and he knew I was fully aware of that as well.

But he didn't look worried. Of course, *hurt* was a far cry from *kill*. I was pretty sure I couldn't kill him. I was equally sure he knew that. I was equally sure he could kill me, and he was probably aware of that same fact. *Damn it.*

"Settle down, princess." He leaned back in the chair and used the knife he'd pulled to start cutting his fingernails. In my office.

Ewww. And no, thanks. I had a cat shifter in my office, holding a knife. I wasn't going to settle down. I didn't lower the blade either. "Do us both a favor, if you would, and tell me why you're gracing me with your presence, cat." *Please…so I can tell you no and you can be on your way.*

"Cat, huh?" He grinned at me, a toothy smile that would look all too at home on a tiger. A lion. A cougar. Any of those. All of those. One of the big predator cats. Why couldn't he be something little? Like a bobcat. A lynx, maybe? Or an ocelot. Yeah. I'd think about him as an ocelot. A little dwarf leopard. Cute, fuzzy. Not at all dangerous.

I stared at him and watched as his eyes flashed again.

No. He wasn't cute or fuzzy and he sure as hell was dangerous. He tucked his blade away and reached for the file folder he'd brought in with him. So innocuous.

The cat shifter sits in my office, clips his nails with an oversized bowie knife and then proceeds to do business. My life is too damn strange. I should have decided to do the tax crap today. Then I wouldn't be stuck here with him.

"My Lady sends her regards and formally requests your assistance, Miz Colbana."

Oh, shit. There was only one person he'd refer to as *My Lady*. And she was as much trouble as the current thorn in my side. Jude was deadly, but at least he was a predictable pain in the ass. The leader of the cats was *not*.

This was bad. This was so very bad. Worse, the man sitting across from me had gone all formal-like, making this sound like an official request. Technically, I could refuse him, but when they got formal and I said no, it was a pain in my ass, because they talked amongst themselves and fewer were likely to look me up later down the road. I already *had* too little business coming my way as it was.

Oh, well. I'd just move. I'd already been thinking about Boise, right?

"I'm afraid my schedule is full." Sliding my blade home, I reached for the phone. "I've got someplace to be in twenty. You'll have to see yourself out, cat."

"We'll pay you fifty thousand dollars. Regardless of the outcome."

"I'm afraid I'll be tied up for the rest of the month." Giving him a vague smile, I grabbed a pen and started jotting notes down like mad—whatever came to mind. *Busy, busy, busy, see*? I don't have time to work for *My Lady*.

I wasn't working for the damn Alphas. And I wasn't—

He dropped something on my desk.

In that moment, I really hated him.

"We all have weaknesses," he murmured. "Me, I like a stacked redhead, cold beer, and pizza. I hear you have a soft spot for kids…can't stand to see them hurt."

"Beer is kind of pointless, seeing as how most of you burn through it before you can get drunk," I muttered, trying to pretend the picture in front of me wasn't getting to me. But it was. It was getting to me badly. Shit, how old was he?

"Hey. I like the taste." He reached over and plucked up the picture, lifting it until it was all I could see. "He's sixteen."

I glared at him. "No fucking way." That kid didn't look like he'd so much as kissed puberty. Skinny as a rail, still soft in the face.

He shrugged. "We tend to mature a little later. He's…hitting later than most. His name is Doyle. He's my Lady's nephew and he's been missing for a week."

Not my problem, I told myself. Taking the picture, I turned it face down and then looked back at the man standing across from my desk. "I can't help you."

"Two weeks ago, he finally started showing signs of spiking." He paused, his eyes narrowing on my face.

Weird eyes. Deadly eyes. They were storm cloud gray, swirling and darkening into black until that was all I saw. "You know what spiking is, little girl?"

"It's when an adolescent shifter tries to change for the first time." They weren't always successful. There were two ways to become a shapeshifter. You got infected. Infection happened with a bite or through unprotected sex. Or you were born with it and actually, being born with it was still being infected with it.

I've heard rumors of a more magically-based shapeshifter race, but the only kind

I've ever dealt with are the biologicals…those who get it through the virus, either by sex, bite or birth.

When a shifter kid spiked, things could get dicey fast. Kids tended to panic and without guidance, there was a good chance they'd lose control during the change.

Panic, excessive strength, animal instincts—not a good mix. Sometimes…that first change killed them. Sometimes the panic and the pain were enough to drive a kid crazy and they'd forget who they were, falling prey to the animal that lived inside their skin. When the beast got control, it didn't give up easily and if that spark of humanity didn't appear, the shifter was executed.

They had a fucked-up lot in life, that was for certain.

But if they made it through those first few rough changes, they generally did okay.

And this poor kid was out there…alone?

"Why did he run?"

The cat shifter shrugged. "We don't know, exactly. Doyle is one of those kids who tend to stand on the outside. Very much a loner."

"You're lying about something."

A faint smile curled his lips. He flexed a hand. I had the odd impression of a cat flexing its claws. "You know, if you were one of us, I could rip your throat out over that."

I readied myself. He was here because his alpha had sent him. That didn't mean he couldn't hurt me a little in the process. And if he decided that was what he was going to do, I'd damn well do my best to bleed him.

He continued to watch me and abruptly he sat up in his seat, leaning forward and staring at me with a wide grin. "It's almost kind of cute. Like a kitten attacking a full-grown tiger or something. Too silly and little to realize how badly it could get hurt."

"I'm not a kitten." Wrapping my hand around the grip of my sword, I flexed my muscles. Relaxed. Flexed. Relaxed. "And if you don't want to hear the truth of what I have to say, maybe you'd be better off telling your boss to find another investigator. I don't live in your world, cat. And the beauty of that? Means I don't have to abide by the stupid, insane medieval crap shit that you all live and breathe." I smiled serenely.

To my surprise, he chuckled. "It seems she had a good read on you. You will get in trouble working this alone." He reached into his jacket and five seconds later, I found myself staring at neat little stacks of green.

Money.

Lots and lots of cold, hard cash.

Oh, shiny…

"Your down payment." Then he smiled. "And don't worry…I'll take care of my own meals and such."

"Wait a second, I never said I was taking the damn job." I continued to stare at the money. Damn, it was enough to set me up for a while. And then some. Abruptly, his words got through to me and I shifted my focus back to his face. "What do you mean, you take care of your own meals?"

"I'm part of the package, kitten. Your bodyguard, babysitter and tattle-tale, all rolled into one." Flashing his teeth at me, he added, "Aren't you pleased?"

Hell. No.

Two hours later, my self-appointed bodyguard was guiding me into the decidedly opulent lair of the Lady.

Somehow, *Hell. No.* had turned into *Okay* without a conscious decision from my brain. I didn't even realize it had happened.

One minute I had been in the process of gathering up the money to throw at his face, and the second...the picture. I had looked back at the picture. The poor kid with stringy blond hair hanging in his thin face, his blue eyes defiant and scared.

Lost.

Sixteen. Out there, alone. Sixteen years old and his body was a ticking time-bomb.

I'd been fifteen when I'd run away from my mother's family. Fifteen, and although I hadn't had to worry about my body going nuts, I had spent the next three years convinced one of my aunts, or worse...my grandmother...might come after me. I knew what it was like to be alone and scared.

"Come on, kitten. She's waiting for you."

Glaring at the back of his head, I pointed out, "I have a name." It wasn't *kitten*. I didn't like *kitten*.

"Yeah. Kit. Not too different from *kitten*." He shot me a grin over his shoulder, one that was faintly demonic, I decided. "It's too late to back out now. You already accepted the money. That's pretty much akin to signing a contract in our world and you know it. She'll take exception if you turn chicken now."

I curled my lip at him.

I'd show him a fucking chicken—he'd squawk like one after I rammed my sword up his ass.

But I wasn't going to back out. After all, he was right; I'd taken the money. And it was about that, right? I could try to pretend. After all, I like money. I didn't get lots of it often and when I did, I go through it too easily. I was finally getting better at budgeting, but man, fifty thousand? I could splurge. A little.

Yet even as I tried to pretend, I knew better. I had a soft spot, all right. A weakness. And it was most definitely for cases that involved kids.

Every time I closed my eyes, I saw that boy's face.

I was sunk. Completely.

"You ever going to tell me your name?" I asked, trailing along after him, eying his muscled back, those wide shoulders. In the back of my mind, some part of me thought: *Pretty...*

And I immediately wanted to punch myself. He was a damned cat. He still hadn't confirmed or denied, but I knew a cat when I saw one. And regardless, he was a shifter, he was somehow connected to the crazy cat clan and that meant *hell, no.*

14

Even if he was hotter than hell.

"I guess I should tell you my name, since I'll be keeping you company for a while…" He smiled as we came to a halt inside a round room—it was draped with swaths of pink silk.

I felt like I'd fallen into a piece of bubble gum.

"And that name is…?"

"Damon."

"Demon? That's fitting." I smirked at him and flopped onto a chair. I put my blade on the couch next to me and drew my knee to my chest, ignoring the pointed look he gave the sword.

"You don't need that," he said flatly.

"I do." I touched it and smiled as the runes danced at my touch. My mother's sword. It wasn't as strong in my hands as it had been in hers—after all, I was half-human, but it was still powerful. And mine. I felt better just for touching it.

My mother's sword. And she knew me.

"She isn't going to like some trained killer sitting in her private quarters with a silver sword," he said. His brows dropped low of those odd eyes of his and he came off the couch, prowling closer. "How did you get it in here, anyway? I saw you lock it up."

I smiled. "We trained killers have our tricks."

And my sword was one of mine…she had been my mother's sword. She would be there when I needed her, or if I thought I might. An aneira warrior wouldn't be easily parted from her blade.

"Put it away," he ordered. "Now."

I closed my hand around the grip. "No."

The last time I'd gone into the lair of one of the damned Alphas, I almost hadn't made it out alive. If he thought I'd go into this one willingly and unarmed, he was out of his pretty skull.

The door opened.

Damon spun around and immediately bowed his head.

I remained where I was. As far as they were concerned, I was just a human—well, they did see me as a trained killer. At least they acknowledged *that*, but I wasn't a shifter, and by the Assembly charter, I wasn't required to follow their stupid laws. Nor would I. As long as I didn't attack her, I was allowed to carry whatever fucking weapons I wanted.

So I stayed were I was, sword in my lap, and watched the lady of the cats came into the room.

She was…unexpected.

Yes. Very unexpected. Diminutive and pale, her hair nearly as blonde as mine. Thick black lashes hid her eyes and her mouth was about as pink as it could possibly get and still be natural. Either she had a damn good hand with makeup or God had just been too kind. She was slender—small waist, petite, but well-enough endowed that I had to wonder if she didn't use her ability to change shape to alter hers in other ways. Some of the stronger ones could do things like that for short periods of time.

15

The Alpha definitely could do something like that.

Pretty as a doll, I decided. And probably every bit as vapid. I couldn't even get a read on whatever animal she was, although I knew she was cat. There was just… nothing there.

It was almost as bad as looking at Jude, although I knew why I couldn't read him. My ability to read people came from their souls. He just didn't have one.

That wasn't the case here. Vampires lost their souls over time after they were bitten, losing them slowly. They didn't just feed on blood—they fed on the psychic energy that came with it, and reveled on the punch of emotion that came with the feeding, since they lost their ability to feel with the death of their soul.

This woman wasn't a vampire. She was…inanimate. Kind of like a doll. Damon had more presence than she did, I remember thinking that.

Then she turned to face me and the power of her gaze almost sent me crashing to the floor.

I gripped my blade, harder, harder, until the grip damn near bruised my hand and it still wasn't enough. She moved and a breath later, so did I. It almost wasn't fast enough but I'd had to rely on my instincts to survive the training of my grandmother and aunts.

I was still holding my sword in the seconds that followed and Damon stood between us, his hands raised in that calming, easy gesture people so often used.

"My Lady, you wanted to speak with the investigator. I brought her so she could talk to you about Doyle."

She backhanded him—if I'd ever needed the evidence of shapeshifter strength, I had it now. He was over six feet and I imagined he weighed two-fifty, at the least. The Alpha? She was smaller than I was. I was five foot five, and she looked to be about three or four inches shorter. Save for the boobs, she was fluff all over.

But that single strike sent him flying across the room, crashing into one of the bubble-gum pink walls. He didn't stay there. Even as she came for me again, he was there.

What the hell—?

"My Lady, you'll be very angry if you harm the one who can help you find Doyle," he said, and his voice had a soothing tone that seemed out of place. But then again, if he was trying to calm her down, the smart-ass mouth he showed with me wasn't the ideal, I figured.

"Damon, are you standing in my way?" she asked. She had a lovely voice. It was like bells tinkling.

Poetic. I was getting poetic in my near-death state.

"I'm just following orders, My Lady," he said, bowing his head.

"You followed orders by letting her bring a blade in here? To threaten me?"

"How am I a threat?"

Damon shot me a dirty look. His left eye was black, his mouth was busted and blood trickled down his face. He was trashed, and he was pissed, and I guess I couldn't blame him. But I didn't look at him. Focusing on the cat alpha, I asked again, "How am I a threat? I bring the weapons I normally carry on a job and if you weren't prepared for that, then I'm sorry, but I don't do my job unarmed, especially not when I'm working with shifters."

"Are you implying I brought you here to harm you?"

Her head cocked to the side and I had the impression of a snake getting ready to strike. Not a pleasant picture. If I lied, she'd know. And if I lied right now, as pissed as she was…damn it, why didn't anybody see fit to mention that the cat alpha was missing a few marbles? Of course, it wasn't surprising, considering how fucking *nuts* all of them were. Maybe it was a pack thing and it all came from *her*.

The pieces clicked into places and I figured it out. She wasn't soulless. She was just a sociopath.

I shook my head. Mustn't enrage the antisocial monster standing five feet away. "I'm not implying anything. I'm treating this job the same as I would any other. I go into it knowing nothing—and that's the way I'd prefer it."

Her gaze, pale, pale blue held mine.

Then slowly, she nodded. When she looked away, I let myself breathe.

"Damon, look at your face…"

From the corner of my eye, I watched. She rose on the tips of her toes, touching his cheek, his nose, his bruised eye. "Oh, you poor thing. Does it hurt?"

I didn't gape, but I wanted to. She'd knocked him into a wall…and she wanted to know if he hurt.

But of course, instead of saying something honest like *Yes, bitch, it hurts*, Damon just shrugged. "I've had worse."

Ten minutes later, they were seated on the couch having tea and I was trying not to stare.

Tea.

For Pete's sake.

"Do you take sugar?"

I stared at the small cup. I'd rather not take it at all. "Please."

She nodded and I waited while she played the hostess. Damon sat across from us, his face healed, but there was still blood on him. I'd have liked to ask him why he didn't bother to go wash it off, but I had a feeling I knew why.

His alpha was a fucking crazy bitch and he was better off not drawing her attention in any way, shape or form.

"So Damon must think you can find my nephew," the lady murmured.

I needed to think of a name to call her. Nobody would give me her name—I had heard rumors of shifters who'd served her for decades who didn't know. She shifted once more in her seat, took a sip from that delicate little mug of tea and then set it down, folded her hands primly in her lap.

I had a suspicion she was posing for me. Like an oversized Barbie doll…ah, bingo. Barbie. It also made her a little less scary in my mind—maybe not in reality, but who cared about reality?

Still pondering the statement she'd made, I finally made myself answer. "I never said I could find him. I don't even know what's going on with him. I just know I was offered a job." Slipping the demonic Damon a look, I resisted the urge to point out that I hadn't exactly been given much of a chance to refuse. I could have walked away from him. Tried harder. I hadn't.

"Are you telling me you can't?" she asked, once more tilting her head to the side. There was something creepy about that. It made her look too...practiced. Like she was mimicking human motions without actually understanding why she was doing it.

"I never said that either. I just don't know anything about the case and I need to do a little more research before I can begin to think about whether or not I can find him." There. That was honest enough, right?

"Are you good at your job?" She reached for her cup of tea again, staring at me over the rim as she took another small sip.

Cautiously, I answered, "Good enough, I think."

"Hmmm." After she set it down, she rose from her seat.

Like he was jerked up on a set of strings, Damon was on his feet. He shot me a narrow look.

I stayed on my ass. That woman might scare me shitless, but I'd grown up around women who scared me shitless and I was done living my life kowtowing to the people who frighten me. If you gave in and did what they wanted, they just pushed for more anyway.

And besides, I wasn't a damn cat. I didn't have to follow their fucked-up sense of hierarchy.

She paced the room and when she turned back, she narrowed her eyes as she saw me still sitting. "You really are a bit of a problem child, aren't you?"

"Yes." I shrugged. "I'm sorry. It's in my nature."

"I know. Your kind have always had that sense of...arrogance." Her nose wrinkled when she said *your kind*. Like we left a bad taste—literally—in her mouth. "I was hoping that you'd be a little less so, since your blood is weaker."

"Well, you know what they say. Blood is thicker than water."

"Is it really, though?" She rubbed one hand against the other and resumed her endless prowl around the room. "They cannot stand you, little warrior."

Little warrior...

I grimaced. Had she been talking to Jude?

Most people didn't know enough of us to really understand what we were. A handful of the older ones did. Others might know the name but they didn't understand, didn't realize what we were...somebody had once called me a watered-down offshoot of a nearly dead race. Not terribly complimentary, but it said it all well enough.

We'd been forgotten, by and large. So it was kind of disturbing that she knew anything about me at all. And even more that she knew of my troubled relationship with my family.

"Whether or not my family can stand me doesn't have much standing on my ability to do the job, now, does it?" I asked, forcing myself to stay focused on Kitty-cat Barbie. Losing focus with her around was a certain way to end up dead. "All that matters is if I can find him or not. Do you want me to try?"

"No." She smiled and as she did, the incisors in her mouth lengthened. That was the only thing that changed and it was awful to see. Pure awful.

She continued to smile even as she lisped out, "I don't want you to try, little warrior. I want you to do it."

Then, as her teeth shifted back to normal, she came back and sat down. "You'll find him, Colbana. And you'll return him to us, unharmed. Or I'm going to come after you and rip out your heart. I'll feast on it after I bury my nephew." She said it in the exact same tone she'd asked me if I'd like sugar, and she said it while reaching for her damned tea cup.

Part of me wanted to point out that her terms weren't entirely fair, but I was outmatched here. Outmatched, outclassed in every way and if she came for me here, on her terms, on her turf, I'd die. From a distance, it would be different and if she wasn't expecting it, it would be different.

But right now, if I pissed her off, I was dead. I rather liked *not* being dead. So I held my tongue and stared at her for a long moment. Then, without looking at the man next to me, I folded my hand around the sword on my lap and rose.

No wonder the damn thing had come to me.

I was in a room with a crazy bitch and a man who'd all but led me to slaughter.

Chapter Three

I'd barely made it out of the lair when Damon grabbed me and shoved me against a brick wall. We were alone in the corridor. Wonderful. No witnesses to see him try to kill me.

"Are you trying to get us both killed?" he demanded, his voice not much more than a growl. The rage I saw in his eyes practically burned my skin.

This close, my blade wasn't going to do me much good.

I banished her, although it felt like I was cutting off my arm. Once I had my hands free, I smiled at him. As he snarled, I reached for the dagger I had stashed inside my jacket before we left. I only had about fifty places to hide them. He would have been hard-pressed to find them without searching me.

This was the only one I'd carried on me. It wasn't silver and it wasn't very big. It wouldn't hurt him much, but if I got away from him, I could call my sword and that one could do some damage.

Assuming I could move fast enough—my head was ringing. Hell, I might be better off doing one of my other tricks. Not that I had many that worked for fighting, but there was one...

"Sure," I said. "I woke up today just hoping some idiot shifter would appear in my office and drag me off to face his Alpha without warning me that I'd either successfully do the job she was shoving on me or she was going to declare open season on my ass. That just sounded like loads of fun, you dolt."

Then, I shoved the blade into his side at an upward angle, twisting it as I went.

It stunned him enough that I managed to get away.

Once I had a few feet between us, I held my breath and just...faded out. My ability go invisible is just a part of me. It's not witchcraft, although it's probably pretty close. It's an ability the aneira alone possess, and I had enough of the blood that even I could do it. Once you tap into that ability, it's as natural as breathing. And it's very useful. Even a predator has a hard time finding what he can't see...at first.

He stumbled, caught off guard and as he did, I back-flipped away. There was a little noise and he could track that, but the second I was far enough away, I stopped with the fancy moves and just walked.

That, I could do quietly, moving into a busier area of the lair, hoping I could get far enough away from him that I'd be harder to track by scent. It worked. For a minute. I ducked through a door and found myself outside in a courtyard, surrounded by people coming and going into the lair.

It didn't last for long. I saw it when he caught my scent and I ducked behind an arbor away from others, out of sight. As he came at me, I called my blade and it was in my hand just as he reached the area I'd picked to make my stand. I dropped the cloak of invisibility just as the tip of the blade pierced his chest.

"Back off," I said quietly.

"You must really have a death wish," he murmured.

"No. Actually, I'm kind of fond of life and it pisses me off that you led me in there knowing what she was going to drop on me." I pushed the blade a little deeper and said again, "Back off."

Instead, he took another step toward me. "Do you really think you can take me? Take any of us?"

"No." I smiled and twisted my blade, watched as a pained look crossed his face as the silver took effect. "But I figured something out...she ordered you not to let anybody hurt me...didn't she?"

His lids flickered.

No other response, though. No other answer.

Smiling at him, I gave the blade another twist. His skin was starting to smoke now—whatever kind of cat he was, he was strong, or he would have already pulled back. "That includes you...and her."

He backed away. "You'll end up dead before this is out and I'll be the one to pay for it," he muttered, disgust thick in his voice.

"Don't worry." I pulled a cloth from my pocket and cleaned the blood from my blade, tucked it away. "I've got a pretty good rep for landing on my feet." Usually.

Damon stared at me. He didn't look impressed.

"All you had to do was leave the fucking sword," he growled. "That was what set her off."

I was tempted to tell him that I *had* left the sword, that she had come to me when I needed her. But why? I might need the element of surprise later on. He obviously hadn't figured it out on his own. "Hey, you saw me lock it up. Not my fault if you can't pay closer attention."

Those rather fantastic eyes of his narrowed.

I shrugged and turned away. I had a job to do. Not one I wanted, but since I wanted to keep breathing, apparently one that was going to have to be done.

"I need to talk to the boy's family," I said.

"You just did."

Stopping, I turned and stared at him.

"My Lady is his only family. He was orphaned. Her brother was his father. His mother dumped the kid on him a few months after he was born and disappeared. Nobody really knows anything about her. The kid's dad died when he was five. My Lady took him in and raised him."

Damn. No wonder the boy ran away.

I was smart enough to keep that bit behind my teeth.

Damon saw it, though. His eyes narrowed and I heard the growl trickling from him. Shrugging, I turned and walked away. Hell, if I was expected to start censoring my thoughts, they might as well kill me now. I'd never survive this.

"Friends, then. Somebody."

"What, don't you want to talk to My Lady again?"

Suppressing a shudder, I continued to walk. "Absolutely. But his friends first. A kid that age, sometimes you get a better feel for them by talking to their friends anyway."

"He didn't have many." Stormcloud eyes rested on my face. "I already explained this. He was something of a loner."

Yes. He'd explained that. But even outsiders tended to have a couple of people they hung with. Not always, but usually. "*Many* isn't the same as *none*. So did he have anybody he spoke with? Ever?"

Silence stretched out between us and I braced myself, prepared to wait endlessly if I had to. Patience wasn't one of my stronger virtues, but I could stand there for hours if need be. It only took about two minutes. Either he was a weird-ass cat or he didn't see the point in wasting time.

"There are a couple of kids," he finally said, inclining his head. "But they aren't going to talk to you."

Yeah. Like that was any surprise. Shooting him a narrow look, I said, "Well, maybe you should tell them it would be wise to. You'd think they'd want him found. And while I might not inspire them to fear…you should be able to."

"Shit, kitten. I think you just said something almost smart."

I didn't grace that pithy comment with a reply. There really, really wasn't any point.

Doyle's friends didn't hang out at the lair—not many of the teens did.

No surprise, really.

What teenaged kid would want to hang around a place where that crazy bitch might show up? The aunt alone was a good enough reason to run away, if you asked me. Hell, if Kitty-cat Barbie was my aunt, I would have run away, too. I knew what it was like to have blood-thirsty relatives who were somewhat lacking in the sanity department.

Mine had been my grandmother, Fanis. The mega-bitch to end all mega-bitches. She could even give Kitty-cat Barbie a run for her money as far as cruelty went, I'd imagine.

Just think about her made me twitchy and I couldn't be twitchy, so I shoved the thoughts aside and studied the long, low building in front of me. It was cordoned off by chain-link fencing, marked with the insignia of the ANH. Perched on the border of East Orlando, it was clearly non-human territory. Humans could go in, but if they did, there was an acceptable risk.

Acceptable risk.

Why did they even bother?

If anything bad happened, anybody inside with non-human blood was still screwed.

As long as all the bad shit happened on our side, it didn't matter.

But if a human was harmed, we were fucked.

Of course, if humans ganged up and hunted us down? Not an issue. That had happened just a month ago up in Atlanta. Eight men had kidnapped a high-school-aged girl. Her mother was a shifter. Her father was human. The girl hadn't manifested.

That didn't matter.

Even though the men had been caught on video as she was forced into a van, nobody was pressing charges. She was still missing and nobody in the human world cared.

If she'd been my daughter, I would have gutted the men. Quietly. Taken my time and taken them out one by one.

One thing about that sign, though, it made it clear to me that was I traveling on dangerous ground. People in there played by shifter rules.

I was now on the job and that meant I'd end up stepping on toes. No safe passage. Didn't matter if I had some bruiser at my back or not. I was going to step on toes.

"What is this place?" I asked as Damon came around to stand beside me.

"Just one of their hangouts," he said easily, a smile on his face.

That smile alone was enough to warn me.

With a critical look at me, he warned, "They won't let you in with weapons. And if you try to sneak that sword in, they'll put you in a world of hurt. Just so you know—they will pat you down. You've got a known face, so…"

"Pat me down? Wonderful." I started stripping out of my gear. I made a show of taking off my sword. Then I held it out to him. "Why don't you lock it in the truck, hotshot?"

The look in his eyes was so full of distrust, I almost laughed. Instead, I just fished my keys out of my pocket and popped the lock, heading to the back of my car and stowing away the knives, my gun, the garrote that worked into my collar. He carried the sword, watching as I put away one weapon after the other. "You'd think you were going to war," he drawled. "Are you afraid I can't keep that cute ass of yours in one piece?"

I kept my head down, letting my hair hide my face as blood rushed up and set my cheeks on fire. I could handle being a little embarrassed. What I couldn't handle was the other reaction.

It had been way too long since I'd been laid.

And he was pretty to look at in a rough kind of way, but there was no way I was doing this. He was just as much trouble as Jude was…

Jude—

Like a whispered summons, I grew painfully aware of his presence. It stroked across my skin, brushed across my mind even as I swore and fought the urge to kick at something. *What in the hell*…I thought. Why now?

Jerking my head up, I turned around in a slow circle. My unwanted bodyguard noticed and he shifted, moving to stand in front of me, effectively blocking my view. I shoved at him. "Would you get the hell out of the way?"

I might as well have been shoving at a boulder for all the good it did.

But it didn't matter. What I needed to see wasn't in front of us.

It was driving down the street and as I turned my head, I saw it.

23

Long, sleek black car. A warning thrummed in my head. Getting louder and louder until it was a roar. By the time the car stopped, I was ready to gouge through my eardrums just to shut it up. *Yes. Problem. I'm aware. Thank you very much, brain.*

The door opened and the roaring faded away as I saw who stepped out. It wasn't Jude. I already knew that. It was early yet for him. Even though I'd long since figured out he could handle sunlight, he didn't bother unless he chose to and only God above knew what motivated him.

I knew the woman climbing out of the car, though, her movements all liquid grace and sex personified.

It was Evangeline, his personal assistant, a woman who hated me with every fiber of her being. If it wasn't for the hold Jude had on her, I had no doubt she'd do her damnedest to kill me. She'd had a hard time of it. Evangeline was a vampire's servant and their blood bond gave her an extra kick, not to mention seeming immortality.

But she was more human than not.

I thought I could probably take her.

My palm itched and I clenched it. If I wasn't careful, the sword Damon held was going to leap to my palm and that sweet little secret was going to be out of the bag. Evangeline pissed me off and I'd like to fight her, but she wasn't a threat until Jude decided he was done toying with me. And I think he was having too much fun for that to change any time soon.

"Hello, Angie," I drawled.

The faint line between her brows was the only sign of her displeasure, but it was enough. I wasn't choosy. I took what I could get. Dismissing her, I went back to stripping off my weapons. The only things left were a couple of knives tucked inside my boots. I placed one foot on the bumper as Evangeline came closer, her movements sinuous and boneless, like an eel's. She'd been one of Jude's since before the mortal Civil War, nearly two centuries earlier. Her humanity died a little more every year. She was almost as graceful, almost as scary as some of the vampires. Almost.

"Jude would like to know why you haven't answered his summons," she said, a pretty polite little smile on her Cupid's bow mouth. And her eyes were pools of seething, ugly hate.

"Oh, that's easy," I said cheerfully, drawing out one knife, laying it in the trunk. I did the same with its mate and then shifted to my other boot. I laid one of the blades in the trunk, but the last one, I held onto as I turned to face Evangeline. "You see, he keeps summoning me like I'm his little dog, or one of his little servants. Like you."

I started to toss the knife. Sunlight danced off the silver surface, casting slivers of light all around. "I'm not."

"He has a job for you," Evangeline said.

"Then he can make an appointment." I shrugged and continued to make the knife dance. "Or he can call me. E-mail—does he know what e-mail is? Hell, he can send you with the information or send it via courier pigeon for all I care. I don't give a rat's ass. But I don't answer to his summons."

"Rat's ass…" Evangeline came closer. "It's ironic that you say that. Considering that he saved you. Your ass, might I point out. From the rats."

"True. But if the whole lot of you had been doing your fucking job?"

She snaked out a hand to grab the knife. I saw it coming and caught the blade, pointed it at her throat, just a whisper from piercing her skin. "I wouldn't have had to do that damned job…meaning I wouldn't have to deal with any of you," I finished. "I could have continued my happy little existence, none of you would know about me and my life would be so much easier. I'm still pissed off over that."

"Please do it." Evangeline leaned against the blade, staring at me and for once, the smile on her face was echoed in her eyes. "I beg you. Draw my blood. Then I can convince my master what an utterly worthless use of space you are…I'll kill you for attacking me and he won't be terribly aggrieved."

I pressed harder with my knife, cocked my head as the tip came ever closer to breaking the skin. "Sugar…killing me won't be as easy on you as you think. Jude could tear me apart…but you can't."

A hard, brutal hand closed around my wrist.

Damon jerked my hand down and shoved me back.

"Leech-lover, go tell your master she's working for the Queen of the Cats," he said, sending me his infamous dark look. "She's not available for anybody else at this time."

"Like hell." The words popped out of my mouth before I could stop them.

He ignored me as he wedged that wide, powerful body between me and Evangeline.

Her eyes widened.

She might not fear me—and that was really, really short-sighted of her, but Damon apparently worried her a little.

"If he wants her, he's going to have to get in line. She's busy," Damon murmured. He leaned in, crowding into her space.

A human would have backed away.

But a vampire's servant was a different matter and Evangeline just stood there, even though something that might have been fear glittered in her eyes. "Is that a fact?"

"Yeah. Why don't you pass the message along?"

"I'm afraid I'm not your errand girl, cat." Turning on her heel, she walked away. "He'll be in contact soon, Colbana. You don't want to keep ignoring him. It won't go well for you."

Yeah, yeah, yeah. I'd been getting variations of that for the past two or three years, ever since I'd decided that life was better without Jude in it. The first few years after I'd met him, I'd gone when he called, feeling like I owed him, but then I'd realized he was trying to put me on a chain. A pretty, polite one, but a chain nonetheless. I'd spent too much of my life caged and I wasn't doing it anymore.

There were times when circumstances jerked me back into his orbit, but usually

I was able to stay away from him. I'd managed to avoid His Arrogance's presence—in person—for going on seven months now. That wasn't going to last much longer, but I also wasn't terribly concerned he was going to go apeshit, either.

He was having too much fun playing with me.

Damon remained in front of me, blocking my view of the car until it rolled out of sight. Then he turned around, studying me with that odd look in his eyes. The one that made me think he was trying to decide if I'd be fun to eat or more fun to just slice to ribbons and play with.

"I think I've seen five year olds with more sense than you," he said flatly. "How in the world are you even still alive?"

"Dumb luck?" I stepped back and nodded to the sword in his hand. "Are you going to lock that up or what?"

He tossed it in. Shut the trunk and then he turned to me. "Put your hands on the damned trunk."

I cocked a brow at him. "Excuse me?"

"You carry more firepower than a Banner extermination unit."

A Banner extermination unit—the slang term for the assassination units out of Bureau of American Non-Human Affairs—was a human group of killers. They went after the non-humans who were deemed too dangerous to exist.

And no matter what, any kill made by the Banner unit was pretty much considered a 'righteous' kill. Thankfully, they weren't used too often—we preferred to handle our problem children on our own. When they did go on a hunt, they went loaded for bear.

I snorted and crossed my arms over my chest. "I hardly carry *that* many weapons."

"Sure. Now turn around and put your hands on the fucking car," he snapped.

"Why?"

"Because I'm going to pat you down and make sure you don't have anything else." He leaned in and all but snarled the words into my face.

He reached for me. I lifted a hand to block but damn he was fast. A split second later, I was face down against the trunk of my car, the metal smashing against my cheek while one big arm crushed against my neck. His other hand jacked my wrist up high between my shoulder blades. My bones screamed and thanks to the pressure he had on my neck, the oxygen in my lungs dwindled down to nothing and panic tried to crowd in on me. Pain and dread gripped me and my free hand itched, so desperately bad. The blade...my sword, she sang to me, called to me...*Ask, just ask...*

No. Not yet—

I lay there, limp, fighting back the rush of fear. If I panicked, it would be worse. It would use up my oxygen and make it that much harder to fight when I had to. And, if I did fight, it would be worse—

No. You're not back there. He's not Fanis—

I battled back the terror, focused on the pain and called up anger. Anger grounded me. Focused me.

No fear. I could still breathe…barely…and he wasn't trying to kill me. He just wanted me afraid while he yelled at me.

My blood is noble. My heart is strong. My aim is true. I am aneira…my heart is strong—

No fear, *damn* it. I could be drowning in it, and he damn well could smell it on me, but I sure as hell wouldn't show it.

As he leaned in closer, his mouth against my ear, I clenched my jaw.

"Listen, you little fool. You're going into a place that we keep safe for our young," he growled. "You got that? And while you aren't exactly what I'd call a threat in our world, our young still aren't precisely ready to defend themselves. You go in there swinging silver or anything else, it's going to piss them off. Some of them may try to shift, which will scare you enough that you might try to defend yourself and you're obviously too stupid to know when to pull back and when to fight. If you hurt one of them, somebody in there will try to kill you. Which means I'm bound, by my word to My Lady to kill them—just because they are defending our young."

He all but spat each word and I knew if he wanted, he could snap my neck in an instant. It was getting hard to breathe, too hard, and I could all but feel the warming in my palm as the magic that connected me to my blade started to waken.

Then it was done. Damon loosened his hold and let me go. "Do you think you can get that into your fool head?"

Shoving upright, I glared at him over my shoulder. "Go fuck yourself," I rasped out and it was like I had to choke the words out through a fucking straw. My face throbbed; my wrist and arm weren't feeling too much better, but my throat felt like it had been pulverized.

Burning hot with rage and humiliation, and yet somehow cold with fear, I placed my hands on the truck and stood there as he did a quick, impersonal pat-down.

One thing was certain.

He was enough of an ass that my long-dormant libido had settled back into complacency.

Hell, he might be on the same level of dangerous as Jude, but he was a few steps higher on the asshole meter. Kind of pathetic. I hadn't thought anybody could outpace the vampire, but this guy had managed to do it in a day.

Now *that* takes talent.

Chapter Four

My right hand itched.

From the minute we stepped foot inside those gates, it itched.

I had no weapons.

I didn't have my sword.

And although I could have the damn sword at any time I wanted, if I let her come to me, it was going to incite riots, according to my asshole bodyguard, and if that happened, he'd have to kill people to protect me.

That shouldn't bother me.

The problem was that it did and he'd figured out exactly what nerve to hit.

I didn't like death.

I'd killed people and I'd do it again, probably before this job was out. I definitely didn't want it to happen if I could avoid it, but what was the problem with me carrying my sword?

"If you go in there stinking of fear, you're going to set them off," Damon muttered.

"Well, if you didn't want me afraid, you shouldn't have set *me* off," I pointed out, then I scowled at the sound of my voice. *Fuck.* I sounded like I'd swallowed a bunch of broken gravel and rusty nails and my throat hurt. It wasn't anything I hadn't dealt with before, but it still pissed me off.

He frowned and looked over at me.

Then he stopped and went to catch my arm.

I backed away. Fast. Part of me wanted to cringe. The body remembers abuse. For a long, long time.

"Don't touch me," I warned him. I wouldn't cower. Not in front of him. I could practically feel the fear bleeding out of me, replaced by anger. *I am aneira—my heart is strong.* And I sure as hell wouldn't cower in front of this bastard.

Something flickered in his eyes, that frown still tightening his face. But he nodded. "Try to keep the fear under wraps, kitten. You don't want to go breathing fear over a bunch of adolescent shapeshifters. They'll think you're hard up for a date," he said, starting back up the path. "If you are that desperate for some rough fun, I can give it to you."

His meaning hit me about five heartbeats later.

I would have laughed if it wouldn't have hurt so much.

At the doorway, I was subjected to yet another pat-down.

This one wasn't quite so impersonal, though. As the man's hands lingered over my breasts, I hissed and drove my head back into his face. Pain bloomed through the back of my skull, but I heard the satisfying sound of his nasal bone crunching. I'd regret it in a second. My head was already pounding and once the adrenaline faded, it would be worse, I knew.

Well, maybe not—I might be dead before the pain caught up with the adrenaline. Either way, I didn't care.

His hand fisted into my hair as I fought to twist away.

"You little—"

Then I was free and Damon was there. "Please tell me you didn't just insult the Lady by taking the liberty I thought I saw," he growled. "That woman is working for the Alpha. An insult to her is an insult to the Lady. Did I just see what I thought I saw?"

Even I could smell the stink of fear crowding the air now.

This time, it wasn't mine. I cocked my wrist, tried to ignore the heat flaring there. Tried to ignore the sword's whisper in the back of my mind.

The bastard who'd groped my tits went to the ground on one knee, blood dripping from a nose that had already healed. "Sir, I…I meant no disrespect."

I stared at him. "You grab my tits and you mean no disrespect."

Damon shot me a dark look. I glared at him and turned away. "Fuck, I never should have talked to you," I muttered. I went to turn away, rubbing the back of my aching head, tacky now with the bastard's blood.

"Get up," Damon growled.

"Sir, I—"

I glanced over my shoulder in time to see Damon hammer a massive fist into the man's face. He went flying into the wall about ten feet away. The concrete block cracked a little. The entire place was made of concrete block. If this was a regular occurrence around her, the décor made sense.

As Damon turned around to face me, I looked away.

So far on this job, I'd had the Bitch Queen tell me I was as good as dead if I failed the job. She'd stuck a crazy bastard on my ass to keep me safe and just a few minutes ago, he'd almost killed me. Thirty seconds ago, somebody had groped my tits.

Fifty thousand dollars wasn't worth it.

"Ma'am?"

It was a quiet, polite voice and I turned, found myself staring into a handsome, lean face. Asian, with liquid black eyes and a courteous smile on his lips.

"If you'd allow me…?"

He gestured.

Oh, yes. They weren't done patting me down.

"Allow me to apologize for Robert," he said as he finished with the pat-down. "I assure you, he will be chastised."

"Yeah. Because after all I'm working for the cat Alpha and nobody wants to piss her off," I snapped. "But any other female who walks through that door would be fair game. I wonder how you all might feel if your sisters, mothers, daughters were treated so."

Something flickered in his eyes and he inclined his head. "Point taken. Again, my apologies and I assure you, such a thing will never happen to you again in one of my establishments, even after your business arrangement with the Alpha has ended. And Robert will be dealt with." He reached into his pocket and withdrew a card.

I ignored it. "Don't bother. I'm probably going to end up dead by the time this job is over anyway."

"If you wish, there is a washroom just through the gates," Mr. Courtesy began. "You could clean up…"

I turned my back on him before he could finish and moved through the gates, heading into the said washroom. The blood was still wet—if I rinsed my hair out in the sink, I might be able to get the majority of it now.

A few minutes later, with damp hair, I met a very brooding Damon out in the hall. We were the only two in the hallway—or so it appeared. I knew better. I could feel eyes resting on me as he crossed over to me. "You ready?" he asked.

I nodded, ignoring the whisper in the back of my head. I swear, I've never gone this long without calling her to me, not when I needed her so bad.

With Damon at my back, I headed down the hall.

He was silent for once.

Thank God.

I should have stayed in the restroom longer. I could have used the time to get my head together. A few hours. A drink. I really should have stayed home and done my taxes.

Sighing, I trolled through the club. That's what this was, I realized. A shapeshifter's version of a rec club. The scents of pizza and raw meat hung in the air, and a quick look in what appeared to be the café explained why. Yes. They could get pizza, or if they wanted…raw meat. Appetizing.

I moved away fast. As fast as I could, because my gut was churning and I didn't want to puke. They might not like that. Down one hall, I heard some odd little yips and whines. Following the sound, I pushed open a door and found myself standing on a grate that overlooked what almost looked like a football arena up with one of those insane garden mazes in it. I caught sight of a furred hide, running at a speed too fast for my eyes to really lock on it. There was a growl, followed by the cry of something dying. And a howl rose through the room.

"Hunting games," Damon said. "Not all of them get out of the city much, so we set up mock hunts in places like this. It spreads out for about a half mile underground and we stock it with game animals."

I didn't respond, just turned away and slipped back out the door into the relative quiet of the hall.

"Doyle's friends were usually more for the arcade or the lounge. None of them were spiking yet, except him. They don't go for the hunts until they can shift, usually."

I continued to walk around.

"The arcade is—"

I found it. It wasn't that hard. Arcades made a hell of a lot of noise and teenaged kids made even more.

Except when I pushed the door open, the noise stopped.

Gazes swung my way and my heart leapt to my abused throat as some of those gazes went predatory.

Damon reached up to rest a heavy hand on my shoulder but at his touch, I moved away.

"Don't touch me," I said again, feeling like a broken record. I stood aside and waited for him to go in first. He had an unreadable look in his eyes, but he circled around and fell in front. I stayed about four steps behind him, eying the people around us narrowly.

Some of the kids in there pressed close. Too close. My hand itched—so badly it burned.

Call me, call…I am here…

The sword whispered to me, the voice as clear to me as if I stood by the trunk where we'd locked her away. It didn't matter what the distance was. I could have her in my hand in a second.

But I wouldn't.

These were just kids. I didn't need a damned sword to deal with kids. *I am aneira—my heart is strong. My heart is strong—*

Keeping my eyes trained on Damon's back, I continued to walk.

Somebody touched my hair.

I heard the gentle clearing of a throat. Looking up, I saw the Asian man from earlier standing on a catwalk over us. He was staring at somebody behind me.

Damon whirled and with a flash of his teeth and a snarl, I was in front of him. "The next person who touches the girl is going to have my boot up their ass, is that clear?"

Whines and weird little mewling sounds flooded the air.

His hand rested on the back of my neck and I tried to jerk away.

"Don't," he warned quietly.

That wasn't enough to stop me, but since I couldn't exactly break that iron grip, I was sort of trapped. Fighting in here would be bad. Very bad. My instincts were pretty clear on that. And, I'd already noticed, nobody was close enough to touch me anymore. Except Damon.

"There," he said, pointing to a small clutch of kids gathered around an old-school video game.

Mortal Kombat…awesome.

I twitched under his hand. "This would be easier if I didn't have a leash."

His hand fell away.

I swallowed. Kicked myself because it hurt so fucking bad to do that. Then, mentally bracing myself, I approached the kids. They knew I was there. "Man, I used to kick ass at that game." I mentally groaned at the ruin of my voice..

One kid, hair dyed black and a gold ring in his nose, flicked me a disinterested look. "Fuck off, nugget."

Nugget. One of the nicer names werecreatures called humans. As in chicken nugget. Snack. Food.

I didn't really smell much different than the typical human, I'd been told. Some

31

could scent magic on me, but it wasn't like the witches, and since most of them couldn't define it and since I didn't look very strong, they just pegged me as one of the watered-down specimens that popped up every now and then. An interesting peculiarity, but nothing to get worked up over.

As long as they didn't pay me much attention, I didn't care.

Moving close to the vintage video game, I peered at the high score.

"Who holds the high score?"

He huffed out that put-upon sigh that the teenaged set perfected. It didn't matter what their race was. "I do. Go away."

Excellent. I could top that score. I used to do better than that. Way better. "Bet I can beat it."

He snorted. "You wish."

"Try me."

With another derisive look, he said, "I would, but my dad doesn't want me touching humans. He thinks I'll catch it."

Rolling my eyes, I said, "Cute, kid. Don't worry. You're not my style. I always wait until the fur comes in before I go chasing them. You're no fun until then."

A dull red flush settled over his face and he turned away from the game to glare at me. Ah, that's better. He was looking at me now. Fishing out one of the bills Damon had used to lure me into this mess, I waved it at him. "Come on. One game. If you can beat me, this is yours."

His eyes widened on the bill, then narrowed on my face before flicking to the man at my back. Nerves danced on his face and I thought, *Please. Just one thing. Let one thing go my way*…If I could get them to talk to me without Damon pulling that snarl-and-growl act, I'd feel like I was in control over something at least. Just then, I desperately needed it.

I beat the high score.

Much to the dismay of the boy and the amusement of his friends.

He sneered at me as I pushed the money back into my pocket. "I ain't got any money, nugget," he said as he flung his long, skinny body down on the couch a few feet away. "So you just wasted your time."

I sat down on the coffee table a few feet away, holding his gaze. "Nah. I love Mortal Kombat. They made a movie out of the game, you know. Kind of sucked but had some fun actors in it. Lots of ass-kicking."

"Humans like you don't know shit about kicking ass." He gave me another one of those sneers. I wondered if he had another expression.

Sighing, I said, "I'm looking for Doyle."

He shot up off the couch. He didn't make it a foot before Damon was there, shoving him back down. "You're going to talk to her, Marcus," he said quietly. "And you're going to be nice about it."

The kid went white.

Sighing, I rubbed my hands over my face. "I hate this job," I muttered. Lowering my hands, I looked at the kid. "Marcus, is that your name?"

That familiar sneer started to spread over his face. I heard a growl coming from somewhere over my head and I swore. "For crying out loud…damn it, kid, if you want to glare at me, I don't give a flying fuck. I just want to know about Doyle. He's missing. And if you know much about him, you know he's probably going to be in trouble if he's not found soon."

Marcus swallowed. "He ran away," the kid said. "The spike was scaring him. Nobody…"

He stopped talking, shooting Damon a look as he suddenly crowded in over my shoulder.

"You're not helping, Damon," I told him drily. Leaning forward, I touched the boy's knee, drawing his gaze back to mine. "Ignore that jerk if you can. I'm trying my damnedest to do it, although it's kind of hard."

Something that might have been a smile danced in his eyes before it disappeared, gone all too quick.

"The spike was scaring him," I prodded. "Did he run away? Was he trying to do something about it?"

Marcus shook his head. "You can't stop the spiking," he said. "All you can do is go with it. My brother went through it three years ago and it was hell. But Dad was with him, and both of them said they'll be there with me when…"

He shrugged. "They'll be there. Doyle was scared. And nobody cared."

He flicked another look at Damon. For a second, the faintest glimmer of accusation lingered there. Then it was gone.

"Do you have any idea where he'd go?"

"Sometimes he talked about heading south. Down to the 'glades." Marcus smiled, a little sadly. "We always thought it would be fun, you know? Heading down there and doing a real hunt. Not this fake shit they've got set up here. But the real deal."

The Everglades were a protected territory. Nobody can hunt there. Not humans. Not us. Why would the kid think to try? Yeah, there were plenty of wild animals, but still.

Although the forbidden aspect was probably part of the appeal.

Sitting out in the car, resting my head on the steering wheel, I tried to work that piece of information through my aching head.

It wasn't exactly a quick hike, going to the 'glades, but if the kid was spiking, he'd already have some of the were traits, including speed and stamina. Eventually, even the carriers grew into some of that. They'd never have the full array of shifter gifts, but they'd be stronger than humans, faster. If he was spiking, he could make that trip pretty fast even if he was on foot. Depending on what breed of cat he was, it might even just be a quick jaunt in the park.

The door next to me slammed shut.

"Chang offers his apologies once more."

I lifted my head and turned the key in the ignition. For the past ten minutes,

Damon had been out there talking with the club's owner—Chang, I assumed. *Yeah, yeah. I don't care.*

"I feel like I should say I'm sorry, too," he added.

I revved the engine and took off flying down the road. I needed to go by my office. Wouldn't hurt to make a few phone calls. I had contacts with the police forces: mortal, Banner and ANH. More than likely, though, one of my ANH or Banner contacts would be the one who would have inside info on anything related to this.

"He asked me to give you this."

Something white appeared in my line of vision.

And stayed there.

As I slowed for a light, I took the card and tore it into tiny little shreds. Dumping the bits and pieces in the cupholder that I used as a catchall, I shot Damon a look. "Do me a favor. You're an asshole. Don't pretend to be otherwise. You're willing to throw my ass under the bus to find this kid. Fine—I get that. The Alpha is ready to murder to find him. Maybe if I had a nephew, I'd be willing to do the same. I don't know. You're willing to rough me up to make sure I understand the rules of your very fucked-up world. Fine. Don't go getting all bent out of shape because some perverted bastard decided he'd grab my tits and shove his dick against my ass."

I shot him a narrow look. He stared at me with a stony look on his face.

"You sent me in there as a target—they see me as human, and I had no weapons, nothing," I said and the words sounded even more stark, thanks to the ruin of my voice. "They saw a target, that's how I was treated. End of story. Don't act all sorry about it when it happens."

Silence fell in the car.

Finally.

Chapter Five

By the time seven o'clock rolled around, I couldn't have been any more desperate to call it quits. The sun was still burning in the sky, there were still calls I could have made, but I had several irons in the fire and that was going to have to be enough for now.

I hadn't eaten since breakfast, my throat was killing me and my head wasn't much better. The ache in my arm had faded fast enough and the headache was stress-related. All in all, if it wasn't for my throat, I guess I'd come through the day well enough.

Spinning around in my chair with my back to the bastard shadow, I took a moment to massage my temples and then I touched the skin of my neck. It felt hot—swollen and bruised, pretty much what I'd expected.

I'd already checked it out when I went to the bathroom earlier. One place he didn't follow me, thank God. I'd taken some Motrin, hoping it would help with the inflammation, although it didn't do much for the pain.

It looked just as bad as I'd figure it would

Angry red marks and ugly black bruises stood out against pale flesh. I now looked like somebody had tried to smash my throat in—imagine that. There was also bruising along the right side of my face where he'd slammed me down against the trunk, but that wasn't anything I couldn't handle.

Shutting down my computer, I pushed back from my desk and started shoving files into my bag. There were various police reports and Banner reports I still needed to work through and I might try to do a little more work in the privacy of my own home, away from this bastard, but for now? I was done.

Checking the time, I thought I should probably go ahead and pop another dose of the anti-inflammatories, so I headed into the small bathroom. I hit the light after I'd shut the door and stared at my reflection.

I don't look like much. Light blonde hair that I kept short. Pale skin. Dark eyes.

Right now the circles under my eyes made them look bruised…rather matched the line of bruises along the left side of my throat where his forearm had smashed against me, the mottled discoloration on my cheek where my face had a close, personal encounter with the car.

Thanks to my sleepless nights, I was color-coordinated with my bruising.

Grimacing, I opened the cabinet and grabbed the bottle of Motrin, popped the cap and shook out triple the dose a human would take. Bad thing about my bloodline was that although I healed a little quicker than humans, it took more for human meds to affect me. I was hoping that would also mean it would take more for the meds to damage my liver, because at the rate I was going, I'd be tearing the hell out of it, otherwise.

I had to chew the damn things up and damn, were they nasty, but swallowing them whole just wasn't an option. Swallowing felt like I was chugging down chopped-up razor blades. It would be better in a few days, I knew. Sadly, from experience. Until then, well, things were just going to suck while my body dealt with the damage. That's all there was to it.

Once I'd dosed myself back up, I slid back out of the bathroom and found Damon standing just outside the doorway.

Those gray eyes dropped to linger on my throat. I turned away.

"I'm calling it a day," I told him.

"About time."

It had been five hours since we'd left the rec club. The contrite Damon from outside the club had disappeared, and his asshole side had returned, leaving me to deal with it all afternoon. I'd been able to think more clearly when he was quiet, but I was on more even ground when he was being an asshole. Didn't know which was the better option yet.

"I'm starving," he said, trailing after me and watching as I slid my sword into the sheath slung around my hips. "Wherever we go to eat, are they going to let you take that in?"

In the middle of slinging my bag onto my shoulder, I paused. "We?" Then I shook my head. "Sorry. You're on your own."

I headed to the door.

A long arm barred my way.

"You seem to forget, kitten…the job and me, we're a package deal." He dipped his head and whispered against my hair, "You're stuck with me, around the clock, until we find the boy."

No. *Hell. No.*

Clenching my jaw, I backed away from him. "No. I have to tolerate you at my back during the day, that's fine. But I'm not putting up with you around the clock." Each word was like forcing glass out, but there was no way I was doing this.

Damon shrugged. "You don't have a choice. If you leave without me, I'll just follow, and I warn you, I'll be mad enough to do something nasty to that car of yours. If you try to lock me out of the house, I'll bust the door down."

While rage sounded an alarm in my ears, I flexed my hand. I didn't need this job that badly. Did I? Shit. I needed this like I needed a damned hole in the head. "I'll call the cops. Tell them you're hassling me," I said. "What then?"

"You can't." He winked at me.

The asshole *winked* at me.

"You see, you accepted the money. Remember that part where that's pretty much just like signing a contract? You agreed to the terms…including the part where I'm a package deal. You call the cops, I'll just explain that I was concerned for your safety and I was doing what I had to do to make sure you stayed under my direct supervision. Face it, kitten. You're stuck with me."

"Cyanide sounds so very appealing right now."

"You can't poison me with cyanide." He shrugged. "Would take a tankload."

"Not for you. For me. Probably the easiest way out of this mess."

If he thought I was going to actually sit down in a fucking restaurant with him, he was out of his mind. As long as I was driving, he'd get what I damned well felt like feeding him. And it turned out to be Arby's.

I sat in the drive-thru while he glared at me. "I'm fucking hungry," he snarled. "You did fast food earlier and you didn't eat a damn thing. We need a real meal."

The Motrin had actually helped this time. I could speak a little easier.

"You want to eat, you get it here. I'm tired and I want to go home," I said, leaning my head back and closing my eyes.

"I need real food."

"Then you're going to have to figure out some other way to get it. This is the only place I'm stopping."

"And if I decide to haul you elsewhere?"

"Try it." I smiled. "Please, try it. The only way you'll get me into a restaurant with you is if you drag me in there kicking and screaming."

I cracked one eye to look over at him. "I'm pretty sure your beloved Alpha frowns on that."

I'd heard a couple of her cats had gotten a little tanked a year ago. Shifters couldn't get drunk–they just burned through the alcohol. But they get high. The drugs had to be made specifically for their bloodline; do it right, though and it could work. These two had gotten very, very wasted.

It wasn't the drugs that had been the problem. They'd behaved…badly.

Shifters didn't like it when other shifters misbehaved in public. They could go as crazy as they wanted on their own turf—it didn't matter if they tore each other to ribbons for *looking* at each other wrong, but in public? Even an argument wasn't nice. These two hadn't argued—they'd tried to get naked and horizontal.

Somehow, I didn't think Damon wanted to drag me into a restaurant kicking and screaming.

"Fine," he growled.

It was a low, angry sound that filled the entire car. If I hadn't been so pleased about finally getting the better of him, I might have been a little scared. Okay, so what if my heart slammed up into my abused throat and I could all but taste the panic crashing through my veins?

I'd won something. So what if it was a piddly little pissing contest. It was something.

"Ma'am…I need your order…" a voice said uncertainly as several people behind us started to lay on their horns.

I said, "Diet Coke."

Then I looked pointed at Damon. He glared at me. "You need to eat."

I groaned and banged my head against the seat's headrest again.

Snarling filled the car and then he finally growled out an order. One that would have probably fed about four humans. I wasn't surprised. Shifters ate a lot. Earlier at

Burger King, I'd watched as he'd wolfed down three Whoppers.

Even when my throat didn't feel like it had been battered into bits, I couldn't eat a quarter of what he did. And I'm not one of those wilting females who didn't like to eat. I was actually pretty damned hungry, but there was nothing here I could eat and I wasn't going to torture myself by trying.

Ten minutes later, we were pulling out of the driveway. He tore into the food and I sipped at my drink, wincing at the sting of it. Home. Maybe a drink laced with whiskey. That would feel good. Then bed.

I'd hide out in my bedroom with my files, maybe a book in case I couldn't concentrate—

A foil-wrapped sandwich got dumped in my lap. "You need to eat."

I lowered my drink to the cupholder. A red light was coming up. After I'd stopped, I unwrapped the gooey mess and dropped the foil onto the console. Then, once I'd taken off, I threw the sandwich out the window.

"Hey!"

I smiled. "Not interested in eating that, thanks."

Yes. I needed to eat, but anything I ate right now would *hurt* and I wasn't about to let this son-of-a-bitch see that.

"Are you always this immature?"

I shrugged and licked some of the cheddar cheese of my fingers. "Depends on the company. When I'm around abusive, arrogant assholes, I tend to get very immature." The pain in my throat was going to be an issue for a few days. It wasn't anything I couldn't deal with, I knew, but I also couldn't keep avoiding eating for the next twenty-four or forty-eight hours, however long it took my body to deal with the swelling.

So I could either suffer and starve for the next couple of days...or I could hit up a friend. It seemed silly to suffer and starve when I had a friend who could do something about the pain.

Decision made, I headed out of town.

I hadn't seen Colleen in a few months, but I figured she wouldn't mind if I swung by this late in the evening.

"Where are you going?"

Drumming my nails on the steering wheel, I said, "You know...I'd really planned on being able to enjoy the silence tonight. After the shit day I've had, I'd really, really needed a quiet night."

"Yeah, well, I'm not exactly enjoying your company, either."

My friend was in her garden.

Colleen spent a lot of evenings there, and even more nights, especially since Mandy's death.

Once upon a time, she'd tried to pretend to live a nice, mortal life, but after her daughter had passed away, Colleen Antrim had given up that pretense. Mortal medicine hadn't saved her kid. Witchery wouldn't have saved the girl, either, but at least witchery wouldn't have made the suffering worse.

Mortal medicine had.

The poor girl had lost so much weight, her hair, her strength...everything. All because they kept holding out hope.

In the end, leukemia had gotten her anyway.

Colleen didn't bother coming out to greet me and I wasn't surprised.

I'd tried to convince the asshole bodyguard to wait in the car, but he didn't. He was polishing up the fourth order of fries and standing three feet away as I lowered myself to sit in the dirt next to Colleen.

"Hi, sweetheart," she said absently, stripping away the dead leaves from a plant I couldn't name. I knew my way around herbs and such, but Colleen liked the really exotic ones. I thought maybe this one was some sort of poppy. I couldn't be sure, but the leaves looked right.

"Hi, Leenie."

She frowned at the sound of my voice. I reached over at touched her hand, focusing hard. Witches were as different from one to another as shifters were. Different abilities, different gifts. Colleen had a gift for healing and empathy—it had made it that much harder on her when she hadn't been able to heal her daughter. She caught the intensity of my thoughts, though, thank God, and didn't speak out loud.

What is wrong with your throat, Kitasa?

Her question came more in images and feelings than actual words, but I picked it up well enough.

Don't ask right now. But can you help?

She went to reach up and I caught her wrist, shaking my head.

Sighing, she just stared into my eyes. *There is a lot of damage. A lot of swelling. The bruising is just the beginning. I'm surprised you can talk. How is your breathing?*

I shrugged. *Hurts to swallow. Hurts to talk. Haven't eaten a damn thing and it's making me cranky.*

A husky laugh escaped her. "Imagine that. Come along."

As we walked by Damon, she gave him an ugly look.

He snarled at her only to have the sound trapped in his throat. Literally. I felt the prickle of Colleen's magic and it made something inside me feel all warm and fuzzy.

I smiled. "Damon...this is Colleen Antrim. Of the Green Road Witches. She's one of their Healers."

They were one of the strongest witch houses in the country. And even an asshole shapeshifter wasn't going to fuck with one of their healers.

I swept in front of her, letting myself smile a little.

And it turned into a full-fledged grin a few minutes later when Colleen locked him out of her house. The door alone wouldn't have kept him out. But the magic did.

As she leaned back against it, the warmth of her wards settled around me and she folded her arms over her chest. "Okay. He can't hear us now. Talk."

"Can you fix this first?"

"There." Her hands fell away and she studied my throat with critical eyes. "It's the best I can do unless you want a full healing."

"I can't." Shaking my head, I got up and went to the mirror. I swallowed tentatively and sighed in relief. It ached a little, but it was more like the injury was a week old instead of hours. Grimacing, I stared at the mottled line of bruises that lingered. They'd faded to a sickly yellow and green that wasn't really any more appealing than the blue and black from earlier. "Can't you do anything about those?"

"Not unless you want a full healing," she said again.

"No." A full-healing would drain me and leave me down for a good twenty-four hours. I didn't know if the crazy cat-bitch would give me twenty-four hours. And... blowing out a sigh, I let myself acknowledge the fact that I wouldn't take time away from the job. The boy needed help. I needed rest and I'd let myself take it, but I sure as hell wasn't going go down for a day just because I had a sore throat. After another look at my neck, I explained what had happened and looked up to find her watching me with resignation in her eyes.

"Just what were you thinking, goading a cat-shifter that far?" Colleen asked.

I shrugged and prodded my throat again. Earlier, the flesh had felt hot to touch, inflamed, I guessed, but it was better now. This was definitely better. "I wasn't trying to. He's just an asshole."

"Pity. He's hotter than hell," she murmured.

"All the good ones."

We met each other's gaze in the mirror and grinned. "The hot ones are either taken, one of the walking dead or not worth messing with."

He definitely fell into the last category.

Flicking a glance at my watch, I said, "I need to go. He's been out there fuming almost fifteen minutes now. If I push my luck, he's probably going to try his hand at breaking your wards."

"Let him try. He'll end up hurting more than he can possibly imagine. It will serve him right." She sniffed.

I shrugged. "Nah. Not worth you having to rebuild them." I grabbed my things from the couch and stood up. "I...ah...I need a favor. It's..."

Her eyes went dark.

There wasn't much that would have me hesitating with Colleen and she knew it.

"What is it, sweetie?"

"The job I'm on. The boy."

"The runaway." She inclined her head.

"Yes."

Her child had run away, too. Her sick child, the one she'd lost.

"Can you ask if anybody has heard anything about him? He's close to spiking. He'll probably set off alarms wherever he goes."

Her face twisted in sympathy. "That's a dangerous mess there, Kit. Why did they drag you into this? Don't you know better than to take jobs like this from the cats?"

"Hell, yes. I..." I rubbed my hands over my face. "It was the boy."

"The boy," she murmured. "What did they do, show you a picture of him? Sing you a sad song about him?"

"Like a song would bother me." I plucked a non-existent thread on my vest.

"A picture, then. Damn it, Kit. How do you land yourself in this kind of trouble?"

"Beats the hell out of me," I muttered.

"Well, it looks like they are already working on that." She reached up and touched my throat.

Truer words…

We made it to the car before Damon spoke.

I enjoyed the reprieve.

But the second the doors closed, he laid back into me. "You don't seem to get this…you're stuck with me, Kit."

"Nope. Not quite getting it yet, sorry."

He leaned in, staring at my face, then he cocked his head, studying my throat, craning his head to look at my face. When he went to push my hair back, I smacked his hand away. Surprisingly, he let me.

"Your voice is different."

"Allergies," I lied. "Colleen's a wonder. I didn't have the tea I usually drink so I came by for a refill and had a cup while we chatted."

"Liar."

I didn't respond.

"You had her heal your throat."

I tapped my nails on the steering wheel and contemplated the night sky as I started the car.

"Shit. I…" The thick slashes of his brows dropped low over his eyes. "You're weaker than I thought. You're not human and…hell. I'm sorry. I didn't mean to do that much damage."

Years of abuse had taught me how to hide my emotions. I hadn't had to use it as much in recent years, but I was going to have to brush those skills back up, I suspected. Starting now.

Without responding, I put the car into drive and pulled off.

"How human are you?"

I turned on the radio.

He turned it back off. "I asked you a question, little girl."

Sighing, I looked over at him. "Where exactly is it in your job description or in that so-called contract that you get to bully me? How much human blood I carry doesn't affect the job I'll do."

He stared at me.

I could feel the weight of it as I sped back toward town.

But when I reached over and turned on the radio, this time, he was quiet.

Ah…finally. Silence.

Chapter Six

There was a time when the town had been called Winter Haven. Full of snowbirds and pretty little houses and condos.

Now it was a hell-hole for some of the wolves and cats and witches who didn't want to fall in line with the local packs, and who wouldn't pay the tithe to join the witch houses. The witch houses weren't a bad thing, per se. They offered protection and the strength of numbers, but you had to live by their rules. Some of us didn't do rules very well.

Those people often ended up in places like this.

I wouldn't call it the *slums*, exactly, because plenty of people here had money.

They just usually came about it in less than ideal ways.

The little sign that used to read *Winter Haven* now read *Wolf Haven*, thanks to some ingenious soul and his clever hand with a can of spray paint. It looked like they'd tried to cover it over with *Cat* and *witch* several times. But the wolves were the first ones who had come here, more than fifty years ago when the human world had first found out about us.

This place had been called Wolf Haven for a very long time.

It wasn't going to get changed to *Cat* Haven just because somebody tried to spray it on a sign.

I parked the car but didn't climb out. This was the very last place I wanted to be. I had good memories of this place…and bad. I'd still been broken when I finally stopped running. This was where I'd stopped. Sometimes, I wished I'd never left.

I could understand why some people thought Doyle might have come to Wolf Haven. A place where almost anybody could lose themselves. Lose themselves… hide. I'd hidden here for a few years myself.

Had hidden here very well, but I'd done it by being inconspicuous, something I couldn't do with the demonic Damon next to me. Tapping my nails on the steering wheel, I stared at the square, squalid building in front of me. TJ still worked there. I liked TJ. She was…well, TJ was TJ. And if anybody had seen Doyle in the area, TJ would know.

It might cost me some money, but that was fine.

"I don't suppose I can convince you to let me go inside there by myself, can I?" I asked.

He shot me a disbelieving look.

"I didn't think so."

I reached over the back seat and closed my hand around my blade. She warmed under my palm. In the back of my head, I could feel her pleasure and it made me smile. "I'm taking my sword. I don't care how many damned shifters we run into, I don't care how many problems you think it will solve for me to be unarmed. I'm not walking through Wolf Haven unarmed."

He stared at me.

I stared back at him.

Minutes ticked away until I finally broke visual contact and climbed out of the car.

Since he wasn't snarling at me or demanding to pat me down for weapons, I had to assume he saw the sense in letting me keep the sword.

He was really going to be happy with me in a minute.

TJ didn't let *anybody* in her place with a weapon.

I locked the car and hoped it would be in the same condition when I got back. I wasn't terribly attached to the damn thing, but it was the only car I had and I didn't have the money to get it fixed if they did a lot of damage. My insurance also wouldn't *pay* for anything that was done to it if I was in Wolf Haven—I hadn't picked up the vandalism rider for it because I just didn't have the damn money.

As we crossed the street, somebody ducked out from TJ's and a grin split my face.

Hey, maybe luck was smiling on me.

"I'll be a son-of-a-bitch."

"You always were," I said cheerfully to the mountain standing there.

His name was Goliath, and like his namesake, he was big. I'm talking big-as-a-mountain big. He had hands the size of dinner plates, a massive, deep chest and when he spoke, his voice rumbled out of him like it was coming from deep within the earth. When he shifted to the half-beast some of them used, he was so damned big, the ground shuddered under his feet when he walked.

Goliath had come to Wolf Haven after the alpha of his pack had tried to kill him. He'd failed—Goliath had beaten the shit out of him. With his own hands. Before he'd spiked. You'd think people would respect that kind of strength, but instead, they'd turned on him and chased him out, threatening to kill him and his kid sister.

Goliath and his sister had settled here under TJ's protective wing. Sort of.

A lot of people came and went around here. Even his sister had eventually drifted off. But not Goliath. He'd never leave TJ.

"What the fuck you doing here, Colbana?" Goliath grumbled, his watery blue eyes peering down at me as I crossed the road.

"Slumming. Wanna run away with me?"

The sidewalk was a crumbled ruin under my feet and I sidestepped a pitted hole as I came to a stop a few feet away from Goliath. At my back, I was all too aware of Damon's presence, hot, edgy and breathing down my neck.

In contrast, Goliath's wolf hovered around him all nice and snug. Curled up like he was taking a nap or something. Big as he was, Goliath was one of the most peaceful, restful people I'd ever met in my life.

"If I did that, TJ would have both our hides." But he smiled at me and reached out, patting my head with one of those plate-sized hands.

I felt Damon tense behind me.

"Knock it off, he's a friend," I said, glancing over my shoulder.

Goliath snorted. "Colbana, kid, you need to watch the company you keep. That's one of the Alpha cat's little toy soldiers. Why you running with him?"

"'Cuz he's pretty?"

Goliath stroked a hand down his goatee and made a strangled sound deep in his throat. Most people wouldn't recognize it as a laugh. "Hell. Nobody is *that* pretty. Find somebody else if you just want a pretty shadow."

"I can't." I grimaced. "I'm doing a job. Speaking of which...I need to talk to TJ."

"Figured. Weapons."

I grinned a little as I heard Damon's snort. Then, as I slid my sword out of her sheath, he swore. "What the fuck—?"

I smiled at him. "I need information and I don't get it if I go in armed."

Goliath tapped his chest. "I'm all the weapon Kit needs." Then he gave Damon a dismissive look. "You are on your own."

I finished stripping away my weapons and turned them over to Goliath who stored them in a chest for just such a reason. He lingered over the sword, stroking a hand down it. "Try to behave this time, Kit."

I blinked at him, giving him my most innocent smile.

He wasn't fooled. Sighing, he locked it up and gestured us through. I was prepared for the magic.

Damon wasn't. I tried to act like I didn't take a little bit of pleasure from his startled grunt, but I didn't pretend for long. Inherent honesty is a flaw of mine. "Keep moving," I said over my shoulder. "Easier that way."

The pins and needles sensation would only get worse if we lingered, although it was enough to drive anybody but the determined right back outside.

Once TJ trusted you, she could have it keyed so that the ward didn't hit so hard, but I'd been gone a long time. Spells didn't have long memories.

As I finally crossed through, the familiar smell of beer, fried food and magic flooded my head.

TJ was looking right at me and she had a cross-bow aimed at my chest. Pretty much exactly like the first time she'd met me. "Well, well, well. Look what the cats dragged in."

"Hiya, TJ."

She sneered at me and laid the crossbow down over the stumps of her legs.

Damon hissed in a breath.

TJ's eyes, glowing in the dim light, shot to him. "What, you ain't ever seen a werewolf before?"

Oh, I was pretty sure he had.

But a werewolf who was missing her legs from below the knees...that was a different story.

The local cat Alpha was a nasty piece of work.

Goliath's Alpha had been a jackass.

But TJ's Alpha had been a sadist of the highest order.

She had been one of his...toys, she'd told me. And she'd tried to run. So he'd made it to where she could never run again, severing her legs just below the knee. A shapeshifter can heal from almost anything. But she hadn't been given the chance because a healer had been forced to heal her, cauterizing the flesh and leaving her damaged legs as they were.

Sometimes I wondered where the bastard was.

I'd liked to find him.

I'd like to kill him.

But I knew he was out of my league…*if* he was still alive. TJ had a way of catching up with her enemies. A fact I'd learned here in Wolf Haven.

As her eyes continued glow and swirl in the dim light, I glanced at Damon over my shoulder and then back at her. "Hey, TJ, it's okay."

She harrumphed. "You got lousy taste in men, bitch."

"Not like that." I hunched my shoulders.

"Then get rid of him. If you can't fuck him, he ain't no use." She grabbed the wheels of her chair and made her way over to the table. "Josie—I need a beer. Get one for my friend."

She gave Damon a dark look. "You ain't my friend."

Damon lifted his hands.

Josie—at least I assumed that was her—was a girl I hadn't met, working back behind the bar. I'd worked there for a long while. Before I was old enough to be legal, truth be told, but TJ had taken care of me. She'd been the first person to do so. As I sat down, I positioned myself so I could see both doors and the bar. TJ didn't bother watching either one. Nobody would get through that door without Goliath approving them.

"Been a while since you came this way," TJ said softly, her eyes resting on my face. "Still running?"

"No."

Josie came over and plunked two beers down in front of us before stomping back over the bar. There were a couple of men hunched over their drinks there but they weren't looking at us. People in TJ's joint made a study of not noticing anybody.

Unless, of course, they were TJ. TJ made of a study of noticing *everybody*.

"So if you're not running, what you up to?" TJ asked, taking a drink from the mug in front of her.

"Working." I shrugged. I glanced around, remembering the day when I realized I had to do something other than pull drinks behind the bar. TJ had pushed that on me. She knew a witch, she told me. They needed grunt work. Wasn't much, but they needed somebody decent, trustworthy…that was how I had met Colleen.

"Hear you've worked your way up…doing shit for the Assembly." Her eyes narrowed. "That can be dangerous. You okay with that?"

"Sometimes." I shot a dark look at Damon. "Lately? Not so much."

"I could help with that." She smiled at me.

Damon's eyes flashed.

Sighing, I said, "Not necessary, TJ." Reaching into my vest, I pulled out the picture. The only reason why it *wasn't* necessary. It was nice, though, realizing she'd be willing to help me out. Of course, if she knew who he was…

Even before I had the picture out, though, she grimaced. "Just keep the option open, Kit. Don't know why you'd wanna work for that crazy bitch in Orlando." She looked at Damon. "Only reason why *he* would be with you."

"Damon, your rep precedes you."

He skimmed a hand back over his head. "Can we hurry this along?"

Flashing a grin at TJ, I said, "He's cranky." Then, as I laid the picture flat, my smile faded. "We're looking for a kid. He's young. Close to spiking. He ran."

TJ reached out and caught the bottom edge of the picture, drawing it close as she hunched over it. "Lots of bad shit happening with kids lately, Colbana. You heard any of it?"

"Seen all sorts of runaway reports, but that's it." Impatience gnawed at me, but I didn't rush her. I knew better. Instead, I studied the mug in front of me. I hadn't taken so much as a sip yet and I was kind of nervous. This was a shifter bar. And although shifters couldn't get drunk the way humans could, if they worked it right, they could get a little bit of a buzz. TJ made her own beer. Think 200 proof. Maybe *400* proof.

Curling my hand around the mug, I lifted it up. One sip had my eyes popping open. "Wow."

TJ snickered. "Couple drinks of my brew and I'll have you dancing naked, Kit."

"Then I'll stop at two." I took one more and eased it away. A comfortable buzz settled in my head and I studied the mug consideringly. If I didn't have to work…

A big, bronzed hand closed around it.

Scowling, I watched as Damon pulled it out of my reach.

"She already said you ain't her friend," I muttered.

"I ain't," he retorted. "But I am your bodyguard."

Then, with a smile, he downed half of it.

"Jerk." I looked at TJ and asked, "Why do I always end up surrounded by jerks?"

She shrugged. "Beats me. There was that one kid from the Banner unit. He was nice."

"Oh." A smile curved my lips. "Yeah. Justin. I liked Justin."

TJ snickered. "A girl would have to be dead not to like Justin."

Sighing, I muttered, "I ain't dead."

Justin had moved on to more profitable, more pleasurable pastures. The kind where he could kill many, many things without getting in trouble for it, and get paid lots and lots of money.

"Josie. My friend needs water. I forget what a lightweight she is."

Balefully, I glared at TJ. "You're the one who ordered the damn beer for me," I pointed out.

"You're the one who drank it."

We grinned at each other for a minute. Then my water appeared and she went back to studying the picture. "He's a nice looking kid," she murmured as I guzzled my water. "If he'd been around, I would have heard."

"Yeah. I know."

"I haven't heard."

"Shit." I finished off the water and then pinched my nose. "What were you talking about, trouble with the kids?"

She shrugged. "Just odd shit. I can't pin it. But they disappear. Not the drift-on sort of shit. When they drift on, I hear where they go. This...it's like they just... aren't there."

"Okay." I reached for the picture and put it back in my pocket. As I stood up, I pulled a bill from my pocket.

TJ glared at me. "I ain't needing that."

"I didn't say you did." I left it on the table as I circled around the table. I'd like to hug her, but I knew she'd hurt me if I did. Instead, I rested a hand on her shoulder.

She covered my hand with hers. "Don't stay gone so long next time, Kit."

"I won't."

As I headed to the door, she said my name. I paused.

The two men at the bar pushed around me and I glared at them as they crashed into me.

TJ curled her lip in their direction and muttered something and then ignored them, focusing on me. "Maybe next time you can plan to crash for the night," she said. "I'll get you wasted and you really *can* dance on the bar."

"Oh, no." I shook my head. "I did that *one* time."

"And it was a fun time..."

Snorting, I headed on out the door. The pins and needles of her containment spell tore into my flesh, no less severe in its intensity on the exit. It was designed to drive people *away*. Odd, really. She ran a fucking *bar*. She should be drawing people in.

But she never lacked for business.

And nobody fucked with her.

Ever.

The spell spat us out in a rush and I stumbled out, groaning as the final slash of it dug into my skin.

A big hand caught me. "Easy, girl."

I glanced up at Goliath. "How do you ever get used to that?"

"Hey...it's keyed into me. Besides, a person can get used to most anything." He grinned at me. "You know that better than anybody, don't you?"

I might have answered that, but I heard a grunt from behind and Goliath's massive hand jerked me out of the way just before Damon could crash into me. "Sheeet," he muttered. "That cat ain't got no grace to him."

I snickered.

Damon just glared at us. But the look on his face was a little...off.

Nice. Magic unsettled him.

A quick look at my car told me it was still in one piece. "You going to be on the clock a while still?"

Goliath shrugged. "Done in thirty. But if you're going to be around, I can hang."
I smiled at him.

A dull flush rose on his cheeks. "Just don't be such a stranger."

"I won't." With a sigh, I turned around and studied the streets. They hadn't changed, yet oddly enough, nothing was the same. People came and went like eddies in the sand around here. I hadn't ever made an impact and that had been the entire point. I didn't *want* to make an impact, didn't want anybody to remember me, to think about me. Just another one of TJ's strays.

"If you're looking for news on a kid, try looking for Keeli," Goliath rumbled.

I slanted a look up at him.

He shrugged. "Keeli…" He paused, glancing at the building at his back and then at me. "She doesn't like TJ. TJ doesn't like her. But the little witch hears things."

"And where can I find Keeli?"

He curled his lip. "Getting high." He waved his hand, gesturing down the street. "She likes Torque cut with coke—you can find her hiding in whatever hole-in-the-wall she can find. But you better be careful. She's just as likely to talk to you as she is to stab you."

"Wow. I can't imagine why TJ doesn't like her. She sounds charming."

Goliath chuckled. He glanced at my car and then at me. "I'll watch your ride. Can't watch you if you're off crawling the streets, but maybe that toy soldier has some use."

I scowled and glanced behind me, realizing I'd mostly forgotten about Damon. At least for a few minutes.

He stood there, glowering, with his arms crossed over his chest.

Goliath opened the chest and I reached for my weapons. "I guess we'll find out."

I wasn't really looking forward to it, though. I'd managed to make it here because I'd made a study of not being *seen*. Not by using that cloak of invisibility, but just by not drawing attention to myself. I was pretty damn certain this guy wouldn't know how to blend if he had to.

Two hours.

No luck.

And it was getting dark.

As we cut back up the street, I had to admit that Keeli, whoever she was, just didn't want to be found.

Okay.

Maybe we'd try to come back—

"Hey."

I heard the low, wasted rasp of a voice and looked down the alley.

Damon caught my arm.

I stopped and glanced at him. I wasn't an idiot.

Popping my wrist, I turned to the sound of the voice and waited.

A shadow moved. "Hear you're looking for Keeli."

"You've got good ears." *Or you've just been in the area for the past few hours*, I thought sourly.

The shadow crept closer. Light reflected off a man's face before he eased back into the shadow.

"I can tell you where to find her…but it will cost you."

Wow. What a surprise, that.

Fishing a bill out of my pocket, I knelt down on the ground and found a rock. I wrapped the bill around it and tossed it into the alley. "There."

Silence stretched out. "That'll do, kid. But…trust me. You don't want me shouting this news. You're looking for news on the Alpha's boy, right?"

Damon tensed at my back.

"What do you know?" I asked, staring into the alley.

I could see him.

Dirty face. Young. Grimy.

He smiled at me.

"I know all sorts of things, girl," he murmured.

My skin crawled, but if he knew something…

I slid Damon another look. His eyes were glowing. His hand gripped my arm. But when I stepped forward, he was right there by me.

They went for him first.

Through the roar of blood in my ears, I heard Damon swearing. That was kind of funny. There were four of them and he was cussing them out?

But then one of them howled… A death scream. One that made the skin on my nape crawl as I slashed through the air with my blade.

She was made like a rapier, but heavier. I could hack away for hours if I had to, and the fool in front of me was bleeding from more cuts than even I could count; he was either too weak or too underfed to heal them well. He made another lunge at me and I drove the blade through his heart, twisting it and jerking upward. Skin smoked as it met the silver and I watched as the life in his eyes faded.

Jerking my blade free, I turned, braced for another attack.

All I saw was Damon. Walking toward me with blood dripping off him, falling in fat drops from his fingers.

"Show off," I muttered.

A flash of white appeared in his face. I almost thought he was smiling.

But that faint smile was gone in another second as shadows came rushing at us from all around.

I found myself shoved to the ground.

There was a rumbling sound—something I couldn't identify.

And another sound—one I could.

The ground was shaking, I thought. As I pushed up onto my elbows, I saw a giant shape rushing into the alley.

Goliath.

Hell was about to break loose.

Then a cat roared and I heard somebody scream. Maybe it already had.

As the fighting raged over my head, I rolled to the side and flexed my wrist. My blade was gone. I managed to get my back to the wall of the busted, broken building behind me, using it for support and shadow as I surveyed the mess in front of me.

Five, six, seven—yeah. Seven scraggly wolves fighting Goliath and Damon. The wolves had shifted. Damon and Goliath hadn't. Two wolves were trying to take Goliath down and he casually caught one, ripped its head off. My gut went a little queasy at the sight.

The second one didn't fare much better.

Damon wasn't quite so casual.

Quick, brutal.

But for every one they took down, several more came crawling out of the shadows.

What the hell—?

Panting for breath, I flexed my wrist and called my blade.

Off to the side, I heard a snarl.

The wolf came for me just as I turned to face it.

I never even got my blade up.

I came to at the bright flare of light.

It wasn't the light that woke me.

It was the pain.

Ripping through my side and eating its way through my veins. I choked back the scream as TJ leaned over me. "Damn, girl. You did it again, didn't you?"

I glared at her. Or tried to. The tears in my eyes were pretty much blinding me.

"Get the fuck *back*."

Well. One thing was clear. I wasn't dying, because if I was, no way would I be hearing that voice. Even if I was going straight to hell, I'd be deluding myself with angel song to the very end. So if I was hearing the demonic Damon that must mean the wolf bite on my side wasn't fatal.

His face appeared in my line of sight and I closed my eyes.

"Stupid little fool!" His voice cut through the pained shrieking in my head. But the hands on my side were gentle. "Shit...shit, shit, this is bad—"

"Chill out, cat. She ain't going to change her skin. She can't—"

TJ, there. I knew that voice, too. Focus. Stay focused on the voices. Focus. Concentrate...the chills hit me in the next moment. Oh, great. First the chills—

"Come on, Kit. Breathe..."

Goliath.

I tried to open my eyes and focus on his face. "You were supposed to be the weapon," I panted out.

I thought I saw a pained look on his face. But it was hard to say as I groaned. The spasms starting ripping me through me.

This was going to be fun…

Three hours later, I finally stopped puking up my guts.

That was when I knew I was done.

It was another two before TJ decided to *let* me leave.

Damon was furious.

As Goliath eased me into the passenger seat, Damon was already behind the steering wheel, staring straight ahead with a flinty look in his eyes.

"Sorry things didn't work out with Keeli," Goliath said quietly, crouching down by the door and staring at me.

I grimaced. "It's okay. If you can just…well. Ask around."

He nodded, but there was a troubled look on his face. "She…I don't know, but I don't think she's here. She would have shown up. Keeli likes trouble, and this…this was trouble. Don't think it was about you, though. Those wolves, they been gunning for the cats and TJ and me a long time. They saw the Alpha's boy there, figured they'd take a shot, I bet. One of them had been in the bar earlier. Left before you all did. Guess they decided to have some fun with him. Then I show up…" He shrugged and sighed. "You just got caught in the crossfire."

"All that for nothing, then."

"Sorry, Kit."

I shook my head. "'S'okay." In the end, it was. Not like a wolf bite was going to do me in. A bad one might make me dog sick while my body dealt with the poison, but that was it.

"We're going," Damon snapped, revving the engine.

Goliath stood, one massive hand lingering on the top edge of the door. "I'll be in contact if I hear any more, Kit. But I don't think your kid has been around here. Don't think he will be, either. Nobody comes here unless they have no place else to go. He had other options."

Did he, though?

I kept the question behind my teeth.

Once we were speeding down the road, Damon said, his voice thick with sarcasm, "That was just a brilliant plan. You got any other ideas? Fun ways to get yourself killed?"

"Oh, please." Closing my eyes, I sank back into the seat. "I didn't even come close to getting myself killed."

"If there'd been a few more wolves, I wouldn't have gotten to you," he growled.

I laughed. "Honey…you weren't the equalizing force there. Goliath was. And TJ. They were the reasons I felt safe loitering in the area," I said, sighing. The pain in my side had settled to a low ache. TJ kept a witch in house. She wasn't trained by the formal houses, but she was skilled.

There would be scars. Scars didn't bother me, though. I could live with them. I had more than my fair share already. And since it was the were virus fighting its way out of my system, any injury I had would heal even faster.

51

It tore through me at an accelerated rate and I hated every second, but it was done fast. Throw in a decent healing and I'd be good as new in a few days.

Just in time to be battered, bit or otherwise abused in another day or two.

Chapter Seven

Two days later, I found a report from the Banner unit.

A witch.

The only name they had for her was Keeli.

I stared at her face—gaunt, with hollow cheeks, circles under her eyes and scars all over her face, like she'd caught one of the diseases that rarely hit humans these days. Chicken pox, maybe.

Drugs had hit her hard.

Death had hit her harder.

They'd found her a hundred and fifty miles south of East Orlando, her body naked, scraped up, scratched up and marked by mosquito bites.

Judging by the condition of her feet, she'd been walking a long, long time, I thought.

I reached for the phone.

"What are you doing?"

"Ignoring you," I said to Damon.

He glared at me and came around to study the report.

He eyes locked on it, skimming it over. "Keeli…" Then he snorted. "Shit, that bastard was trying to work you over."

"No." I dialed TJ's number. "Must be sad, Damon, not having friends you can trust."

The hand resting on the table curled into a fist.

I looked away as TJ answered.

"Hey, TJ. I need to ask you a question…"

Keeli's death was so far the only thing I'd uncovered.

Four days in and I hadn't found much of anything about the boy I'd been hired to find. The boy I *had* to find if I didn't want a death warrant placed on my tail.

I was about ready to just throw myself off the top of the Epcot Center just to get away from it all.

The only problem I wasn't sure if it would kill me. Wolf bites wouldn't do it, and neither would nearly being strangled. Would that jump? Nah. Probably not. It would just hurt. And probably hurt like hell.

I wasn't human enough to die easily.

The sound of the phone ringing was enough to shatter what remained of my frayed nerves but I pretended not to hear it. No reason to act as though I had, after all. Somebody was calling Damon on his phone and it might not have anything to do with me.

Except I recognized the odd, blank look that came over his face when he was talking to *My Lady*. Shit. That title was enough to turn my stomach.

There was both an upside and a downside to these conversations. He'd be taciturn and quiet for hours. Awesome. The downside? He'd be even more of an asshole after the silence passed.

Not so awesome.

Pushing open the front door, I leaned against the doorjamb as he carried on his conversation behind me. Reports being checked, had investigated a number of possible areas in East Orlando where he might have gone—no luck at this point.

Yes, yes, My Lady—I'm so very sorry…

I tuned him out. I didn't need to worry about the asshole behind me because there was a problem in front of me. Walking toward me with a small smile on his pretty face.

The rays of the setting gilded his features. Golden hair, made silver by the bright light. Long, lean easy grace. Lovely green eyes.

There he was…Jude in the flesh. Out in the bright light of the evening sun.

But why now?

"You keep refusing to come when I call. So I do as you said to Evangeline. I came to you," he murmured into my mind.

I tensed, mentally going on retreat, but it didn't help. He was still a presence crowding into my skull, one I couldn't shut out no matter how hard I tried.

As he came to a stop in front of me, I tried not to gape at him. Tried not to glare.

I also, to my disgust, had to try not to drool.

Jude was a sexy, sexy work of art, one that got better with age, but I didn't want to think about that. Didn't want to think about him at all, really.

"I wish to hire you," he said quietly, keeping his voice low.

That didn't stop Damon from hearing him.

I heard the shifter's voice trip over the phone, then steady. *Yes, yes, My Lady, everything is well…*

I stepped aside and gestured. The small, inner office was spelled—work by some of Colleen's fellow witches. It would work well enough.

And *hello*…I could piss Damon off.

He came off the couch the second he saw Jude.

I waggled my fingers at him.

"I assure you, we are making progress, My Lady. Ruling things out is part of the process," Damon said, his voice calm and easy even as he swiped out a hand for me.

Jude blocked it, summarily shoving me forward.

Good grief. I stumbled into my office just in time for Jude to slip in behind me and shut the door.

That was all it took to activate the spelling.

I'd have to open it for anybody to enter. Unless somebody busted the wards. A witch could do it. Weaker shifters couldn't. Vamps were incapable—wards were earth magic, living magic. Vampires couldn't break them if they tried. Sadly, Damon was a strong shifter. Give him enough time and I knew he could break the damn ward.

"Well, well, little warrior," Jude murmured, turning to face me. "You pick unusual company these days. That's Annette's most favorite toy. How did you get so lucky? She doesn't like to share her toys."

Annette. The cat-bitch's name was Annette. It didn't suit her. Kitty-cat Barbie was so much more fun.

I sneered at him and dropped down into one of the chairs.

"He's not a toy I'm interested in playing with," I muttered. Then I mentally cringed, knowing exactly how Jude would take it.

Yep. Seconds later, his hand stroked over my cheek. "I'm glad to hear it, little warrior. I'm not particularly good at sharing myself...and I'd hate to have to share you with that."

I batted his hand away. "Newsflash, vamp. I'm not yours."

"So you keep insisting." He snagged the only other piece of furniture in the room, another chair, and swung it around. He straddled it and stared at me as he rested his arms on the back. "Why are you working with cats?"

"A job. Money. Same reason I take any job."

His gaze flickered down to my throat. "It's a job that's gotten you in trouble already. Is it paying well?"

"Not well enough," I muttered.

A fist slammed against the door and I groaned as I felt the magic of the ward crackle. "Open the fucking door, Colbana."

"He has a nasty temper," Jude murmured.

Absently, I touched my throat. "I can handle it." To be fair, Damon hadn't laid a hand on me since that first day, except to push me out of the way a few times. It had been necessary more than a few times, and not just when we'd gone trolling down in Wolf Haven.

"I heard the Alpha's nephew was missing."

I shot Jude a dark look as the pounding at the door increased. Damon shouted, "Colbana, open the door or I'm going to wring your fucking neck again."

Sighing, I leaned forward and buried my face in my hands.

A hand touched my knee. Cool as death. I knocked it aside.

Too bad I couldn't brush aside the whisper in my mind.

"She does not tolerate failure, Kit. Why did you take this job?"

I shoved up out of the chair.

The hell would I answer him.

Jude continued to watch me while Damon banged away on the door. Each time he did, the magic sparked. He'd break the ward soon. It would cost me money to put it back up if he broke it. "I can't let him break my wards. I need the safe room."

"Look at me."

I shouldn't.

But I did.

The green of his gaze started to glow.

"If you fail her, it's likely she will try to have you killed. You already know this."

With a short nod, I acknowledged that. What was the point in denying it?

"I can help you. Not many can stand against the cat Alpha. But I can."

Rolling my eyes, I stared at him. Why in the hell would he?

I knew I amused him, but my amusement factor wasn't going to get me that far in life.

He came out of the seat. *"Would you like a way out, Kit? It will not cost you much."*

"Uh-huh." I wasn't about to become another one of his servants.

A faint smile canted Jude's lips upward. *"I have enough of those. Just…"* He brushed his fingertips along my bruised neck. *"One taste. For now. Another when you require my assistance…should it come to that."*

I tensed. *No.*

"Why not? It's just a taste, Kit. And it will not harm you, nor bind you…and if it comes to it, it could be the very thing to save to you."

Why in the world would he be willing to fuck with the Alpha Cat just for a taste of my blood?

A smile pulled his lips back from his teeth and the glow in his eyes started to go red.

"Fucking with her is reason enough. But you…you amuse me, as you already know. And you are…unique. Now…do we have a deal?"

The banging at the door grew louder and something that looked like lightning whipped around the room.

With a curse, I shoved my wrist into his face. The wrist would have to work. My throat had been abused enough lately.

Jude smiled.

It had hurt.

Plain and simple.

There was nothing erotic or seductive about it, although I know they can make it pleasant.

I don't think he wanted it to be pleasant, and I'm actually happy with that.

He did seal the wounds; another thing I was happy about, despite the fact that it only made it hurt more.

The entire exchange lasted maybe fifteen seconds.

I had maybe another thirty before Damon would break the wards.

Jerking away from him, I went to the door. Under my hand, the door knob buzzed. The magic responded to my touch and the abused wards faded away. Since they hadn't been broken, once they had enough time, they'd rebuild themselves and be as strong as they had been before the bastard had started beating on them—the beauty of things made from the earth. They healed.

I opened the door and then found myself on the ground, shoved there by Jude's hands just in time to avoid a punch that just might have caved my head in.

"You should show more control, cat," Jude said icily as he helped me to my feet.

Damon's face was fixed in an awful snarl. And something…I bit back a curse as I stared at him. His face was awful. The bones were stretched and terribly wrong and he looked…bigger. Nearly a head taller, broader, with the cloth of his shirt stretched too tight over his chest and shoulders.

But as I stared at him, the bones shifted. Melted back into place. "What kind of little fool locks herself in a room with a vampire?" he asked, panting out the question.

"One who has business to discuss with him," I said dryly. "And you were on the phone."

"Business…" Damon shook his head. "You're otherwise engaged for the time being."

"Hmmm. Yes, so I've heard," Jude said. Then he reached into his pocket and pulled out a folded slip of paper. "A retainer, Ms. Colbana. For when you're no longer so occupied. I'd appreciate a call at your earlier convenience."

Damon went to snatch the check away.

I managed to get it first.

I was not going on retainer for that jerk.

Except if I didn't take the damned check, Damon was going to think he had something to do with it. Shoving it into my pocket, I turned away and headed over to my desk. "I'll be in touch when I can, Jude."

Absently I flexed the wrist he'd bitten. He hadn't taken much. I couldn't even tell.

"*I can—*"

I tensed.

His voice was heavier in my head. Fuller.

Oh, *shit*.

Seconds later, he was gone.

"What in the hell did he want?" Damon growled.

I dropped down into my seat, determined to ignore the creeping sensation of dread crawling through my stomach. I wasn't going to freak about this. Nope. Wasn't going to do it. Folding my hands across my belly, I stared into Damon's dark gray eyes. "You heard him. He wants me available for a job when I'm done with this."

"You shouldn't work for vampires. They're dangerous, slippery creatures."

"Yes, and it's so much better working for cats, Hell, for werecreatures of any kind for that matter," I muttered. "In the past four days, I've had a number of them try to attack me, I've got a nasty scar on my torso—"

"Hey, Wolf Haven was *your* move, not mine," he interjected.

"Yes, but we were attacked by weres…not vamps, not humans, not my kind. Weres." Narrowing my eyes at him, I leaned forward and added, "My so-called bodyguard has almost crushed my throat. Every time I go into a business, I get patted down and twice, I've had somebody grab my tits—"

He slammed his hands down on my desk so hard, I felt the damn thing vibrate. "Twice?"

I stared at him.

"What in the fuck does that mean?"

The phone rang.

I reached for it only to have him grab my wrist. "What in the fuck does that mean, Colbana?"

"Do you want me to do my job or not?" I snapped.

"Answer the fucking question."

The call rolled over and a familiar voice filled the air. "Heya, Kitty girl, it's Lincoln down at Banner Central. I heard you were looking for a runner. I don't know if this is the one you're looking for…"

Damon let go of my wrist.

As I reached for the phone, I glared at him. "I really wish I'd never laid eyes on you," I muttered.

He glared right back.

Chapter Eight

I don't pray much.

But as we drove to Banner HQ, or Bureau of Non-Human Affairs Headquarters for the Florida Region, I was praying, and praying hard.

Lincoln had some info on a runaway.

Actually, what he had was a body.

And if it was the body of the kid I was searching for, I was going to need Jude's help in the worst way.

A way out. That was what he'd offered me and as much as I hated to accept it, if it was the *only* way out?

Fine. I'd take it.

The question was, how fast could he get to me?

Maybe I should have asked him that.

"Tone it down," Damon said from the seat next to me. He was drumming a hand on his knee, staring out the window. "You're driving me nuts."

I ignored him as I started to mentally plot my escape route.

He still underestimated me. That was a good thing. So far, in the past few days, I'd played it quiet, never once calling my blade to me even when I wanted it, when I all but thought I was going to die. So he didn't know I could summon it at will. That was an ace in the hole.

I hadn't needed to pull any of my other little tricks, either. Most of them just included the subterfuge skills, invisibility and all of that—skills suited to assassins and thieves, but useful all the same.

He could track my scent if he had to, but I knew that and I could compensate, and scent trails only lasted for so long.

All I needed to do was buy time to reach Jude.

Granted, I'd be going from one problem to another. If I was alive, though, I could figure a way out.

Alive was better than the alternative.

It was a mantra I had told myself very often during a certain point during my life. It had gotten me through hell before. I could rely on it to do the same again. Alive was better than the alternative and if I was alive, I could figure a way out.

Okay.

So that was the plan.

Stay alive.

Absently, I flexed my wrist again. It didn't hurt anymore, but I'd swear I could still feel the press of his fangs, and I didn't like it—

Suddenly, Damon's hand on my arm.

I hissed out in pained shock before I could stop it. Clutching at the steering wheel with my left hand, I tried to keep my focus on the traffic. "You prick, I realize a car wreck isn't going to damage you much, but it will hurt me pretty bad. Would you stop it?"

"You drive like a fucking racecar driver," Damon snapped. "Pull over."

"I'm trying to get to Banner HQ, remember?" I jerked on my arm. "They might have the kid there? On ice?"

"Pull over," he said again. "Or I'll fucking make you."

I sighed and pressed on the brakes, easing through the traffic until I could turn off International Drive. I ended up in the parking lot of one of the many vacated restaurants, although judging by the looks of it, it wouldn't stay vacant much longer. Lately the packs had been buying up all the land and turning out some seriously profitable enterprises for use among the were packs.

"Okay, asshole." I pulled over. "What now?"

He didn't respond.

Instead...he reached over and grabbed my left wrist. The one Jude had bitten. I hissed out another startled breath as he jerked it to his nose.

My heart beat jacked up to about ten thousand beats a minute, or so I thought, as he opened his mouth. Oh, hell no—

But all he did was inhale.

"Did you let him bite you?"

"What the hell?" I twisted my arm and tried to pull away.

"Did you?"

Again, I tried to pull away from him but it was like trying to pull something out of concrete. "You son of a bitch, you seem to forget something...I'm working a job for your Alpha. That doesn't mean I owe you answers on every damned thing I do."

"You little idiot." He jerked and thanks to the seat belt, I thought he was going to pull my arm out of its socket. "You don't get vampires very well, do you? Once you let them bite you, they own a piece of your fucking soul. He can call you, whenever he wants. Can whisper into your dreams...and you can't fight him. You can't say no."

"Oh, please." I sneered at him. "He's been fighting his way into my dreams for years now and I've been saying no just fine."

Damon's eyes narrowed.

"You haven't fed him?"

"What I have or haven't done isn't your concern. But here's the thing." I jerked on my wrist, and as I expected, he jerked me back, until I was nose to nose with him. "I'm about ass-deep in alligators right now, and not because I invited it or wanted it or even did anything to warrant it. I'm trapped. Whether I like it or not. And if I don't find this kid, I'm looking at my own death...I figure it might not be a bad idea to have a way out. If that way is a vampire? So be it."

"You really are a clueless fool." He shook his head. "Just how sheltered a life have you led to think that a vampire is better than death?"

I leaned in, pressed my nose to his. "Sweetheart...you don't know anything about the life I've led. But one thing I've figured out? As long as I'm alive? I've got a chance to get out of whatever hell I've landed in. If your bitch-queen kills me because you all couldn't keep an unhappy kid from running away? Well...I can't turn things around if I'm dead. As long as I'm alive, I've got that chance."

The storm clouds in his eyes darkened to black. Flared. "You need to watch how you speak of her."

"You're right. She's the Queen Bitch, not the bitch-queen. Absolutely, I'll give respect where respect is due." I tugged at my wrist again. "Now come on. Let's go see what's going on."

He didn't let go. "You haven't answered me. Did he bite you?" His thumb stroked over the inside of my wrist and for some reason, it struck me. There was something almost gentle about his touch. "If I'm going to have to protect you from the fucking vampire on top of everything else, I need to know."

I curled my lip. "I've been dealing with Jude in my life for six years. I think I got this."

I carried a picture of Doyle in my back pocket.

I'd made a copy and tucked it in my pocket the day I accepted the case.

Maybe it was silly, but I wanted to remember what I was risking my life for. Who.

A kid.

A nervous, scared kid who wasn't even sure he could survive the change from human to were.

He had blond hair, sleepy-looking eyes and the promise of what would be a killer smile. So much promise. And what was more...he had kind eyes. The kindness in his eyes hadn't been lost on me.

It seemed that the cat shifters could do with more kindness in their ranks.

Chang had seemed the decent sort. A few others hadn't been too bad. But most of them were caught up in the power play and it pissed me off that somebody who might have been one of the nice ones could be lost to them.

I knew his face now. He was mine. I'd do everything I could to find him and if I couldn't find him, it would be because there was nothing left to be found.

On the way down to the cold lower level of Banner HQ, I slid my hand into my pocket and tugged out the picture of Doyle, rubbing it with my thumb. I didn't look at it. There was no need. I knew his face well enough now that I could draw his picture. More than once, I'd found myself doing just that.

He didn't look like his aunt.

Queen Bitch.

Would death be kind—?

No. I can't think like that...can't, I can't, I can't....

A hand came up and closed over my neck as the elevator doors opened. The people trickled out, but before we could follow them, Damon hit the button to shut the doors and then he just held it. "Are you trying to push yourself into a panic attack?" he asked, dipping his head and growling right into my ear.

I drove my elbow into his stomach.

I might as well have been hitting steel for all the good it did.

I did it again anyway.

He swore and spun around, shoving my back against the elevator doors.

My hand itched—*bad, bad, bad.*

"Listen, little girl," he snarled.

He reached for me.

I darted aside.

When he reached for me again, the blade was just there.

He stilled. The only sign of surprise was the slight widening of his eyes.

"Stop it," I whispered, pointing the blade at him, leveled at his throat. "I'm tired of this, do you hear me?"

"You should put that thing away before you hurt yourself."

I leaned in enough that it was pressed against his throat, watched as the tip pierced his skin. As smoke drifted from his wound to curl in the air, I glared at him.

"How did you get it past me this time?"

"And you keep calling me the idiot." Blood stained the tip of my sword red now. The blade liked it. She wanted more. A lot more. "You saw me lock the damn thing up in the lockers upstairs, cat. Or are you blind?"

His nostrils flared, a growl rumbling through his throat.

"The two of us need to come to an understanding," I said flatly. I twisted the blade, watched as it pushed a little deeper into his throat. "I'm dead if I don't find this kid. If he's down there on a slab, I'm dead, all because your crazed queen needs to blame somebody and it doesn't matter if he's been dead for ten minutes or ten days."

His lashes flickered.

"Now I'm not going to whine about how unfair that is. Nor am I going to bitch about the fact that if you all had been doing your job by that boy, maybe he wouldn't have run," I added. "The bottom line is…he did run. And I've got a soft spot for kids. This is a well-known fact, a card your Alpha knew and worked to her advantage. Now…if that's not him, we've still got a job to do. If it is him…well, I'll deal some other way. But nevertheless, there's a job to do and it's not going to get any easier with us at each other's throats."

He snarled and pushed himself closer, driving the blade a quarter of an inch into his throat. "You think I want to be working with some crazy little bitch who can't control her emotions?"

"Well, you worked with your Alpha," I pointed out with a polite smile. "Face the facts. I'm not were. I respond to fear, anger, grief and all the other emotions. Those are my shortcomings, having human blood. You should have been prepared for that. If you're not equipped to deal with it? That's *your* shortcoming as one of the more alpha cats in the damned clan." I smirked at him. "I keep hearing about your vaunted control. All the shifters are supposed to be in control. It's what guides them through the spiking, adolescence. If you can get through that and not lose your marbles, it's supposed to be smooth sailing."

Damon glared at me.

"It seems to be a myth, if you ask me." I twisted the blade and watched as blood trickled down. Flesh continued to burn and he just stood there. Oh, he had control, all right. He had it in spades.

"Is there a point to this or are you just really into having me wring your neck?" His voice was a growl too deep. The storm clouds in his eyes had changed, too— shifting to that eerie luminescence singular to felines. The pupils were changing.

Pushing too far. Oh, well.

"The point is…if you want this job done, you have got to get off my ass. I can't do it with you growling at me. I can't do it with thunderclouds over my head and I can't do it if I'm worrying about an ax falling on my head at the first wrong move, if I'm worried about anything other than doing this damn job."

Those eyes flashed again, and then, to my surprise, that eerie, flickering glow melted away and he stared at me with a human gaze. "Are you done?"

"Possibly." I twisted the blade once more. Maybe I really *was* crazy. "Are we going to keep doing this or are you going to let me work?"

He reached up and closed a hand around the blade.

Shifter flesh met the enchanted silver and started to smoke. As he pushed it away, he leaned in and said, "You can work, little girl. But sooner or later, you and I are going to have a reckoning."

"I can't wait."

It wasn't Doyle.

Staring down into that battered, unrecognizable face, I couldn't really even find any relief over the fact that it wasn't the kid I was searching for.

Yay. I got to live a little while longer.

But this kid was dead, and he'd died horribly.

"It's not him," I said to Lincoln, still staring at his battered face.

"How can you be sure?" Lincoln stood next to him, his dark face dubious.

"For one…the hair is the wrong color. My kid is a blond. And… He's not a cat. I think this boy was a wolf." Even though life had left him, I could sense that fading energy. He hadn't been dead long enough for it fade completely and I could still see it, hovering over him like a creature in mourning.

I could almost hear its grieving howl echoing through the air as I crouched down by the table, studying the disaster that had been his face. "Shit, what did they do to him, Linc?"

"Tortured him, poor kid," the cop said, his voice heavy and tired. "How can you tell he's not a cat? Our tests haven't come back yet."

I shrugged. "I just can."

"You're certain?" Lincoln asked.

Rubbing my temple, I sighed. "Certain? No. Not one hundred percent, but…"

"He's a wolf," Damon said from behind me.

Lincoln looked at him, then at me.

I shrugged. "Meet my bodyguard. One of the cat shifters. My gut says this is a wolf, but his nose would know for certain."

Lincoln narrowed his eyes. "Bodyguard, huh? Who exactly did you piss off enough to need a bodyguard?"

"You know me." I rose and started to circle around, studying the boy's body. Spying a box of gloves on the table, I snapped a pair on and reached for his hand, eying it closely.

"Yeah. I know you. So the better question would be who haven't you pissed off."

I glanced up at him and saw the concern in his eyes. I shrugged. I wasn't about to go into detail here and there wasn't really any point anyway. How did I explain that I was working an impossible case where I was making people angry and the bodyguard was both my ball-and-chain and my life preserver? Linc would be worried enough to ask questions and those kind of questions wouldn't help him, or me.

He'd probably be safe since he was human, but I wasn't taking a chance. I liked Linc. He was nice to me and unlike a lot of humans, he didn't treat the NHs of the world like shit. He was decent.

"Look at his hands," I murmured. The tips of the kid's fingers were raw, the nails nothing but nubs, bloodied and dirtied.

"They had him trapped somewhere," Lincoln said. He pulled on a pair of gloves himself and moved to the opposite side of the body, lifting the hand and showing me those fingertips were in the same condition. "He tried to climb out. For a long, long while."

Just thinking about that made me quake. It wasn't a good thing to think about right now, so I decided to handle it in the most mature way possible. Denial.

Conscientiously, I continued to study the boy's fingers, the scraped and bloodied raw tips. "He should have healed, though."

"Not if they were starving him." Damon came to stand beside me. A muscle jerked in his jaw. "It would be hard to say if he had gone through his first change or not, but if he had spiked or was going through the first few changes, he'd have to eat more than twice what a shapeshifter normally eats—building up reserves. And we eat a lot."

Lincoln glanced up, then back down, keeping his attention focused either on the kid's lifeless body or me for the most part. "So they probably had him a while." He nodded. "Narrows the victim list down some."

"The wolves will know who he is," Damon pointed out. "Contact them. They are probably looking for him."

I curled my lip. "Not everybody cares when their kids are missing or abused," I said.

Weakling...your mother should have strangled you with your cord when she had you...

I twitched as the voice of my grandmother whispered through my mind. Damn it. I usually managed to avoid thinking about her—sheer determination on my part, but something about this case was plucking at those memories.

Screw her. I am my mother's daughter -*my heart is strong. My heart is strong-*

"Shifters take more care with their kids," Damon said, that familiar snarl in his voice.

"Uh-huh. You saw a lot of care down in Wolf Haven, didn't you?" I could have pointed out that I'd seen what a lovely parental unit Doyle's aunt appeared to be. Definitely all full of sunny smiles and hugs, that one. But I decided not to bother.

Making another pass around the body, I studied his hair, his feet, noticing the shredded skin of his soles, the scrapes and bruises on his hands and legs. None of it told me anything. At least not yet. Just part of the puzzle for now.

Stripping off the gloves, I looked at Linc. "You going to call the wolf pack?"

"Planned on doing it after you left." He smiled lazily. "I fumbled my way to that conclusion after you said wolf. I trust your instincts, Kitty girl."

I heard the sarcasm in his voice, although I wasn't entirely sure if Damon did.

"I assume their people will take it over?"

Linc shrugged. "That's up to them. The body was found on common ground, outside of the wolf pack's registered territory. But if he's theirs, they have jurisdiction."

I nodded and turned away. As an afterthought, I turned back. "Hey, can I give you my card? That way, you'll have my cell. If you hear anything unusual that might tie into the runaway I'm looking for, maybe you can give me a call." Just in case that wasn't working, I gave him a gamine smile and tried to flutter my lashes.

Linc lifted a brow.

Flirtatious and charming. Obviously not my milieu.

"Sure, Colbana." He stripped off his gloves and accepted the card I held out, giving me a solemn nod.

Linc was a sharp one, sharp enough that he'd probably pick up on the things I couldn't say in front of my unwelcome bodyguard.

As I headed back out, I paused long enough to grab the sheet and pull it back up over the boy's battered, broken body. "I hope somebody finds who did this," I said to Linc. "I don't care if it's you, or the wolves. But somebody needs to suffer for this."

Linc met my eyes, nodded shortly.

Without another word, I left.

Damon, thankfully, was silent.

Colbana.

The message popped up on my phone sometime past eleven that night.

Sprawled on my bed, going bleary eyed as I combed through yet another batch of runaways, I grabbed the phone with one hand and flipped the sheet over me with my other. I was just barely fast enough.

The door to my room opened a micro-second later.

I was dressed. Workout shorts, a tank top, decent enough, but still. Studiously ignoring him, I read the message and tapped back a reply.

The one and only.

That's a relief. Can't handle two of you, Linc texted back. *So, exactly why did you make a point of giving me your cell number when I've had it for three years now? I mean, I called you to ask you out about once a week for a year.*

I smiled a little as I deleted the message before replying. Linc had picked up on that, all right.

The shadow fell across my bed, although I didn't hear him.

Rolling around, I casually settled with my back against the headboard and glanced up. "Any reason you're in my room?"

Damon leaned a shoulder against the bedpost, stared at me. "Who is the message from?"

"A guy."

Black brows ratcheted up. "You really think you got time to mess with that shit right now?"

"Hey, when you got an itch…" I shrugged and sent Linc back a reply. *Just need a favor. When the results come back on the kid, can you email me them to my old email? Not the current—somebody reads them over my shoulder right now. He's also trying to read my texts, BTW.*

I deleted that message as the asshole in residence pushed away from the bedpost and prowled closer.

Sure thing, gorgeous.

I rolled my eyes.

Two seconds later, the phone was out of my hand.

"You asshole, give me my phone back."

Damon read the message, then went to scroll back through the other messages. "Why are you deleting the messages?"

"None of your damned business!" I snapped. Rolling to my knees, I went to snatch the phone way.

I stopped as he lifted a hand and rolled out of his reach in a backwards shoulder roll before he could so much as touch me. Coming off the bed, I kept it between us as I stared at him.

He'd warned me there was a reckoning coming and while I figured it would happen sooner or later, I'd rather not have it happen just yet. My palm itched. Absently, I twisted it as the bones popped.

Damon wasn't messing with my phone anymore. He threw it down on the bed and glared at me. "Would you quit acting like every time I move, I'm going to attack you?"

Call me…I'm here, I'm here—

The sword was on my bed and she burned unnaturally bright.

He glanced at her and said, "If you even move toward that thing, I'm going to bend it into knots."

I curled my lip at him. "Like you could."

He leaned forward. "Is that a dare, little girl?"

66

"No. It's a plainly stated fact. Now…why don't you do us both a favor and get the fuck out of my bedroom?" I jutted my chin out, rotated my wrist again as the itching and heat flared. The sword flashed brighter. I usually wasn't this close to her without having her in my hand.

I couldn't help it, though. Ever since he'd spouted off that little piece about a reckoning, I'd been on eggshells, just waiting for whatever the hell he had in mind. If he thought he could leave another mark on me, I'd bloody him.

He leaped over the bed. I backpedaled and faded into nothingness, going invisible as he came for me.

This was one time where his sense of smell might not help.

The entire room smelled of me.

"Considering how mouthy you are, you're a damned coward." A smirk was on his lips as I brushed by him, just barely missing his outstretched hand. He moved back over by the bed and settled on the foot of it, that sly, Cheshire cat grin curling his lips as he reached behind him, closing his hand over the grip of my sword.

My breath hitched in my chest.

Mine—

His eyes flickered my way. No, he couldn't see me and tracking me by scent was harder. But he heard that. I couldn't stop the way my heart reacted when he touched my blade. Couldn't stop it.

"Don't like seeing me play with your toy, huh?" He lifted her and caught the tip in his other hand. Muscles flexed. "How about if I twist it up a little?"

He couldn't. Others had tried.

But she was mine—

She flared, bright as the sun, and disappeared. I dropped the invisibility as she settled into my hand. "Keep your damned paws off my blade, cat."

He was staring rather dumbly into his hands.

A rather queer look settled over his face as he lifted his head to study me. "So that's how you do it."

Was there really any point in responding to that? I twirled my wrist, satisfaction settling inside me. Having somebody else touch this blade was like having somebody combing through my underwear drawer or something. Maybe even worse.

"That's why you're always popping your wrist or wiggling it when you're worked up, isn't it?"

Staring at him, I held her at ready. "Are you going to leave me alone or not? I've still got reports to go through and I'm tired."

"What's your range on calling it?" He stood up, still eying the sword. "Are there other weapons or is it just that one?"

As he took a step closer, I lifted her. "Please stay away."

"I thought we had a truce," he murmured. A smile tugged at his lips.

If I didn't know what a bastard he was, I might have almost believed the smile. "Doesn't mean I want you getting close to me."

He eyed the sword, then me. "You can't really hold it like that forever. I can just stand here until you lower it. All I want to do is talk, Kit."

"I can hold it a lot longer than you might think." Memories of drills danced through my mind. Fanis had broken the bones in my forearm when I was eight because my guard got shaky. When the same thing happened at fourteen with a heavier weapon—a battle-axe—she'd broken my right humerus and my collarbone. I knew how to hold my guard, and despite what he thought, I was stronger than humans.

"So you're going to stand there and have a pissing contest over nothing rather than an answer to a question?" His smile widened and his gaze dropped, staring at my tits as though the close-fitting tank top wasn't even there. "Okay. I'll just enjoy the view."

Hissing, I lowered the blade and spun away.

Spying a T-shirt thrown over a nearby chair, I grabbed it and stalked over to my bed. Once more, I kept it between us as I put the blade down. "Take it again, and I'll just call it back," I said flatly, jerking the T-shirt on over my head.

I didn't even have time to gasp for a breath.

He was right there.

A hand on my neck held me in place. Swearing, I flexed my wrist. "Go ahead," he said, his voice gruff. "I'm not…"

I tensed as I felt his hand catch the hem of the shirt I'd pulled on.

"What in the holy hell happened to your back?"

I clenched one hand into a fist. Closing my eyes, I just stood there.

Seconds ticked away, bled into minutes.

He didn't ask again.

Finally, he let go.

I didn't open my eyes again until I heard the door close behind him.

I didn't move for probably ten more minutes. I wasn't sure if I could. If I moved, I just might shatter.

Chapter Nine

"Such a little weakling…"

Fanis stood over me.

Aneris Hall. The aneira stronghold. The royal family's home. My grandmother's home.

I cringed on the floor of the room where they'd locked me, cradling my aching arm to my chest.

"The healer has to re-break the bone," she said, moving to pace around me.

I wanted to cry, but I didn't dare. I knew better.

"She said she could give you an elixir so you would sleep through it but I will not allow it."

Biting my lip, I tried not to beg. There was no way I would beg. The last time I'd begged…my back still had the scars.

"Do you not have anything to say, granddaughter?"

I shook my head.

"Good."

She stood by as the healer broke the bones. And as I screamed, she smiled.

You are dreaming…

I flinched at the sound of his voice.

Jude was the last person I wanted to see witnessing those dreams.

"The absolute last?" he murmured, stroking a hand down my arm. The one she'd broken.

Forcing my eyes to open, I found myself lying on the bed. The dream world was almost painfully vivid and I gasped. I could smell the lingering stench of burnt popcorn—the family next door had burnt some a few hours earlier and it had yet to fade. There were also the familiar scents of lavender and vanilla, coming from the scented rocks Colleen made for me.

And Jude. Sitting by me, stroking a hand up and down my arm.

"You can see into my dreams now?"

He shrugged. "Bits and pieces, yes."

"Wonderful." I struggled to move, figured it would take a few more minutes, but to my surprise, I was off the bed and moving in a blink. "Whoa. That's unexpected."

Jude smiled. "I tap into your energy when I break into your dreams. Now that there is a link between us, I don't have to do that and there is no drain on your resources." He dropped his chin on his fist as he eyed me narrowly. "You're an odd bird, Kit. Most humans can't move for hours when I do this. I'd expected I'd have more control over you now that I'd tasted you but…"

A faint line appeared between his brows. "It appears I don't."

"I'm not human."

He shrugged. "You are…in part. You're not witch, and you're no shapeshifter. The aneira even show as human in any testing that is done on them, did you know that?"

I shrugged. "And this matters to me…why?"

"Just as I said. You're an odd bird." His head cocked and a smile curled his lips. "You're about to have company."

I frowned. Two seconds later the door opened and Damon came prowling in.

He moved to pause by the bed and when he looked down, I did the same thing. I had to remind myself that I wasn't *really* moving around my room. I was just dreaming. In reality, I was in the bed. Still, it caught me off guard to see myself, lying there. Vulnerable.

The last thing I wanted to be around Damon.

Rubbing a hand over my chest, I focused on the naked back of the shapeshifter instead. He wore a pair of low-slung workout pants and if I didn't hate him, I might have enjoyed the view very, very much.

"It figures the bastard sneaks in while I sleep."

"Don't get your maidenly honor all worked up. He is worried," Jude said, shrugging, his tone bored.

"Worried." I snorted. "Probably trying to think of a way to kill me and still get his Alpha's nephew home."

"No." Jude shook his head. "His emotions aren't murderous." His lids drooped low, only the thinnest sliver of his glowing green eyes visible. "Your heartbeat slows in dreams and this connection would slow it even more. He's listening. Takes his job seriously, this one."

I glared at Damon's naked back. "His Alpha made him promise he wouldn't allow any harm to come to me while I was working the job. He actually *let* her bash his face because she was pissed off at me. By the way, do you know she's crazy?"

"Annette? Oh. Yes." Jude's smile went cold. "She's very, very crazy. And you…you little fool…went to work for her."

I was getting so tired of men calling me a fool.

"Is there any reason you're here?" I asked tiredly.

"I heard your dreams. The terror in them…I could feel it. Taste it." A strange light appeared in his eyes. "I wondered what could push you to such fear, little warrior. You've always been so foolishly brave."

Disgust, humiliation and rage crowded into my throat.

Jude just watched with that sly little smile. "Ugly, awful dreams you have. It's no wonder you hate her."

"Stay out of my dreams," I said quietly.

He shrugged. "We all have our nightmares, Kit. Yours are just a little more recent than some. Besides, I wanted to test the strength of this new bond we share."

"There is no bond." I stared at him.

"Nothing I can hold you to, of course." The smile widened and the faint light in the room reflecting off his fangs. "But there's a connection now, little warrior. And sometime soon, you'll be glad of it. By the way, I heard stories of several runaways. Groups of them, actually. You should focus your investigation to the south."

Way to derail the conversation, I thought sourly. Runaways. Blowing out a breath, I shook my head. "To the south? Just where to the south? The Keys? Cuba? South America?"

"Hmmm." As he uncoiled off the bed, I tensed.

He closed the distance between us and tugged on the hem of my shirt. "I'm glad you're dressed. You don't need to sleep in the skin around one like him. Save that for me."

I smacked at his hand but he was gone before I made contact.

And I woke up to find Damon standing over my bed.

Groaning, I grabbed a pillow and flopped over onto my belly. "What the hell, you jackass?" I muttered, shoving my face into the pillow.

The dream was still echoing in my mind. Loudly.

Jude had seen my dreams. My nightmares. My fucking grandmother.

Groups of runaways.

In the south.

And now Damon was in here, staring down at me.

"You weren't breathing right."

I pulled the pillow over my head. "I'm breathing now," I grumbled.

South. Was Jude jerking me around or had he really heard something?

"Your heart rate was too slow."

"I was willing myself into a catatonic stupor. The only way I can really get any sleep with you in my home."

"What was going on?"

Swearing, I flung the pillow away and twisted into a sitting position. "Would you leave me alone?" I glared up at him and wished that I wasn't able to see so clearly in the dark. It was a handy skill for a born killer, but still.

Seeing in the dark made it that much easier to see that he was, indeed, naked from the waist up.

And...wow. I hadn't seen that in the dream. He had a tattoo on his chest. A vivid, rather tribal looking creation that spread up over his entire right pectoral, across his shoulder and curving down over his right bicep. I stared at it for a second while some part of my brain tried to wonder how it was possible for him to even have a tattoo—tatts weren't that much different than scars, implanting the pigment under the skin...shifter bodies rejected shit like that.

So how was it even possible?

Then he crouched down, eyes on level with mine. The storm clouds, for once, weren't so brooding and angry, but the look on his face was just as disturbing to me as the anger, although for different reasons entirely. I'd rather he be angry with me.

"What's wrong with you?" he asked softly. "You sounded like you were having a nightmare, but then it just...stopped."

"Apparently the leave-me-alone thing falls on empty ears," I muttered. Fighting free of the blankets, I clambered out of the bed and stormed toward the bathroom. "Just what in the hell did I do to deserve having a death sentence on my head and a couple of psychotic cat shifters breathing down my neck, on top of all the other shit I've dealt with?"

I made into the bathroom and slammed the door. Magic shimmered as wards settled into place. Flipping the lock, I grabbed a spare pillow and a blanket out of the closet. I had a safe place in my office. And another one here. It was the bathroom, the smallest room in the house, the easiest to secure. Not the nicest place to spend the night, but I could do it.

As I settled down in the bathtub, I called my sword.

I could hear him moving around, heard the door shut. But I didn't bother getting up.

I hadn't stopped having the nightmares until a few years ago.

When they'd gotten really bad, I still ended up in here, certain that I'd awaken and find Fanis standing over me.

This was one place I almost felt secure. Miserable enough to some, I figured.

But for nearly thirteen years, I hadn't ever had a bed to sleep in. After my mother died, I'd been pretty much treated as a stray dog in my grandmother's house. And the dogs had been fed better.

After I'd fled Aneris Hall, I'd been so busy running, I ran until I was too tired to go any farther so I dropped where I was. Often, I hadn't even had a warm place, or a blanket, or pillow. At least here, I had those…and safety.

Not to mention the psychotic cat sleeping out in my living room.

I woke to hear my phone chiming.

Shit.

I hadn't thought to bring it into the bathroom with me.

If it was Linc…

Muscles shrieked and protested as I climbed out of the tub and stumbled into my room.

Damon was already standing in the doorway. Storm-cloud eyes studied my face as I snagged my cell from the bedside table. It wasn't Linc. Good. That was good.

Colleen.

Call me.

Okay.

I'd call her. But caffeine first.

Knuckling at my eyes, I headed toward the door, only to stop a foot away as I realized the bane of my existence was still standing there. Balefully, I lifted my eyes and glared at him.

A faint smile, there and gone, twisted his lips and he stepped aside.

Coffee.

Cyanide.

For me. For him—he said it would take a tank load, but maybe Colleen could work up something that would work. It was possible, right? Had to be.

Five minutes later, I was thinking clearly.

Clearly enough to realize he wasn't hovering at my back.

Nor was he in the living room where he normally slept. He'd already made up the bed—thank God he was fairly neat. His clothes had already been packed away, which meant he'd been up for a little while. A T-shirt was draped over the back of the chair close to me, along with a towel, so he must have been in the guest shower when the text woke me up.

But he wasn't out here now and he wasn't in there—

Storming into my room, I found him leaning against the wall just outside my bathroom, staring inside.

"You slept in the bathtub."

"Yes." I cradled my coffee and took a drink, burning my tongue. Didn't matter. I had caffeine. That immediately made the day a little bit easier to face.

Storm clouds flashed in his eyes as he shoved off the wall and faced me. He crossed his arms over his chest and I briefly found myself distracted by the way muscles played under his golden-brown skin. *Pretty—*

No. *No.* Not pretty...asshole. *Capital* asshole.

"Why did you sleep in the bathtub?" he asked, a growl edging into his voice.

"Because I didn't want to talk to you and you wouldn't leave me alone. I figured you'd at least give me five minutes to pee in peace and quiet and when you didn't barge in immediately, I thought maybe that would be the ideal place to sleep."

A muscle jerked in his jaw. "I left you alone because I figured you wanted to be left alone. You weren't in there pissing or anything else. You could have come out."

"Oh, like you've been so respectful of my privacy or anything else." Another drink sent more caffeine pulsing through me and I imagined I could see the cobwebs blowing away. Jude. The dream. South. And those kids had said something about the Everglades...

"I left you alone last night, didn't I?" he snapped.

I took another drink. "A fluke. Although if you're really trying to grow some manners, you could always leave me alone again. I need to change."

I needed forty-five minutes in my gym. I needed to call Colleen, but I had to work that dream out first or I was going to go crazy.

Such a little weakling...

Yeah. Better to work it out now, than lose my mind later.

I'd much rather work out alone, but that wasn't going to happen. At least he was busy with the weights he'd had delivered. They had shown up on the second day of our not-so-ideal arrangement and half of my space was surrendered to his equipment. I would have hauled the crap onto the front lawn if I thought it would accomplish anything.

It took a good twenty minutes before I managed to clear my mind enough to fall into my routine. Sweat dripped, muscles burned, and finally, my mind felt clear.

The sword that felt like a part of me sliced through the air.

Everglades.

Groups of them—

Just kids.

Children—

Child. Weak, ignorant child—The crack of a whip slicing through the air. *If it kills me, I'll make you something stronger.*

My breathing hitched in my throat.

Hold that weapon steady, Kitasa—useless waste. Oh, dear. You dropped your guard—

I stumbled as her voice rang through my mind and I remembered the sickening, wet crack of my bones breaking. The ghostly ache danced up my arm.

"Shit."

I stopped in the middle of the floor and brought my hands to my face. My right hand still clutched my sword and I squeezed it, tighter, tighter.

Get out of my head, you evil bitch, I thought, half desperately.

"You know, whatever those demons are that are eating you up…"

I gulped in another breath of air and lowered my hands, ready to tear into him, ready to turn around and bury my blade in him and screw the consequences.

I turned around. Saw him standing three feet away. "Seems to me you managed to leave them far enough behind. If you can pick fights with vampires, crazy cats and entire packs of rats, I'd think you could deal with whatever those demons were, too."

Then he went back to his weight bench.

"Bad vibes. I want you to know, going in, I've got a bad, bad feeling about this," Colleen said when I called.

I had two cups of coffee and a pastry nearly as big as a plate in my belly and I suspected I'd need more sugar and more caffeine just to get through this. "I get nothing but bad vibes about this entire mess," I said into the phone as I leaned in and studied the donut case.

Chocolate.

That was the ticket.

Pointing to one liberally smeared in it, I smiled at the lady behind the counter. She wasn't paying any more attention to me than she had to. She gave me the donut and then went back to staring at Damon.

Human. Even if I hadn't been able to tell just by looking at her, I would have figured that out after she continued to stare at him for the first thirty seconds and didn't look away even after he pointedly shoved his sunglasses onto his head and glared at her.

Another shifter wouldn't have done that with him. Hell, most of them would have been cowering the second he walked inside.

"Okay, we both have a bad feeling about this," I said. "Glad we have that established. Now that we do…why am I calling you?"

"Three witches from one of the outer houses have seen…something."

The outer houses were basically subsets of the main houses. Green Road was huge and its outer houses covered most of the south. "Oh? And how does this have anything to do with me?"

"All ties into kids. One of our girls went missing, but we were able to find her and get her back. She's still in seclusion and I don't know what all happened, but I thought it was kind of odd, especially after I heard another witch—unaffiliated—disappeared a week later. She hasn't been recovered yet. She's seventeen."

My skin started to crawl. Unaffiliated witches didn't practice with a house. It wasn't common, but it happened. And it wasn't a good thing, either. Witches were more vulnerable on their own. They pretty much *defined* the phrase *strength in numbers*. One or two witches alone, especially young ones, were easy targets. Warriors were far and few between. Now one warrior witch was a sight to behold, but still, even they needed to be trained.

Sitting up a little straighter, I braced my elbows on the table as Damon slid into the booth across from me. He had a massive pile of toast. Just toast. And milk.

"What else?" I asked, staring at those neat little triangles of bread.

"I heard from a contact that somebody from the wolf pack had a kid go missing, too. I can't confirm, but…"

"I can." Images of a boy's battered face flashed through my mind.

Four teenagers. Wasn't exactly a pattern, but…

"You can, huh?" Colleen made a little humming sound under her breath. "Curiouser and curiouser."

"Well, I can't confirm he was with the wolf pack, but I do know that a wolf kid was found. I saw his body the other day." Made me think about the tests I had yet to see. Needed to log into my other email. While Damon sat there contemplating his mountain of toast and listening to my phone call, I pulled my tablet out of my bag.

"So four kids. All NHs," Colleen said.

I thought of Keeli and murmured, "Maybe five."

Hell, considering all the reports I had to go through, there could well be more. But no way to know yet. Yeah, decent parents would report the runaways, but despite what Damon said, not all parents were decent and that didn't change just because somebody was a shifter. They were still people, and people often sucked.

Colleen continued to speak as my tablet powered up.

"The witches in the outer house are located near the Everglades."

My gut roiled. "The Everglades."

"Yeah. One of them thinks she saw the witch, the day before she disappeared. After I sent up an alert about the kid you're looking for, I got a call. Came in late last night. The witch says she saw the boy you're looking for."

Damon's cup clattered onto the table.

I saw him reaching for the phone and jerked up a hand to stop him.

"Saw him?" These were witches we were talking about. They could see them with their eyes…or other ways.

"That's all I got out of her. She won't tell me anything else. Says if you want more, you have to go to her."

I blew out a breath as I logged into my email. "Okay. So I get the feeling I'm planning a trip to the Everglades."

"Yes. And now…why aren't you more surprised about that?"

Sourly, I stared at my donut. I wasn't hungry for it now. "A little birdie told me."

My e-mail loaded and I didn't even have to skim through it. There was a bunch of junk, a bunch of spam, a bunch of old contacts. I'd changed the e-mail because of all the spam, junk and shit. But the one e-mail that I did need was right there at the top. Linc. Damn, the man really did know how to come through.

"I'll be in touch, Colleen," I said, disconnecting the call and putting the phone down.

I clicked on the e-mail and started to read.

"The Everglades." Damon was staring at my bowed head.

"Yes."

"Was that your witch friend?"

"Yes."

Lab samples. Soil.

My gut churned as I read some of the notes Linc had thoughtfully thrown in. Several different kinds of dirt…soil. Whatever. The specialist who had done the tests thought it might be consistent with the sort found in the Everglades.

Spinning the tablet around, I shoved it at Damon as I drank the rest of my coffee.

A muscle worked in his jaw when he looked up at me. "Why am I reading lab tests on a dead wolf kid?"

"Because it appears he was down in the Everglades," I said. "And because, as I'm sure you heard since you were listening in, one of the witches affiliated with one of the outer houses down there thinks she saw Doyle. A couple of the witch kids have also gone missing. All in that general area. There's a connection, so it looks like we've got a road trip."

"It's a drive." He nodded shortly. "We should get going."

"We need to make a stop first." I shouldn't have had the coffee. My stomach was already pitching. The last thing I wanted to do was go back the rec club. "I need to talk to Marcus."

"Why?"

"Too many coincidences. All these kids tied into the 'glades. I want to know if there's a connection."

Damon narrowed his eyes. "If there was, the kid would have said. He knows better than to lie when I'm around."

"He might not have lied." I shrugged as I slid out of the booth. "There's a difference between lying and not telling everything you know. And he might have thought he was doing his friend a favor."

"By not telling you what you needed to know to find him?" Damon was on his feet now, too, crowding into my space under the pretense of carrying on a private conversation in a busy place.

Instead of tipping my head back to stare at him, I busied myself scooping papers and reports into my bag, shutting down my tablet last. "Kids don't always have that vaunted foresight. For all we know, the kid thought he was doing Doyle a favor by keeping quiet, even assuming he knows anything."

"How does not helping bring him home protect him?"

Useless waste—the sound of the whip whistling through the air. I turned around and looked up at him. "You know what the holy hell happened to my back? My grandmother did it to me. While my aunts watched. The first time happened when I was eight. The second, when I nine. It was a yearly, sometimes monthly, occurrence until I ran away when I was fifteen. And if somebody had tried to take me home? I would have either killed them…or myself."

Slinging my bag over my shoulder, I headed outside.

Maybe the Queen Bitch hadn't beaten that boy, but somehow I knew life at the lair hadn't been easy for him.

I'd figured that out just by the look in Marcus' eyes.

Chapter Ten

Marcus wasn't at the club.

We found him at his house and his dad didn't want to let me in.

If it wasn't for the bruiser at my back, I knew I wouldn't have gotten in, either.

"He's starting to spike," the man said, staring at me with narrowed eyes. "A human girl—a pretty one—walking in there isn't going to help. Especially once she starts smelling scared."

"I'm not going to freak out on him," I said. "I just need to ask him a couple of questions about Doyle."

"He doesn't know anything." The father shook his head.

"I think he might know more than he realizes."

"Are you calling my kid a liar?"

Oh, for crying out loud. Mildly, I pointed out, "That isn't what I said. I said, very clearly, I think he might know more than he thinks. I found out some information about some other missing kids and I need to ask him a few more questions."

"And when he starts coming after you because you smell like dinner or sex, what are you going to do?"

"He's not going to get within a foot of her," Damon said, edging in front of me. "But, Conley, you're going to let her in, and you're going to do it now before I decide to get pissed off."

A growl trickled from the father's throat. "You can't threaten me for protecting my kid."

"She's not a fucking threat to him."

"She's human! And when he scares the shit out of her—"

"She doesn't have the sense to be scared," Damon snapped. "Trust me, I've seen her in action. And I won't let the kid get near her. Now let her do her job."

I rubbed my temple as the headache pounded, ever close. This job was proving to be so much fun. Maybe Colleen could brew up some sort of tonic for the permanent headache I was living with.

It took a few more minutes and once Conley agreed, reluctantly, he looked me over with a critical eye. "Just how good are you with your weapons?" he demanded.

I cocked a brow. "Pretty damn good."

"She'll take them off," Damon said.

Conley shook his head. "How is your control?"

Serenely, I smiled. "Well, unless it's the jerk at my back...it's generally flawless. I don't draw down unless I absolutely have to. Don't worry, I have no absolutely no desire to harm your child."

Another thirty seconds passed and then he nodded. "Keep your weapons. If you're a fighter, you'll feel better with them on, meaning you're not going to walk around in a cloud of fear. That automatically makes things better from the get-go. Just don't draw them."

I laid a hand on the sword, stroked the handle. "I'll leave the sword someplace else…it's the most obvious one."

Behind me, Damon snorted.

Conley went to say something, but I shook my head. "It's fine. And I appreciate the gesture."

He shrugged. "I was one of the Assembly's exterminators before I had a family —my wife was one of the Banner cops. She wouldn't go anywhere without a weapon. I understand fighters."

I left the sword on the kitchen table after he gestured to it. "He's downstairs. It's quiet. Dark. We soundproofed it for just this purpose after we found Erica was pregnant. The less stimulation a kid going through the spike has to deal with, the better. Keep this short and quick, Ms. Colbana. Please."

I nodded.

Then he opened the door and slid through. "A few minutes with him first." He looked at Damon over my shoulder. "You come in first and stay between them for the first couple of minutes."

After the door shut behind Conley, I looked at Damon. "It gets tiresome having you constantly refer to me as being too stupid to be scared," I said, focusing on that instead of what I was getting ready to do. Baiting him felt almost normal.

"Having you constantly refer to me as the asshole or the jerk gets pretty old, too. I've got a name."

"You do? Damn. I thought for sure you'd introduced yourself as Lord Asshole the first day." Sighing, I shook my head. "Your name must have slipped my mind."

Turning away from him, I focused on the back window and let the minutes tick away.

Long, empty minutes.

Five of them. And then Damon moved, lingering at my back just long enough to murmur, "Do not come out from behind me until I tell you to, baby girl. You hear me?"

I glared at his back. "Excuse me? Baby…"

The door opened and he stepped inside.

Scowling, I reminded myself to yell at him later.

It was dark.

I smelled sweat.

The musk of cat.

Fear.

Automatically, my palm started to itch, but I ignored it. I was just going to talk to a scared kid.

"Stay up on the landing," Conley called from somewhere in that black maw.

I followed the sound, or tried to, from what I could see around Damon's wide back.

"Ask what you want to ask," Damon said quietly.

"Marcus."

I heard a weird little clicking sound.

"Hey, Marcus…I…ah."

A panting sound. Something whipped by the ground just in front of the landing. Fast. Too fast. A big, warm arm came around me. I would not acknowledge that Damon's presence felt a little comforting just then. No way, no how.

This was just a kid.

My heart is strong—

"Marcus, I need to know if you know anything about the 'glades."

A strange little growl came from below my feet. I looked down. Through the metal grate, I saw him.

Fur was sprouting on his face. Melting in. Growing back. An endless, odd little wave that was disturbing as hell to look at. Muscles rippled, bulged, out of place on his still-skinny frame. It was freaky as hell.

But in the dark, dank light of the room, I saw one thing clearly enough.

His eyes were still scared.

Sinking to my knees, I smiled at him through the metal grate. "Hey, kid."

"Nugget." His lips peeled back from his teeth. "You wanna come down here and keep me company?"

"Can't. I'm still looking for Doyle."

Damon sank down next to me, the caged energy of his presence wrapped around me, too close, too close—

Marcus closed his eyes and I watched as his nostrils flared. Breathing in the scents. "You don't smell just human," he said abruptly.

"That's because I'm not. Doyle, Marcus. I need to talk to you about him," I said gently. "Can you help me?"

"He had to run," Marcus whispered. "Had to."

Then he started to shake his head, fear entering his eyes as he darted a look at Damon. And the fear grew.

A knot settled in my gut.

There was something he wanted…maybe even needed to tell me, but he wouldn't, not while Damon was there. And Damon wasn't going to leave me alone with the kid. I knew that as well as I knew my own name.

"I'm going to hazard a guess," I said quietly. "You don't have to say if I'm right or if I'm wrong. You don't have to say anything, and you're not in trouble for this, because it's just some stupid half-human running her mouth."

I felt Damon's body tense.

"He didn't feel safe at home, did he?"

Snarling flooded the room and the blur tearing across the room didn't stop until he was lost in shadows too thick for me to penetrate. "Okay, okay," I said quietly as fear rose up thick enough to choke even me. "We don't have to talk about that. But the 'glades. Marcus, I need to know if he ever told you about the 'glades. I think he's in danger there. Other kids have gone missing."

There was no answer.

Not in words, anyway. Not for a long, long time.

But he did start to whine. Low, weird noises, like a sob trapped in a throat that just couldn't cry the way a human needed to.

"You're walking a dangerous line," Damon whispered in my ear as I unlocked the car.

"Had to ask."

"And when Conley talks?"

Blowing out a breath, I jerked the door open. Or tried. I couldn't back up enough to open it because Damon was still *right* behind me. "Why in the hell do you have to hover three inches away from me all the time?" I dropped my head against the car. "Don't you people know what personal space is?"

"Yes. And I have this weird fascination with invading yours." He brushed the hair off the back of my neck and I tensed as I felt the pad of his thumb slip over one of my scars. "You haven't answered. What are you going to do when Conley talks?"

"He won't," I said shortly. "It serves him no purpose and the boy is already too scared to say anything. It would only risk his son getting hurt if he said a word about the boy suspecting the ward of the Alpha being unsafe in his own home. And if most of the cats really are protective of their young, I suspect it would be...frowned upon...for her to be abusive. Would be bad if he ran away from home because he was afraid of living with her, huh?"

"That's not what the deal is."

I snorted and turned around. "Like hell." Glaring up at him, I said, "I don't know whether you feel obligated to lie like that or if you really believe it, but she hurt him."

The storm in his eyes spread over his face as he lowered it to growl at me. "I don't lie, baby girl."

Oh. Yes. "Stop calling me *baby girl*, asshole."

Sidestepping away, I jerked the door open. It slammed into his midsection. He grunted a little and I smiled as I wiggled into the car through the narrow opening. "We need to get going. I want to go by my place and pack a bag."

Somehow, I didn't think we'd find all the answers we needed in a couple of hours.

Ninety minutes into the drive, the phone rang.

The ringtone was Aerosmith's *Crying*. An old classic. I used to love the song, then I made the bad mistake of programming it for any and all numbers associated with Jude.

Sighing, I put it on speaker. Since Damon would hear the conversation anyway, I might as well keep my hands on the wheel. That way I wouldn't have to fight with him for control of the damn phone if he decided to join in on the conversation as he'd tried to do several times.

Bad enough on city streets but when I speeding down the interstate at over ninety miles an hour? Even worse.

"Colbana," I said.

"Kit…"

Jude. He'd deigned to call me himself. Wow. Wasn't I special?

His voice rolled over me like a hand sheathed in a silk glove and I hated the fact that goose bumps broke across my skin.

"Hello, Jude, bane of my existence," I said sourly.

"Darling Kit, the sweet nothings you whisper to me…I treasure each and every one."

"Oh, bite me." Then I snapped my mouth shut and mentally swore.

Next to me, Damon closed his eyes and shook his head.

On the phone, Jude laughed. "Kit, I count the days until I do just that. Tell me… is that miserable bodyguard of yours there? I hear another person breathing."

"What do you want, leech?" Damon said, his voice flat.

"Pleasant as always," Jude murmured. "Are you taking care of my Kit, Damon?"

"I'm seeing that a contracted employee of the Cats stays safe." He shot me a narrow look. "I couldn't care less about taking care of anything of yours."

Ouch. "As much as I love being talked about like I'm a toy or something, can we please not? Jude, what do you want?"

"I sent Evangeline to your office to speak with you, but you weren't there."

"I'm often not there." I cut around a truck and arrowed back into the right lane. "My job involves me leaving the office a lot."

"But I don't feel you so strongly…"

I hissed as I felt that whisper in the back of my mind. Faint. Very faint. But there.

"How can I protect you when you don't let me know you are leaving…?"

I wanted to snarl at him. Wanted to hang up the damn phone and tell him not to call. To stay out of my damned head.

But Damon was staring at me oddly and Jude was talking—

"Are you going to be back in the office today? I had information about the upcoming job," he said, his voice cool, polite. So very Jude.

"No. I'm out of town, probably for a few days."

"Where?" Out loud, he said, "When can I anticipate your return? I need to get this information to you."

Blowing out a breath, I said, "I'm following up a lead I received on earlier about my current job. I'm not going to be available for your case for a while yet, so Angie is just going to have keep her britches on."

"You're going south…very well. I'll keep watch."

I curled my lip and disconnected the call.

"He seems a little too protective of you," Damon said.

"I've noticed," I said dryly. *And you have no clue.*

"Why is that?"

"Apparently he finds me as amusing as you find me irritating."

"Not possible," he muttered, settling low in his seat and blowing out a sigh. "Not possible at all."

Chapter Eleven

The outer house of the Green Road met at a ramshackle old place that looked like it had been built to withstand hurricanes, wild witchcraft and werecreatures of all kinds.

And it looked like it had done all of those things and more.

I slid my sword into my sheath before I started toward the house.

"You think they'll let you take that in there?"

"Yep."

The disbelieving look in eyes was enough to have me biting back a laugh.

"The Green Road witches are crazier than most of them," he said, keeping his voice low. "They only allow combat if you're one of their warrior-trained ones, and everybody else is expected to be a pacifist. You carrying a blade in there is practically a declaration of war."

"Really?"

He dragged his hands up and down over his face. "You just like seeing me have to fight over your cute ass."

"Do me a favor and quit referring to my ass in any way," I said.

He pushed around me as we reached the door.

"Damon, damn it."

He paused and shot a look at me. "Wow. You did remember my name."

The door blew open before he could knock.

The woman there was almost as tall as he was, nearly as wide, and her hair blood-red, streaked with pink and blue. Her eyes were greener than mine and her lips were black.

Just looking at her made my eyes hurt.

She stood there, glaring at Damon.

This could get ugly, I decided. I saw the magic dancing over her like a bird mantling its wings. Damon hadn't been wrong. Green Road was full of powerful witches and most of them were pacifists. But their warriors were mad-powerful and they took their job of protecting the non-fighters very, very seriously.

This was one of the warriors, I could see it on her.

It could be amusing…a talented witch was a match for a strong shifter. Maybe even an even match. Hell, in the right situation, a warrior witch was almost an army. Of course, this wasn't one of those situations. Still, it would be one hell of a fight.

But damn it all.

I cleared my throat. "Hi. Colleen Antrim was supposed to send word about me. My name is Kit Colbana."

Her green eyes cut my way. I felt the weight of her gaze like an anvil dropping down on my head. She studied me. I could feel the pressure of her magic riffling through me, tasting me, taking me in. "You went after Mandy," she said quietly.

"Yes." I bit my tongue on the rest of the words. *I went after her when you all wouldn't.* Colleen had broken away from the witches when her daughter was born without magic. The witch who had headed the Green Road at the time had been a bigoted piece of work and Colleen hadn't wanted that around her daughter. When she'd reached out to them for help, none of them had responded.

A few more seconds ticked away and then she nodded. "You're good people. Shame the kid died." She stood aside and said, "Come on in, Kit. You're welcome here."

I edged around Damon and headed inside.

He made to follow, only to freeze at the door. I'd felt the magic ripple and accept me, but it had closed immediately after. Sighing, I turned and looked at the witch. She was still studying him.

"Who is he?" she asked.

He glared at her. "Damon Lee. Cat clan of Florida."

The witch acted as though he hadn't spoken, looking over at me. I realized it was up to me whether he came in or not. And since we were in a house of witches, they could rebuild any ward he might try to power through. *Sweet, sweet justice*, I thought…

But, shit. I'd told him we were at a truce. And whether or not he intended to hold to it, I didn't give my word easily.

"He's kinda sorta my bodyguard," I said tiredly. "And I kinda sorta agreed to work with him on the job I'm doing." I looked at him through the weight of wards I couldn't see. "I can't ask you to do anything you're not comfortable with, but he's not going to hurt anybody who doesn't threaten him or me, and I'd rather not listen to him bitch at me—if you'd let him in, I'd appreciate it."

"Hmmmm." She continued to study me and then she shrugged, flicked her wrist. I felt the wards shift, saw the faint flicker in his eyes. As he came through, I turned my back on him.

"Some of the girls don't get out much. They can use the eye candy."

I couldn't help it. I laughed. "Well, he's pretty to look at, but tell them to keep their distance. He's kind of toxic up close."

"Not an issue. Shapeshifters are a pain in the ass and the males are even worse, especially when they are in rut." She headed into the gloom of the house and I followed along, frowning over that last statement. "I'm Kori, by the way. Colleen and I were trained together. She's good people. Thanks for…well, Mandy. Some of us should have been there. We weren't."

I kept my mouth shut.

The only thing that would come out wasn't going to endear me to her and I didn't want to see if Damon could fight his way out of a house of angry witches if I pissed enough of them off.

In the door of a massive library, she stopped and turned to face me, a smile on her face. "Nothing to say to that?"

"Nothing to say."

"Oh, you got plenty," she mused, shaking her head. "You just hold your cards close to your chest. Smart girl."

Behind us, Damon made an odd, choking sound that might have been a smothered laugh.

"I just know when to hold them sometimes," I said, sliding him a dirty look.

Kori smiled. "Maybe that's what it is." She nodded to the library. "You want Jo. She's in the stacks." Then she pinned a hard look on Damon. "You don't want to go in there. Maybe you're her bodyguard or whatever, but Jo isn't one of our fighters. The girl can take little Jo blindfolded, even with magic. You will scare her. If you go in there, she'll shut down and whatever information you want from her? You won't get."

Damon lifted his hands, moved two paces and leaned back against the wall, folding his arms over his chest.

Day-yum. I actually got to get away from him for a few minutes. I gave Kori a bright smile. "Hey, mind if I hang around here for a few days?"

She laughed and then headed down the dark hallway. "I'm on kitchen duty tonight. You all are welcome to eat with us if she doesn't freak you the hell out, Colbana."

In the stacks.

I thought it would be easy to find her.

It took me almost thirty minutes.

Because she wasn't on her feet and she wasn't on the floor.

She was hovering in midair, arms wrapped around herself and rocking, mumbling and muttering.

"Ah...hey, Jo."

She tensed. The rocking grew more frenzied.

Licking my lips, I looked around, spotted a table. I started to strip off my weapons, all of them. Once I'd stripped them all away, I looked back up. But she wasn't there.

Aw, hell.

"Jo..."

I searched the air above me, but she wasn't anywhere—

A flicker of movement just out of the corner of my eye had me turning and I saw her drifting around the edge of the bookshelf at my back. I caught her just as she moved into the next aisle, clutching a book in her thin, pale hands. "Jo. I'd like to talk to you."

She glanced at me and her eyes were awful.

Black, empty and void of...everything.

Swallowing the knot in my throat, I managed to squeeze out, "It's about the boy you saw."

Slowly, she drifted down, down, down...then she stood and shook her head.

When she looked at me again, there was…sense. I guess. Something of self in her eyes and I sensed…witch. Her power. Earlier there hadn't been much of anything. Just cold.

"The boy," she whispered.

"Yes. You saw him."

"No." She shook her head and gestured broadly at nothing. "They saw him."

"Who are they?"

Her eyes went black. "We are."

The skin on the nape of my neck crawled and I hoped like hell I didn't let the fear I felt show. "And who are you?"

"We are we. And we saw him. He's dying. You can't save him because you are not looking. He's no longer the predator…just prey. Just meat. Like we were."

She blinked and the moment shattered. Jo stood there looking at me with lost, sad eyes. "I'm sorry. Did they talk to you?"

Numbly, I nodded.

"I hope they helped."

Then she gathered up a stack of books I hadn't noticed and slid out of the library.

Helped?

Um. No. Not really.

As I left the library, another witch was waiting. She was as lacking in color as Kori had rocked it—hair so blonde, it was practically white, skin so pale I don't think she ever went out in the sun, and her eyes were so pale a gray they seemed nearly colorless. Her clothes were white. Everything. White.

A polite smile curved her lips as she nodded at me. "I'm Es."

"S. As in the letter?" Immediately, I winced. "Sorry."

She chuckled. "Colleen told me you were…well, I'll be polite. But it's fine. It's E-S. But yes, it sounds like S the letter. I'm the mother here."

Witch houses had a leader. A mother, or if the most powerful was a guy, the father. I hope I managed to keep my astonishment hidden. Nothing about her screamed power—shit, Kori's strength had made this woman seem like…nothing.

Another one of those polite smiles curved her lips. "I wouldn't be much of a caretaker if I intimidated the hell out of every witch who came to me, would I?" she said gently. She looked down the hall, gazing in the direction Jo had run. "Many of mine are…broken. They need a quiet hand, Kitasa. I imagine you can appreciate that."

Blood crept up the back of my neck, up my cheeks until I knew I all but glowed with it.

She was studiously looking the other way. "After all, you deal with many victims in your line of work."

Nice lifeline to offer there. But I wasn't buying it. Colleen had sensed the very same thing on me the day she'd met me. And just like Es here, she'd pretended otherwise.

Swallowing the shame and disgust rising inside me, I shouldered around her and headed for the front door. Damon was already at my back when she called out, "There are a few other witches you might want to speak with, aneira. This goes... deeper, I suspect, than you realize."

I twitched at the sound of the formal title on her lips. Stopping in the middle of the hallway, I jammed my hands into my pockets and stared at the dirty toes of my boots. I wanted to leave. Hell, I wanted to just fade away, lose Damon and take off running. If I ran hard enough, I'd eventually lose them. I could get lost in the world. I'd done it before.

But the problem was sooner or later, one of them would find me.

My grandmother had been happy enough once I was out of her hair and she didn't have to see me.

But the cat bitch wasn't going to be so easily satisfied. She'd hired me to do a job.

If it had been any other job, I might have been willing to risk it.

Screw *might*.

I would have done it.

That kid's sad, lost eyes haunted me, though.

Pulled me in.

Wearily, I turned around and found myself staring at the wall of Damon's chest. "Can you move, please?" I said.

He stepped aside. But he didn't stay there. As I headed down the hall, my ever-present shadow was at my back.

"Tate," Es said, gesturing to the witch behind the two-way glass. "She's got a way with fire. One of our younger ones and just so you know...she hates anybody who isn't a witch. If it hadn't been a witch child she saw, she wouldn't have cared. Now, take notice...she would have seen it, but she wouldn't have cared."

"She saw a kid being kidnapped?" Damon demanded.

"No. She saw a kid getting into a car." She gave him a sidelong glance. "Tate notices everything and she'll notice more about you than you could possibly imagine, including what you had for breakfast, the fact that you're in rut, and the fact that you hate your Alpha. If you don't want her seeing anything that I just saw, you might want to lock it down so very tight, even you can't see it."

I snorted. "Es, you have to get your eyes, or your witch-whatever checked. He's slavishly devoted to that woman."

"Oh, he's enslaved...to something," Es murmured. "But that doesn't mean the same as devotion."

Then she turned those colorless, powerful eyes on me. "She might go kinder on you, but I don't know. You're not human and you smell like magic. She's young and her parents were mortal...she might think you have some witch blood in you. She won't know your bloodline."

"Very few do."

Es nodded. "True enough. But it may not matter. I'll be there with you because if she gets angry, I'll have to be the one to run interference." She looked at Damon. "You'll have to get her out if she gets angry."

"If she's that dangerous, why is she here?"

"Because we need our warriors," Es said simply. "I hope to focus that energy. If I can't, I'll have to destroy it."

She opened the door a moment later and a blast of heat licked over my flesh.

"Tate. We have company."

"Company can get fucked," the woman said. "I'm working."

"You work all day." Es smiled as she gestured at me. I walked into what felt like a smoldering, sweltering hell. "This woman only needs a few moments."

Tate stopped for about five seconds. Her gaze lit on me. Her hair was buzzed, cut so close I could see her scalp. It was dark, though, very, very dark, and her skin was a warm, mellow gold. She wasn't even sweating. Thirty seconds in there and I had already soaked my shirt through. Her eyes were bronzed, like melted pools of the metal, and energy crackled, snapped around her.

Damon came up behind me and his energy practically smothered me. I felt like I was drowning in it.

Tate snorted. "If the little dolly can't talk to me without her boyfriend, screw it. Busy, Es."

She whirled in a graceful pirouette and I watched as streamers of fire danced around her.

"Pretty light show," I said. "You boning up for a gig on Broadway or what?"

She stiffened and the fire died away. Her eyes narrowed on my face. "Excuse me?"

I shrugged. "Well, a few minutes ago you were all combative and serious shit. Now you're dancing. Figured you were showing off and I might as well show my appreciation. It's very pretty. You should add some music, though."

"How about I show you pretty and melt your sword?"

Why in the hell did everybody always try that? I wondered. They were going to bend it, break it and now she threatened to melt it. "Think you can?" I asked, glancing down at the blade.

"Oh, I know I can."

The arrogance and laughter in her eyes goaded me. "How about this—I have a couple of questions, and they are easy ones. If you can't melt the sword in thirty seconds, then you answer the questions."

"Fine." Then a smug smile curled her lips. "But you have to hold it."

"Tate…" Es stepped up. "If you harm somebody I've invited into my house, I'll be very displeased."

Tate didn't look concerned.

Es rested a hand on my shoulder. I looked over at her and shook my head. Damon swore and grabbed me. I shrugged him off and drew my blade, holding it out in front of me.

I smelled of magic. I knew that.

But there was more magic in the top two inches of my blade than I had in my entire body. It was just a quieter magic. One nobody ever really saw.

"Have at it, firefly," I said, smiling.

I felt the heated jolt. Three seconds in, the metal heated enough to I was starting to feel it. But the blade held up fine. Ten seconds in, my hand started to burn.

By twenty seconds, Tate was no longer smiling. I could smell my own flesh scorching. I dealt with the pain the same way I'd always dealt with it—I blocked it out. I'd blocked it out to survive, to get through whatever in the hell I had to get through. *I am aneira—my heart is strong—*

"Enough," Es said after the thirty seconds ended. Tate kept going.

"I said enough!"

Power ripped through the air, icy and white, cutting off the stream of Tate's power and I gasped as the backlash travelled up the blade. She was glowing—white hot. And pleased. She liked magic. Loved it.

Before any of them could notice, I banished the blade and had to clench back a scream as the hilt all but ripped away from my burnt flesh.

Black dots danced in front of me.

A hard, brutal palm gripped my arm, fingers digging into my flesh. Damon shook me a little. "Okay, witch. She won. Questions now."

"Fucking cheat," Tate spat out. "That was an enchanted blade."

"I never said it wasn't. And you never asked."

My palm throbbed. Screamed.

Think past it—have to think past it—

"The witch," I said, falling back on instinct. Shock was trying to settle in and I knew if I wasn't careful, I'd pass out right there. Not good, not good. "The kid who disappeared. The car. What can you tell me about them?"

A frown darkened her face. "What do you care about them? She was unaffiliated, alone. Her dad was an asshole and wouldn't let her come here, even when he was told it wouldn't cost him anything."

Green Road operated on a tuition and tithe basis. But kids who couldn't pay to attend the schooling could still come on a scholarship basis. Many of the witches were very, very wealthy, and most of them believed in taking care of their own.

"The kid. The car," I said again. "Anything you can remember?"

"No car. SUV. Florida plates." She rattled off a number, one I couldn't recall for the life of me, but it didn't dawn on me to ask her to repeat it. "Humans with her. I figured she was whoring for money. Some of us have to."

"She was just a kid," Damon said, his voice full of disgust.

"So was I," she said. "Didn't stop me."

"Anything about the humans?" I asked, cutting in.

"Snakes. The whole lot of them. The kind you just want to see die." She smiled and leaned toward me with a conspiratorial wink. "They were the kind I used to burn in the backyard, up until my dad found out what I was doing. Then he tried to beat the fire out of me. Literally. So…I burned him."

"Bully for you."

Chapter Twelve

Es was speaking.

I barely heard her.

I was cold. All over cold.

A hand came over the back of my neck and shoved my head down between my knees. "Breathe, kitten," somebody rumbled, a familiar voice.

It tickled something in my memory. Kitten. Didn't like that.

"...*something for her hand...*"

Voices roared around me, echoing in my ears.

A softer one, that didn't make much sense. Then his. Damon. Demonic Damon. Pain in my ass.

"I don't care. You're going to either heal her hand yourself, or you're going to get somebody in here to do it for you, or I'll take it personally."

A soft laugh tinkled through the room. Dimly, I realized this wasn't good. I needed to think past the pain that seemed to be snaking up my entire arm. It was a burn. I'd been burned before. Granted, never this bad. And shit, I had to get it healed, but I could call Colleen and she'd help me. Somehow. She'd help.

I made myself sit up, staring at the black and red meat that made up my hand.

"Calm down, Damon," I said. The thin, high sound of my voice didn't sound very reassuring. Clearing my voice, I tried again. "I'm fine."

"Your hand looks like a Texas barbecue gone bad. You're not fine."

"No. No, you're not," Es murmured. "Child, you suffer from an excess of great stupidity or great bravery. I'm not sure which."

She came around to me and nudged Damon aside. "Move over, cat. I'll fix her."

He glared at the back of her head but fell silent.

She settled in the chair next to me. "You know, we've measured her ability to generate heat...for short periods of time, she can put out over fifteen hundred degrees. You understand how dangerous that was?"

"My blade can take it."

"Humph. The blade, yes." She caught my hand and turned it, forcing the cooked meat of my palm upright. "But look at what it did to you."

"Hey, it got me the information I wanted."

"Silly child...I could have gotten you that, if you'd given me time," she murmured. Her fingers were cool on my wrist.

"But Doyle might not have time. And the next time I need to ask her something, maybe she'll be a little more likely to give it to me if she views me as more than just dirt on her boots." I groaned as I felt the first brush of her magic. "I may not be her equal, but she knows I won't roll over like a dog for her, either. Her kind respects strength."

"True enough. But you took pain...and Tate isn't capable of that. I don't know if she'll respect you for that, or hate you." She deepened her hold and then looked at Damon. "You might want to hold her shoulders."

My breath started to come in harsh, heavy pants. "This is going to hurt, isn't it?"

"Yes. You may scream. Nobody will hear you but us."

"No." I scrambled at my waist for my belt but pain and panic made me clumsy.

"Child, we need to hurry. The longer we delay, the more risk there is for permanent damage."

I nodded jerkily, still clawing at my belt.

"Shit," Damon muttered, hauling me back from the table.

He crouched in front of me, trying to see what I was doing. "Why are you messing with your belt, Kit?"

"Knife." My teeth were chattering now. Shock? The pain? I didn't know.

"Bad time to decide to stab me," he said. "You couldn't fight off a puppy right now."

"Knife..."

"Okay, okay..." He worked the knife sheath off my belt and pulled out the knife, but I knocked it aside and reached for the sheath.

His face tightened in a scowl and he held it for a second. Finally, though, he let it go.

As he eased me back to the table, I shoved the leather between my teeth.

In the back of my mind, I could hear the echo of a laugh. *Scream for me, granddaughter. It's the only time I enjoy hearing your voice. Scream...let me know how easily you break.*

As the bright edge of pain broke through me, I bit the leather and struggled to hold back the screams.

Scream...you useless waste.

I woke to darkness.

Cool, complete darkness.

My body felt too heavy to move and I groaned, struggling to lift a hand to my face, but even that took too much energy.

Groaning, I muttered, "Great. Just great."

"Tell me about it."

Gurgling out a yelp, I tried to scramble out of the bed, but I couldn't even move. A full-fledged healing wasn't much different than coming off a bad case of the flu. It was short-lived, and after I had a meal and a few hours of rest, I'd be okay.

Oh, and I needed to get the hell away from the bastard lying in the bed next to me.

Damon leaned over and snapped on the lamp on the bedside table. It brought him entirely too close to me. If I could have shrunk into the bed, pulled away, jabbed him with a hot poker, any of those things, I would have.

As it was, I couldn't even find the strength to reach for the damn blankets. And I was cold.

He stayed where he was, on his elbow, peering down into my face. "How do you feel?"

I closed my eyes.

A soft laugh drifted from him. "That good, huh?"

I flexed my hand, rotated it.

"You go ahead and call your sword, baby girl, if it will make you feel better, but you'll just drop it. You can't hold it right now and you know it."

I opened my eyes to glare at him. "Fu…"

Well. That went well. Clearing my throat, I managed to rasp out, "Fuck off."

"Nice manners." He reached over and caught my wrist, dragging it in front of my face. "She fixed it, completely. Don't worry, once you can drag your pretty tail out of this bed, you'll be good as new."

I closed my eyes again.

"You know, I had no idea a full healing would hit you so hard. The quiet is nice."

I kept my eyes closed.

After a few minutes, the pervasive weakness took over and I retreated back into sleep.

Let me in, darling…

I felt Jude whispering at the edges of my mind.

Grunting, I turned away and tried to block him out. The chill of his presence was something I just didn't want right then, although if he pushed, I didn't know if I could fight him off.

I was too tired.

What is wrong? You feel sick. Or ill—

I continued to ignore the press against my mind, struggling to wake up, but the bonds of sleep were…powerful. Too powerful. And that cold chill pressed so close. Shivering, I wiggled away from it, instinctively seeking out the warmth I felt in the bed.

Warmth.

Strength.

Part of me knew exactly what that warmth and strength was.

The rest of me didn't care.

As strong arms came around me, the cold chill faded away and I sank back into a dark, dreamless sleep.

"Scream."

The whip came flying through the air again.

I'd bitten my lip bloody and I knew I'd scream again.

But not yet—

94

"Scream, you useless waste."

A broken whimper escaped me as the edge of the whip came around, the tip licking the bottom curve of my breast.

"You tried to enter the Dominari."

I tensed, certain for the next lash of the whip.

It didn't come.

"You actually think you can *run* the Dominari."

Her voice was a mocking, ugly laugh as she came close. Her hand shot out, fisted in the long tangle of my hair, jerking my head back. "Why do you bother?"

Because I'd fail.

The race was brutal and cruel, and of the twenty or so students who ran it every year, nearly half of them had to be rescued or they'd die on the course. Of course, they always called for help. I'd screw up. And when I faltered, I wouldn't call for help. I planned to go out there and die. It was my best chance at escape.

"You know you can't survive such a…Oh. Oh…now I see."

Her mocking laughter surrounded me and once again, the whip lashed through the air.

Once more, I woke and I was unable to move.

It wasn't weakness that kept me pinned immobile, though.

This time, it was arms. Massively muscled arms that held me sprawled atop a massively muscled chest. One arm was banded across my upper back. The other hand cradled my head.

Cradled—

I tensed, squeezing my eyes closed. Okay. This was awkward. I didn't know entirely why I was sprawled across Damon's body, or why he was clutching me like an overgrown doll, but he wasn't cradling anything. Probably debating on the best way to snap my neck when My Lady told him to.

"Go back to sleep," he muttered.

I shoved against his chest.

Those arms didn't loosen one single bit.

He heaved out a sigh and rolled and now, instead of sprawling across his body, I was pinned under it and that wasn't any better. Not at all. Startled, I stared up into his face. The storm clouds in his eyes were sleepy and his short hair was about as mussed as it was ever going to get. "Can't you ever just do what you're told?" he asked irritably.

"What in the hell are you doing?"

"Well, I was sleeping," he drawled. "And it was the first peaceful night's sleep I've had since the kid disappeared, too. Hard to sleep soundly when I'm keeping one ear cocked for whatever harebrained scheme you've got cooked up, but since I figured you'd have a hard time getting out of the bed without waking me, I figured it was a good time to let my guard down."

"Why in the hell are you in my bed?"

"Easy." He sprawled on top of me, pressed far, far too close for comfort, seemingly completely content to do so. "It's not your bed. The witches only had the one open room and I wasn't about to sleep on the floor when there was a giant king-sized bed up here. You're a little thing. How was I to know you'd end up on top of me?"

Blood crept up to my cheeks as I tried to wiggle away from him.

The arm he had around my waist was putting a damper on that, though.

And against my belly, I felt something else—

Oh, hell.

Asshole. He fell into asshole territory and he's not getting out of it. *You don't sleep with assholes.*

Something brushed against my neck. The pads of his fingers.

"Let go of me," I whispered. Although I wasn't exactly expecting him to listen.

It was something of a surprise when he rolled away and did just that.

Scrambling out of the bed, I all but fell on my ass in my hurry to get away from him. "Look, I don't know what in the hell your problem is, but you need to get over it," I snapped.

That cagey grin lit his face. "Oh, you know what it is. You just don't want to think about it."

I opened my mouth. Closed. Opened it again. Then, still not sure what to say, I decided to err on the side of caution and closed it. Stumbling to my feet, I looked around the room. It was simple, done in dark wood, a dresser by a window covered in heavy drapes. I caught sight of my reflection and then yelped as I realized I was only wearing a shirt.

And not one of mine.

One of his, if I guessed right.

"What the hell…?"

A heavy sigh came from the bed. "Don't go getting all riled up, baby girl. You needed to sleep in the worst way and you weren't going to get it dressed in that combat gear you call clothing. I promise, I didn't even look. Well…much."

"You…" I shoved my hands through my hair. "You're an asshole."

He came up off the bed and prowled closer. "Yeah. Yeah, yeah, yeah…I know. I'm an asshole. An abusive one, and now you can even add a perverted one to the list of my sins." He dipped his head and I stiffened.

Move—my brain screamed.

My legs wouldn't cooperate.

Heat bloomed inside my belly.

"Here's the funny thing, though, baby girl…you're the one who all but climbed on top of me during the night. You had your arms wrapped around me, practically your legs."

I swallowed, blood rushing to my face.

A big hand curled over the back of my neck, his fingers pushing to tangle in my hair. I felt the warm puff of his breath against my ear as he whispered, "I have to admit, it was one of the nicest handfuls I've had in quite a while. But don't worry. I behaved myself completely."

That heat curdling inside me threatened to explode. Slowly, I pulled away.

Without looking at him, I snagged my bag. There was a door a few feet away. I was praying it was a bathroom. But even if it was the hallway or a closet, I didn't care. I needed to get away from him.

Before I did something really, really stupid.

Chapter Thirteen

The last witch hadn't been able to shed much light on the subject, other than the fact that yes, she'd seen another witch. One who was missing, in this general area.

It hadn't been a black car, though.

It had been a busted-up, steel blue van.

Something about that niggled the back edge of my memory, but I couldn't figure out what.

"Now where, baby girl?" Damon asked as he tossed our bags into the back of the car.

I ignored him as I pulled a map out of the glove box. He came up behind me as I was unfolding it. The wind kept grabbing at it and he leaned over, pinned it down on one side, while I held the other.

"What you looking for?"

"A sudden, blinding flash of insight," I muttered. Since I wasn't really expecting that to happen, I pulled a pen from inside my black vest. He'd referred to it earlier as combat gear. It wasn't. It was just…useful. Very useful. I bent down and marked an X on the map. "First sighting."

Finding the next was harder.

I marked it and put a tiny little two next to it.

The third and fourth had been practically on top of each other.

I starred the fourth—something about the van was still bugging me.

"Why the star?"

"The van." I fisted a hand in my hair and stared at the map, although I wasn't seeing it. In the back of my mind, I saw a dusty blue van. Where, though…where did I remember seeing it? In person? On the news? Hell, for all I know, it could have been one of the hundreds of MP reports I had to churn through. Shoving my hair back from my face, I stared at the starred X. "Something about the van is bugging me."

His hand stroked up my back.

I was so busy concentrating for a minute, it didn't occur to me to notice.

But as he rubbed his thumb over my nape, I tensed. Swallowing, I closed my eyes. "Damon…why in the hell are you touching me?"

"I think we've already established this," he said, his voice low as he leaned in over the map, studying it with the same intent gaze I was. "I think you know, if you'd just let yourself think about it."

I set my jaw. "I have no idea what you're talking about."

"Uh-huh." He tapped a point on the map. "We should go visit the park. Since we're here. Take a hike or something."

"A hike?" Shrugging away the hand at the nape of my neck, I started folding up the map. "I'm sort of in the middle of working a case that I need to solve unless I want the Alpha Cat to try and rip my throat out."

He reached up. Laid a hand on said throat. "I'll take care of your throat, Kit."

"Uh-huh. So reassuring from the man who all but crushed it a week ago."

That look darkened his eyes, the one I couldn't quite comprehend. "I'll take care of it," he said again. "And we need to go on a hike. I caught weird smells on the wolf kid. Maybe I can track them."

I trudged along behind him, swatting at mosquitoes, cursing the heat, still feeling too damned tired and wondering how long we'd be out here. We'd spent most of yesterday in the woods and had collapsed at a little roadside hotel only to get up at dawn and return.

He'd wanted to check out the northern part of the park, but my gut told me to go south. So here we were. And I was miserable.

Thirst nagged at me and I tugged the bottle from the pack I carried. I emptied it in three long drinks and added it to the small collection in my bag. Rummaging through the pack, I unearthed a granola bar, but before I could tear into it, I found myself trapped between Damon's body and a bent, gnarled tree that felt rough against me, even through my T-shirt and the material of my vest.

Swearing, I jerked a look up at him. "L—"

A hand covered my mouth and he looked down at me, shaking his head.

Storm clouds swirled in his eyes and the pupils swirled. Flared. And as I watched, the bones in his face started to shift.

Swallowing, I nodded.

He backed away, lifting a finger to his mouth.

Yes, yes. I get the point.

He held out the pack he'd slung on his back. His hand was human when he started the motion, but furred, clawed by the time I caught the pack. The damn pack was more than twice the weight of my own. I shifted my balance and swung it onto my back. He pointed to the tree and mouthed, *Stay.*

At least that was what I thought he said.

Hard to say…because the bones around his mouth, the shape of it…everything was changing.

Slowly.

I decided it was easier to watch a shift in full speed rather than this. Muscles appeared in places where they didn't belong and bones broke, realigned, formed, as fur spread and flowed along his body.

He stripped out of his clothes as he changed, the slow shift giving him the time to get of them without them falling to shreds around him. And it was all so completely silent. Completely eerie.

I still couldn't hear whatever had caught his attention.

Even when he turned his back, standing on two massive legs, more than double the width they'd been only minutes earlier and prowled forward, I couldn't hear anything.

Dark golden fur, almost the same gold as his skin, spread across his body. There were spots of deep, dark gray, nearly the same shade as his eyes, all across his arms, shoulders and legs.

He almost looked like a wereleopard I'd seen once, but that didn't seen quite right.

Cat. I could only think cat.

As he disappeared into the trees, I dealt with the bags. I managed to shove them into the branches of the tree, hooking the straps around another branch to keep them from tumbling out of place. Out of the way, off the ground, and I didn't have to worry about tripping over them.

That done, I gathered up his clothes and wedged them on top of the bags. Once I'd done that, I drew my blade and faded.

There was no way I was standing here in this hot, oppressive forest for anybody to find me.

Especially when I didn't know just what had sent him prowling off into the silence alone.

A breeze kicked up and that's when I heard them.

Dogs. Baying.

Voices...

Backing up against the tree, I held my breath.

I could climb the damn tree if I had to get away from the dogs but then I could end up trapped. I didn't know if they were coming—

So focused on the dogs, I didn't notice the bigger, quieter problem.

She tore through the trees, naked and trembling, young and terrified. I can see the mantle of her energy hovering over her—an overgrown housecat, I thought, spine arched, hair on end, swiping out at anything that moved. Too terrified to fight well.

I dropped the invisibility and moved forward.

She saw me—briefly, I realized that something about her face seemed familiar. Very familiar...*blue van*, I thought dumbly.

Oh, *shit*—

This was the girl that had gone missing from Atlanta, I realized. *A month* ago. Son of a *bitch*—

But even as my brain processed that, she started to scream.

"Shhh." I struck out and grabbed her wrist, whirling her around and slamming her against the tree. I caught her off guard, just enough to stun her, the only reason it worked. Mind whirling, I grabbed the shirt Damon had shed from the pile of clothing and shoved it at her.

It fell to her feet.

She just stood there. Trembling. Abruptly, she just collapsed, curled in on herself and moaning like a cornered animal. I guessed that wasn't too far off.

And all the while, the baying of the dogs got closer.

This was bad.

Very bad...

100

When Damon sprang through the trees, I had never been so glad to see him. Glad enough to see him that I just might forgive him almost anything. He saw the girl, saw my sword. In his half-form, a weird look that might have been a smile split his monstrous face.

"Foolish enough to fight," he rumbled.

I lifted a brow and then looked to the girl.

He picked her up, hefted her over his shoulder. "Just humans. The dogs are a problem, though. You hide," he said shortly. "And be here when I come back."

Just humans…nothing I couldn't handle, I figured. But yeah, dogs are a problem. While I could outrun any human on earth, dogs were a different story. Sighing, I glanced up into the limbs spread out over my head. "Can you boost me?"

I'd barely gotten the question out before I was scrambling up through the branches. I hauled the bags as I went, stashing his as best as I could in foliage and slinging mine back into place. As long as I was wearing it, it would fade away when I did.

He stared at me for a long, hard moment and even after I faded from sight, he lingered for a moment. Then he was gone.

I calculated two minutes before the dogs burst into the clearing.

They paused, sniffing at the tree and tipping back their heads to howl like the devil.

Shoo, I thought, glaring down at them.

A couple of them were staring right at me, but they couldn't see me. They could smell me, yes, and hear me, most certainly, but they couldn't see me.

When the humans stumbled out behind them, I clenched the blade even more tightly. Two, three, four…five.

I waited with bated breath for another one, but that was it.

They all gathered around the dogs, peering up at the tree. "What the hell's the matter with them?"

Tall guy. Blond, dirty. Looked like he hadn't bathed in a month. Stank like it, too.

"Maybe she hid up there, thinking to throw them off."

Dirty-Blond sniggered. "Won't work. I bet she tried the swamps next. Hope not, though. Gators don't like cats being around them. If they get a bite of her…"

Another one, short and stumpy with stringy hair, shook his head. "She's still too strong. She won't get caught by a gator." A smile split his face. "We'll be looking for her for a while. And if we catch her before the other team…"

Teams.

I studied each face. Committed them to memory.

I didn't mess with humans. I stayed away from them because they could bring too much trouble down on us.

But these weren't humans. Not if they were hunting kids.

That made them monsters.

"Come on. We need to get moving. If somebody else finds her, we have to pony up the dough. Not this time."

They moved off into the woods. I settled deeper into the tree and drew my knees to my chest. Part of me wanted to climb down and go after them. If it hadn't been for the dogs, I might have.

I could take five humans.

But the dogs evened the odds in their favor just a little bit.

Too bad I hadn't brought my bow and arrow.

I wouldn't make that mistake again. Of course, if I'd realized we'd be dealing with something like *this*, I damn well *would* have brought it.

Live and learn, Kit. Live and learn.

Night was falling by the time I saw the brush and branches swaying. It had been a couple of hours, easy.

If this wasn't Damon, screw him—

Rising, I stared down as the trees parted and I found myself staring down into feline eyes that reflected the fading sunlight.

He was searching the tree for me. I faded back into sight with a sigh and groaned as a headache slammed into me. Swaying a little, I started to work my way down. "It's about time," I muttered.

Exhaustion made my hands clumsy but I determinedly kept on climbing. By the time I stood on firm ground, my muscles were trembling and my head was pounding in time with my heart.

"When you said wait, I didn't think it would be for hours." I shoved my blade into the sheath, staring at his alien face.

He was silent.

Not like him.

I couldn't be a total bitch to him without him mouthing off right back.

"Ah...Damon?"

He took a step toward me.

I backed away.

Fur and muscle melted away and I found myself staring at a much more familiar face, into storm-cloud eyes.

"The girl is okay, right?"

He gave a short, single nod. "With the witches. Called Es—played up on her duty to the Assembly."

Okay, so he'd spoken two sentences there. "Okay...so what's with you?"

His hand shot out and I found myself plastered against him two seconds later. "You stayed."

"Damn it," I snapped, shoving against his chest. Hard and hot, my hands slid against the smoothness of his flesh without budging him an inch. "What did you think I was going to do? I barely even know where I am."

"You're a little fool," he muttered.

Then he buried his face against my neck and I shuddered.

"I never know when you're going to show sense or do something that will end up with you dead…or worse."

I could feel the heated puff of his breath against my skin and that shouldn't feel so good. It shouldn't feel so good at all.

Asshole. Territory. He was asshole. Territory.

I couldn't…

My breath hitched in my chest as he lifted his head, staring down at me with eyes that burned. Storm clouds shouldn't burn so hot. But his eyes did.

Couldn't breathe, couldn't breathe—

He dipped his head.

Oh, shit—

But he didn't kiss me.

Instead, I felt the hot brush of his lips moving along the skin at my throat. Starting just under my ear, moving along the flesh, slowly, thoroughly, until he had kissed, stroked, marked.

"The bruises are pretty much gone, Damon. Don't you think it's a little late to try and kiss it better?" I managed to squeeze out.

"Can't do it anyway," he rumbled. "Damage done can't be undone. But I can sure as hell regret it."

A few seconds later, he let me go.

I stumbled away and turned my back, shoving my hands through my hair. Shit. My brain was a whirled-up muddle and I didn't even know how to process this.

Swallowing, I decided the best way to handle it was not to think about it. At all.

If I didn't think about it, then I could pretend it hadn't happened.

Except every inch of my throat burned.

And every inch of my body ached.

"We should get the hell out of here," I said hoarsely. "I need to talk to that girl."

It was a hike that took forever.

My muscles were a mess already just from the endless crouch in the tree. It wasn't anything I hadn't had to do before, remain motionless for hours on end, but I wasn't bred for hiding in a tree and it had taken a toll.

On top of that, remaining unseen was *hard*. It was meant to be done for short periods of time, not for hours on end. I almost felt like I had a hangover, but I hadn't had the fun of getting drunk first.

And then, of course, half of my brain was trying to think about what had happened earlier—*especially* the part of my brain that was controlled by my long-unused sex drive…and maybe some other part of me that was stupid enough to be drawn to the bastard. The other part of my brain was in furious denial.

All in all, I was in no shape to be hiking through the Everglades National Park.

I needed food. I needed a bath. I needed sleep.

What I didn't need was the exposed root in the middle of the path that tripped me up and sent me sprawling. My exhausted body just couldn't react in time.

Damon, obviously, didn't suffer that problem and a microsecond before I planted my face in the dirt, hard hands caught me, one gripping my arm, the other snagging the backpack. He had me back on my feet with a speed that left my head spinning and I groaned, burying the heels of my hands against my eye sockets and praying for oblivion.

The pounding at the base of my head increased.

"What's wrong?"

"Nothing." I did *not* want to talk to him. I did *not* want him being nice and the tone of his voice was too close to nice right now.

Swallowing, I willed myself to think past the pain. I bullied myself into moving. I made it another twenty steps before I stumbled again.

"All right," Damon snapped. He'd been hovering at my side despite my attempts to keep some distance between us and I hadn't gone down, but I felt like I was moving through quicksand, each movement agony and it was getting harder to stay upright. "What in the hell is wrong?"

His hand closed around my neck when I tried to turn my head aside.

Oh...there he was. Dominating, pushy bastard.

"Nothing," I lied through my teeth. Then I smiled.

He snarled. The sound that came out of his throat wasn't the kind of sound that should come out of *anybody's* throat when they still wore human skin.

Arching my eyebrows, I said, "Sorry, cat. You'll have to do better than that. Hey, I know...you can try wringing my neck again. That's your favorite threat, anyway."

"How about this...you either tell me what is wrong with you, or I'll throw you over my shoulder and haul your cute ass back to the car."

I sneered at him.

Then I found myself plastered against him for the second time that night. Thoughts fizzled away and I was having a hard time breathing. That was bad, too, because my heart was beating so hard and all that blood rushing to my head...now I was getting light-headed.

His hand stroked down my back, rested on the curve of my hip with his fingers gripping my butt. "Here's your last chance, kitten. You can tell me...or I'll just assume you want me getting that up close and personal with your anatomy."

"Fine." I drove a fist into his stomach.

He let me go, but it was more to humor me than anything else, because there was absolutely no strength to it.

I didn't have any left. It was nothing short of a miracle that I was able to stay upright. Stumbling backward, I sagged against one of the gnarled trees and glared at him through tangled, sweaty hair. I needed a bath. Scratching at one of the numerous mosquito bites, I thought about just heading on down the path another fifteen feet until I tripped over the concrete blocks that had replaced my feet. But I was pretty sure he'd do exactly what he said and I wasn't certain my pride could handle it. Maybe if I rested for five minutes...just five minutes.

Slipping off the backpack, I rooted around through it but I'd gone through all the water. And the granola bars. All that was left was a lousy pack of gum.

Miserable, I let it drop to the ground before covering my face with my hands. "I'm tired," I said flatly. "In case you haven't noticed, I'm not exactly built for crouching in a tree for hours on end. And I had to do it while staying unseen—it's hard to maintain that for long periods of time. I feel like I've been run over by a truck. My head feels like it's about to explode, I can barely move my legs, I haven't eaten, I stink to high heaven and I feel like I'm going to fall on my face—oh, wait, I've just about done that."

Seconds ticked away. I heard the rasp of a zipper. Then his voice, as flat as mine. "Here."

Dropping my hands, I looked up and saw the bottle. It was one of his, half empty.

I crossed my arms over my belly and looked away.

"Take the damn water or I'll pour it down your throat. And in a minute, I'm going to give you an energy bar and you'll eat it, or I'll shove that down your throat along with the water," he warned.

"You need the water as much as I do," I snapped.

"This isn't as hard on me as it is on you." He continued to hold the bottle out. "Were, remember? And I grabbed something to eat on the way back."

I flicked a glance at him, saw a look in his eyes. Decided I didn't want to know what he'd snacked on. Seeing as how there wasn't a restaurant around for miles... yeah, I didn't want to know.

Snagging the bottle, I popped it open and guzzled. Nausea rolled through me, but I battled it down, breathing shallowly until it passed. It was another sixty seconds before I thought I might not start to puke. And there was no way I wanted to do that.

"Just so you know, if you try to make me eat a damn thing, I'm just going to hurl it up," I said. "I need to eat, but I can't do it right now. I pushed myself too hard A faint sigh escaped him. "Fine. But we've still got five miles to go. And we can't do it with you stumbling every other step, Kit."

"Just give me a minute. I'll be okay."

The baleful look in his eyes told me that he very clearly didn't believe that.

I glared back at him.

There was no way I was spending those five miles flung over his shoulder like a sack of flour.

Okay, so the alternative was that I spent it curled up in his arms while he carried me like a damn toddler.

"I'm going to get sick," I told him after the first few minutes.

"Okay. Just give me a warning."

I lapsed into silence for about five minutes.

"You're still one of the biggest assholes I've ever met."

I said that while looking at my knees, because I wasn't going to crane my head to look up at him.

"Don't worry. You're not the first person to tell me that. And rest assured, baby girl, you're one of the most stubborn and headstrong females I've ever met. Probably *the* most stubborn."

"Don't call me baby girl. I'm not *that* stubborn."

"Uh-huh." He stroked a thumb down my arm. "You know, seeing as how you can't walk and we still have about twenty minutes to go before I can get us to the car, why don't you start thinking through the next step?"

I made a face. I wasn't about to tell him that thinking downright *hurt*. Right then, though, *everything* hurt. My brain felt like it had been ripped open and fried and then sewn back together.

"The girl was a cat," I murmured, closing my head and trying to relax a little. That, oddly enough, wasn't terribly hard, as long as I didn't think about it. Damon was carrying me, both packs and he wasn't even winded. I sent my blade back to the car because it was just too awkward to try to carry it like this, plus, it just felt too heavy right then. I couldn't even carry my sword, and he was hauling me around like I weighed nothing.

"Yes." His thumb was still stroking the sensitive skin of my shoulder where he held me. "How can you always tell?"

"I just can." Even though thinking was so very painful, I made myself do it. "Remember that girl from Atlanta who went missing a month ago? There was video of some guys grabbing her in broad daylight?"

I glanced up at him and saw the muscle twitch in his jaw as he said flatly, "It's her."

"Yeah. That's the van I was thinking of. I knew there was a blue van I needed to remember." Blowing out a breath, I tried to find some way to hold my head that wouldn't add to the ache, but the only thing that worked just wasn't doable. Leaning against his chest felt so nice, but…no. Just no. "What kind of cat is she, can you tell?"

"Smelled like a lynx. Hard to be sure—she's still in the middle of her spike so her scent's chaotic. Why?"

I shook my head and then groaned as it sent pain sparking through my skull all over again. "Just thinking it through. Isn't that what you told me to do?"

He rubbed his cheek against my hair. "Maybe you should just rest instead. You did enough today, Kit. That girl will go home because of you."

"No. You're the one who said hiking."

"But I'm not the one who planned on heading south."

I closed my eyes. In the back of my mind, there was a vague, odd sense of unrest. Too much left undone. Doyle was still missing. So were the other children. "We have to come back here tomorrow," I said quietly.

Damon's arms tightened on me. "I know."

I didn't remember reaching the car.

I didn't remember getting to a hotel. Not exactly a posh place.

I definitely didn't remember how I ended up in bed.

But I woke up sprawled on top of the coverlet, done in stunning shades of puce and vomit-green, to the smell of food. My belly rumbled and I popped one eye opened in time to see Damon at the door, shoving bills into the hand of a delivery boy.

Food.

There was food.

I sat up just as he shut the door.

The hotel room boasted a small kitchenette, and over on the counter, I spied four pizza boxes, three cardboard takeout boxes, and some sort of foil tray. I jumped out of bed, but before halfway there, I stopped.

My belly was rumbling, but I smelled bad enough to kill a dead horse.

I needed to shower before I ate.

Still…

Okay, I compromised and flipped open the top box of pizza, snagging one slice and practically inhaling it as I headed for my bag. A quick shower. Then I'd eat.

I wanted to soak for a month, but I didn't have that luxury. So a shower. Then food.

"How are you feeling?"

"Tired, dirty and hungry," I said around a mouthful of pizza.

A faint grin twitched the corners of his mouth. "Sit down and eat. Then shower."

I shook my head. "I have to shower." I couldn't sit down when I was dirty like this. It was a miracle I'd even been able to get what little rest I'd gotten when I was this filthy.

She's a pig, Rana. I set my jaw as another memory worked its way free. My dear old grandmother. *You know how humans are, and she is no better.*

Nights spent sleeping in the dirt. Skin all but black with it. I'd itch until I bled and she didn't care. My clothes would fall to rags—

"Stop it," I muttered, forgetting for a moment that I wasn't alone.

"Kit?"

I shook my head as the pizza lodged in my throat like a stone. Carefully, I made my way into the little kitchenette and snagged a plate, laid it down. "Try to leave me some food, cat," I said, not looking his way.

I had left behind that hell the year I found the courage to run.

I needed to remember that.

Chapter Fourteen

Six hours of sleep did wonders for me.

That, and a meal.

I'd managed to make myself eat and then I collapsed.

Morning came too early, and I would have slept more, if it wasn't for the fucking phone going off.

I recognized that ring and I wished I could have just buried my head under the blanket and hide away from the world.

Damon, like me, tended to use ringtones for various people.

There was only one person who didn't have a ringtone—the Queen Bitch herself, and hers was just the plain, regular, old-fashioned ring. The sound of it was like an ice pick in my ears and as much as I wanted to hide my head under the covers, I didn't.

As I heard Damon greet her with his formal, "Good morning, My Lady," I sat up and mimed like I was gagging myself.

He stared daggers at me.

I rolled my eyes and climbed out of bed, making a beeline for the bathroom. I still felt like the dirt, and sweat, and stink from yesterday clung to my skin. Shower. Long and hot, then more food. Thankfully, the headache was gone. I used the toilet, but somewhere in between washing my hands and stripping off my clothes, there was a hard, demanding knock at the door and it opened before I had a chance to jerk my shirt back on.

"Do you mind?" I glared at him.

He stared at me, a deadly look in his eyes.

He had the phone in his hand. "She wants to talk to you. A couple of warnings—I told her about the girl. She wants to know what progress is being made and she's not pleased that you haven't found Doyle yet."

"Yeah, well, I'm not exactly dancing in circles about the fact, either," I said, glaring at him. I clutched my shirt to my chest. "Can you give me a minute?"

"No." He took the phone off mute. "Here is the investigator, My Lady. I apologize for the delay."

He shoved the phone at me without another second and I suspected if I didn't take the damn phone, he wouldn't be above hogtying me and forcing me to talk to the crazy bitch.

Turning my back to him, I lifted the phone. "Colbana."

"Kit..."

She practically purred my name.

The soft, throaty sound of it shouldn't have sounded so deadly, but it made me shudder. I had to battle back the metallic taste of fear crowding my throat before I could even respond. "What may I do for you this morning, Alpha?"

"I'd like to know why you haven't found my Doyle, Kit."

"I'm looking. I think we're getting closer. There are—"

She interrupted me. "I don't want to *hear* anything except that you've found him." Then, contradicting herself and showing what a crazy bitch she was, she said, "Why exactly did you rescue some throwaway lynx yesterday instead of searching for my precious nephew?"

Throwaway. My palm heated. The woman wasn't even here and I wanted my blade. I wanted to cut her. I wanted to hurt her. Popping my wrist, I imagined it. Imagined actually *doing* it, although there was no way in hell I could. Not on my own. I'd taken some weaker shifters on my own before and I could do it again.

She wasn't a weaker shifter.

She was Alpha as all get out and there was no way I could take her. Well, not unless I played really, really dirty.

But it was fun to dream. I carried those happy thoughts as I formulated my reply. "I believe there's a connection and I'm using every tool at my disposal to find your nephew, Alpha. At this point, the girl is another tool."

Seconds ticked away. Long, long seconds.

"I hear you've spoken with witches. Are they more tools?"

"Some of the most skilled ones I have at my disposal," I answered honestly. "I believe one of them may have seen Doyle and I'm searching the area, looking for signs."

"I see." She made an odd sound, one of those noises that was just too deep for a human throat and it made the hair on the back of my neck stand on end. "Hurry up and find my nephew, precious, would you? I miss him. Now…put my boy back on the phone."

I held the phone over my shoulder and waited for him to take it.

He did. But if I thought he was going to leave, I was in for a rude awakening.

He continued to stand there.

Inches away. Too close for comfort. For sanity.

"Yes, My Lady."

My blood was roaring in my ears, too loudly for me to make out what the bitch was saying.

And then he touched my back, stroking the tip of one finger over one of my scars. It was one of the longer ones, from the top of my back, near my right shoulder, cutting diagonally down to stop just above my left hip.

"Of course, My Lady. She is."

He touched another scar. Shorter, this one. He rested his finger on the bottom edge of it, stroking it up to where it disappeared around my side, ending just below my left breast.

"Yes. I'm aware…." A few moments of silence. "I'll remind her. I—"

He went silent. From the corner of my eye, I saw him lay the phone on the counter by the sink. "She wants me to remind you what's going to happen if you don't find him," he said, his voice flat.

And still he continued to trace the scars.

I closed my eyes. "That's not the easiest thing to forget. Tell me, Damon... exactly who is going to be the lucky one? Is she going to do the deed?"

"The Lady doesn't like to get her hands dirty," he whispered, his voice a low, rough rasp. He traced another scar, one that curled around my hip. When he reached the end of it, he kept his hand there.

"I bet." Swallowing, I turned around, holding my shirt to chest. "What exactly is your position in her pack?"

He blinked and I noticed that he had ridiculously thick black lashes. He studied me through them for a long moment before he finally said, "Pretty much an enforcer. I handle security. Problems."

"And if I don't find her nephew, she'll decide I'm a problem."

A muscle jerked in his jaw. "I can't tell you what the Lady will decide."

"But you know how she's likely to think." I reached down and closed my hand around his wrist. "I'd rather you not keep touching me."

It was like trying to drag away a boulder.

"Stop it," I half-shouted, shoving at his chest. "Would you get the hell away from me?"

"Not in a thousand years," he muttered.

When he moved again, it was to pull me against him and move, spinning me around so that the bathroom door was against my back. "You'll find the kid, Kit. That's all there is to it." He pressed his lips to my shoulder.

"It's been almost two *weeks*." The futility of it was getting through to me. "Two weeks. And in case you haven't noticed...if he's involved in what we saw yesterday? He may already be dead."

"No. Doyle is smart. He's determined. You'll find him. But..." A shudder wracked his body. "If you don't—"

I turned my head and made myself open my eyes, made myself meet that intense gaze.

I had to acknowledge this.

I wanted him.

He was bad for me, I knew this.

He was bad for me the same way too much coffee was, the same way too much chocolate was, the way everything good and sinful sweet thing was...and I wanted him anyway.

The problem was that if I failed my job, his Alpha would order him to kill me, and I didn't have a chance in hell against him.

Nor was he going to *ignore* that order. I knew enough about the fucked-up hierarchy of the werepacks.

They just didn't ignore orders. If they did, they died.

"If I don't find him, she's going to tell you to kill me," I said softly. "And as..." I paused, closed my eyes and searched for the right word. How in the world did I describe the feel of his body against mine? The way I somehow felt safe around him —*safe* around a man who could kill me in a blink, safe around a man who'd damn near crushed my throat within a few hours of meeting me? Oh, this was insane.

"As *insanely* interesting as this feels? There's no way I'm going to even think about getting horizontal with a man who may well decide to kill me in the next few days, the next few hours, the next few minutes..."

His eyes flashed.

He leaned in.

My brain damned near exploded as he caught my lower lip between his teeth and nipped me. "Pretty little kitten, we don't have to be horizontal. Right like this is fine," he growled against my mouth. Then he shifted and whispered against my ear. "I decided quite some time ago that I wouldn't be killing you. It doesn't matter what the outcome of this job is. And anybody who tries is going to have to go through me. Nobody and nothing is going to hurt you as long as I'm around. Nobody hurts you when I'm around, you got me?"

His hands glided up my sides. It was a sensation that sent all sorts of hot, trembly little sparks crashing through me and for the longest time, I couldn't think. It got so, so much worse as the heels of his hands glided over the outer curves of my breasts. "You got awful quiet there, little kitten. Cat got your tongue?"

Dumbly, I just stared at him.

He might have been a cat, but the smile that lit his face just then looked decidedly wolfish.

"Actually...I haven't had that pleasure..." he muttered against my mouth. "Yet."

Seconds later, he stroked his tongue across my lips.

A gasp escaped me.

One of us shuddered. I don't know if it was him or me.

But then he pushed his tongue into my mouth and I wrapped my arms around his neck. Bad for me or not, he tasted too damn good to deny. His groan rumbled against my breasts and it was sheer amazement, the way it felt.

A big hand cupped my butt, boosted me higher. Wrapping my ankles around his hips, I arched against him. Through the thin cotton yoga pants I'd worn to bed, I could feel a thick, heavy ridge. His jeans held him confined and it was a damn good thing, because I could already see me trying to rip away my clothes and just wrap myself around him. Desperately. Hungrily. Forgetting everything else—

No...

Something important—

Groaning, I tore my mouth away from his and shoved against the muscled wall of his chest.

"This is insane."

His hands closed around my wrists.

"Life isn't exactly supposed to make sense, baby girl," Damon said quietly.

Shaking my head, I closed my eyes. I needed to think. Needed to think—

"If you don't find him, she'll want you dead," Damon murmured against my temple. "So we need to focus on finding him."

I stiffened. Well. That was a good way to throw a pall on things. Twisting away

111

from him, I moved on clumsy legs until I had a little bit of space between us. A very little bit. I glanced around and then shivered at the cool kiss of air on my naked flesh. Scowling, I looked down and saw my shirt on the ground. I bent over and grabbed it, hauling it over my head. "I wanted a shower," I muttered. "I just wanted a shower and I wanted to eat."

"You just took a shower last night," Damon pointed out.

I shrugged, absently scratching my arm. Even though there wasn't anything on me, I still felt dirty.

He noticed.

Dropping my hand, I crossed my arms over my chest and glared at him. "Are you going to let me shower?"

He stood there for a minute, studying me. "We're talking, baby girl. Very soon."

"I can't wait." I bared my teeth at him.

His hand snaked out and he caught the front of my shirt, hauled me against him. A kiss so hard, so quick, it left me breathless. "Keep doing that, kitten," he whispered. "And we'll just go complicating an already complicated mess. Now shower, so you can eat and we can talk and start trying to figure out the other options we've got."

"We've got *two*," I told him. "I find Doyle or I die."

"There's only one acceptable one. We find Doyle. But there are going to be other ones. We start figuring those out. Today."

I showered down, from head to toe, washed my hair twice and felt mostly better. Physically, at least.

Emotionally, mentally, I was still a mess. As I stood there slicking on lotion, I had to acknowledge an ugly fact—I was going to be a mess until this job was over and done, and maybe even for a while after.

Assuming I survived.

Of course, if Damon was to be believed, he didn't want me dead.

Not thinking about that right now, I told myself. Instead, I focused on the mundane task of digging through my bag for clothes. Tan tank top, sport bra, tan BDUs. A little bit cooler version of what I'd worn yesterday. I had some shorts I could wear, but that wasn't going to happen, not if we were going to head back into the Everglades. No way, no how was I going through there in shorts. It was stupid enough going out there in a tank top, leaving my flesh exposed for the mini-vampires also known as mosquitoes.

I grabbed the clothes I'd slept in and draped them over the shower rod. We needed to wash clothes if we were here more than another night. With my hair still wet, I left the bathroom.

Damon was standing at the window, talking in a low voice on the phone.

His conversation carried on, consisting mostly of grunts, repeated intermittent use of the words *yes* and *no*, and an occasional *hmmmm* thrown in for variety.

Hard to figure out who he was talking to, but I knew it wasn't the Queen Bitch.

His voice just didn't have that blind adoration, that *yes, ma'am, I'll kill whoever you need me to kill* obedience to it.

I opened the fridge and spied the box of pizza sitting there. We'd polished off two and half pizzas last night—I'd actually eaten nearly an entire one, plus some spaghetti and buffalo wings.

Pulling it out, I saw there were only two pieces left. But there was some spaghetti. He must have had some, too, because it had been half full last night and now there was just enough for me to have a bowl. That was fine. All I needed, really. Breakfast of champions: pizza and spaghetti. The carbohydrates would do me good, I figured.

I nuked the pizza, but ate the spaghetti cold, guzzling two cups of coffee while I waited for him to finish up his phone call.

By the time he had finished, I was done eating, had my socks on and was lacing my boots. "We should have ordered another pizza," I said.

"We'll get something from one of those fast-food joints you love so much," he said, watching as I started slipping my weapons into place.

"Don't bother on my account. I got enough."

He prowled across the room and settled on the bed just a foot away from me. Too close. Too close—

Trying to ignore him, I pulled on my vest, wrinkling my nose a little. It was stiff with sweat but it had too many places to hide weapons for me to *not* wear it. "If we're here past tomorrow, we have to stop long enough for me to wash my clothes." I settled it into place and reached for my garrote, working it into the collar.

"Do you always carry that many weapons on a job?"

I shrugged. "Depends on the job. If I'd figured yesterday's hike would turn out like it did, I would have brought *more*."

He stood up, laughing a little as he reached out and hooked his hands in the front of my vest. "Kitten, just how many more weapons can you *carry*?"

"My bow." Bitterness twisted my gut as I thought about the sleek, pretty carved piece I'd left at home because I hadn't planned on needing it. Plus, I still had to abide by U.S. laws and if I was caught carrying something as conspicuous as a bow and arrow in a national park, I'd be in major trouble. The sword, I could easily convince the authorities was part of my job, and the other weapons I carried weren't hunting weapons, but anybody who looked at the bow and arrow would think I'd gone into the 'glades to hunt—

Hunting—

"Hunting," I murmured.

Memory flashed through my mind. The boy. The wolf who'd been found. *They had him trapped somewhere…He tried to climb out. For a long, long while.*

"Hunting games…"

Would they?

"What are you mumbling about?"

I turned away from him, my mind whirling. In a rush, I finished with my weapons. I didn't strap my sword on yet. It wasn't easy to drive with her in place and it wasn't like I had to carry her for her to be handy. "We need to go," I said, shoving my hands through my damp hair. "Whatever we need to talk about, we'll do it on the road. But we have to go by the witches' house. I need to talk to the girl."

"She wasn't exactly in talking shape," Damon said, still studying my face.

"Maybe the mother and her healers worked wonders."

Chapter Fifteen

"It's you again."

I smiled at Kori, although I suspected it fell something short of charming.

The other day, her brows had been...well. Normal, I thought. Today, they were intersected with bare patches, like she'd decided to either wax or shave parts of the brows, but not others.

And instead of pink and blue in her hair, it was green and orange. She really, really made my eyes hurt.

"Hi, Kori."

She just grunted and then looked past me. "I guess I have to let your boy in, too."

"He's not mine," I said, trying not to think about the way his hand rested on the small of my back. Trying not to think about the way he'd had his tongue halfway down my throat earlier.

"He's not, huh?" Kori started to laugh. "Anybody told *him* that? Or you, for that matter?" She stepped aside and gestured down the hall. "Healing hall down at the end, through the mirror, on your right."

I blinked at her. "Did you say through the mirror?"

With a blinding smile, she said, "You heard right. It's always good to make sure we keep our weak and sick well hidden. In case somebody was lucky enough to take me out." Then she winked. "But trust me...nobody is that lucky."

"Okay." I wasn't going to challenge her in any way on that. Hell, I still had the memory of my cooked hand dancing large in my mind. Tate had done me some serious damage. Yes, it had been for a purpose, but still, damage was damage and Kori could wipe the floor with Tate.

"Hey, kid."

I paused and looked back at Kori.

She came closer, all long, muscled limbs and coiled grace. Tightly coiled grace, like she was ready to spring to action. She caught my hand and lifted it, studied it closely. "Takes balls to face somebody like Tate the way you did," she murmured. "She's not..."

A sad look entered her eyes. Then she shook her head. "Not all there."

I didn't know how to respond to that in any way that might not piss her off so I just kept my mouth shut.

"We need fighters," Kori said quietly. "But we don't need cruelty."

"Nobody needs cruelty."

Kori shrugged. "It has its place at times in our world." She let go of my wrist and then backed away. "Our house is here when you need it, kid. I'll be ready."

Again, I didn't know how to respond. It was an offer too generous for a mere thank you, but it was all I had. With a short nod, I said, "Thank you. If you ever need a sword…well, it's not magic like you have, but I'm damn good with it."

"I bet you are." She grinned and nodded. "Go find the little cat. I think the mother finally got through to her earlier, but…"

She craned her head around, studied Damon. "You might want to leave the boy elsewhere. He'll scare her."

"I know how to handle kids going through the spike. And just so you know? The boy has a name," Damon said.

"Yeah. I think you growled it at me before, but I forgot," Kori responded. "If I was at all interested, I'd ask you again what it was…but you don't really want me knowing yet. If I take that much interest in *your* name, it would be because I want to fuck you or kill you."

I managed to swallow my laugh.

Barely.

Down at the end. Through the mirror on your right.

I stared at the mirror and twitched at the massive amount of energy that hovered over it.

"It's just a mirror," Damon said, standing behind me.

"No, it's not."

"Yeah, it is. If they had the girl around here, I'd smell her and I don't…"

I listened to his words trail off as I pushed my hand through the glass.

This was amazing…

"Son of a bitch," Damon said from behind me.

I took a step forward. Then another.

I was halfway through the doorway when his hands closed over my shoulders. I could smell it now—it was like a sick house. A hospital. Like the healing hall back at Aneris, where I'd lived the first fifteen years of my life. Some of the healers in my mother's family had practiced a magic that was much like a witch's ability to heal and I could recognize the herbs just by scent alone.

All the time I spent at Colleen's had only added to that ability.

Rosemary, mint, alder bark, cardamom, Solomon's seal.

"Damn it, Kit."

I glanced back and looked at Damon. "Come on, are you afraid of a mirror?"

He hadn't been holding me as tight as he could have and I took advantage of it, twisting out of his grasp to push completely through the glass. His fingers swiped through, brushing over my hair, but I was inside the room now.

If he wanted me, he'd have to follow.

"Oh, he wants you."

I searched the gloom for Es, moving away from the glass. I found her sitting by a narrow bed. "What?"

"He wants you, I said." She smiled up at me. "I believe it's already been mentioned that he's in rut."

116

"Yeah, yeah." I glanced back over my shoulder, a little surprised that he hadn't come through the mirror yet. "Several people have used the phrase, but I'm not too familiar with it. What, is he in heat or something?" I wrinkled my nose at the thought. "That would get weird."

She started to laugh. "Oh, it's more complicated than that. Don't worry. He's not going to go spraying the grass where you live or anything. If he decides to mark his territory, it will get more personal."

"Gee, that sounds so very reassuring." He still hadn't come through.

"Magic unnerves some of the shifters," she said quietly. "Even though they are as much a product of it as we are."

"I'm not very magical." I could go invisible and I could call a sword. That was it.

"That's it? You almost always have luck on your side. You have an uncanny insight into things. And you can *see* magic," she murmured. "And you see it better than most others. Like her...what do you see when you look at her?"

I looked at the girl on the bed, kicking myself for not noticing earlier.

"I see a girl who's been hurt," I said flatly.

"That's not what you see."

Sighing, I stared again.

"She's hiding," I murmured. "Like she's curled up in on herself and won't come out."

"Yes...she fears her change now. Even though she's spiking...ah, there he is."

I looked back and saw a hand appear through the wall. It wasn't a mirror on this side. Just a wall. Seeing a hand poke through it was...odd. Very odd. It disappeared a second later and then a moment later, he came running through like he was ready to mow down anything in his path.

I applauded—quietly.

The mother chuckled.

Damon snarled at me.

"He keeps doing that like it's supposed to mean something," I said, turning back around to face her.

She smiled at me. "This is what I mean by it's so much more complicated. Don't worry. It will make sense in time. Come. I want you to talk to her."

"She's sleeping," I said.

"Yes...a deep, deep sleep. Your voice won't wake her. But you may help her. Come. Talk." She patted the bed by the girl's feet. "Talk...and I may be able to show you what you wanted to ask her. There are...awful things in her mind. Awful, Kitasa."

I blew out a breath but before I could take a step, a hand clamped around my neck. "Not smart," Damon growled. "She's spiking."

"She's *sleeping*," I pointed out. "And she's not going to do anything. Whatever those bastards were doing, it terrified her so much, she's fighting the spike."

"You can't fight it."

"Not indefinitely," the mother said. "But she's trying very hard. Don't worry so much, Damon. I can tell if she's going to stir and certainly you're fast enough to protect your own...aren't you?"

"I'm not his," I said. "Geez, are you all deaf?"

Damon's hand tightened, just a little, then he let me go. Somehow, it didn't surprise me that he hovered at my back, just an inch away as I settled on the foot of the bed at the girl's feet.

"Do you know her name?"

"Lesil. Her name is Lesil," the mother said quietly. "She was leaving school. Unhappy. The students there are unkind. She was trying not to cry when a car drove up. She knew the boy inside. He made her smile. Said he would buy her dinner. She wanted so badly for somebody to offer her a kindness..."

I knew what that was like.

"You've seen what happened to her?" I asked softly.

"Healing can be a deep, intimate experience."

Bile churned in the back of my throat as I lifted my gaze and met her eyes. "Who healed me?"

She inclined her head. "You were injured in my house. A visitor. By one who is still a pupil. Naturally, it was my responsibility."

Humiliation, rage, bitterness churned inside me.

Looking away from her, I focused on the girl. "There's nothing intimate about seeing somebody's most painful moments, Mother," I said quietly. "It's just another humiliation. Another dishonor."

Her hand touched mine. "I know you think so...but you were never dishonored, warrior. The dishonor is, and has always been, theirs."

I just shook my head.

"Tell me what I need to know to stop this." Focus on the job. Just the job.

Not the witch sitting next to me, and not the man behind me, staring at me with eyes I could practically feel searing me to the soul.

"He took her. There is a drug for shifters that incapacitates them—it's called *night*. I believe that is what he gave her, but I don't know because all I can experience is what *she* experienced. There was clarity and happiness, and she looked at him and smiled, laughed as she stole some of his fries, then she took a drink. She realized that something was wrong...got out of the car. It gets fuzzy, but she stumbled around. There were men, a van. Then...darkness. When she woke, she was in a hole."

I closed my eyes, fighting as memories swirled too close.

"You will not enter the Dominari, Kitasa. You will not shame this family—"

"I'm going to try, Grandmother." I'd stood up to her. I was fifteen and by our laws, I could enter if I chose. I had no sponsor and it would be grueling work alone, but I'd run it. And when I didn't make it, I'd drop down...and die.

The awful, lovely smile that spread across her face. "You will not." Hands grabbing me, dragging me.

"...she wasn't alone."

I gasped as I settled back into my mind, the memories of that time falling away. Swallowing, I shook my head to clear it and looked at the mother. "What?"

"She wasn't alone," the mother said patiently. "There were others with her. She could tell the weres by scent, but she can't recognize magic yet. Hasn't seen enough of it, I don't suppose, to know the taste of it, the feel of it. So the others, she thinks they were human. I wouldn't know if she is right or wrong."

I watched her sleeping face. It was a help, but it wasn't—

"I have images in mind," Es said softly. "They take them out. Run them, while men chase them. For...*sport*." She spat the last word out like it was something vile.

Everything inside me went cold.

"So that's it then. That's what it is. They take kids and hunt them down." I'd been right. It was all about a game. A sick, twisted game. Fury gripped me. I wanted to shriek with it. Instead, I tugged out Doyle's picture.

I showed it to the mother.

"Did she see him?"

She stared at the picture.

Then she looked at me. "I don't know. There is a boy, blond, handsome. But he's...changing."

I shot Damon a look over my shoulder. "This *is* a recent picture, right?"

"Yeah." Then he shrugged. "But if he's spiking hard, he could change fast."

"Not that fast..."

He cocked a brow. "The spike can hit some pretty weird. Like two or three years of growth spurts shoved into two or three weeks. It's why some of us have to eat around the clock—why that wolf kid might have been in such bad shape. His body didn't have the physical reserves to heal him because the spike was using them all up."

Okay.

Okay.

Blowing out a breath, I looked at the girl.

The mother had wanted me to talk to her—

"You were in hell once," she said quietly. "You know what it's like to fight your way out. And survive."

Closing my eyes, I rested a hand on the girl's foot. She flinched at the touch, but I didn't move away. "Hey, Lesil. You need to wake up. I...uh..." Blood crawled up my neck and I had to fight not to cringe at the shame and anger twisting, vying for control inside of me. "You got away from them, but if you don't wake up...*they still win*."

Then I rose.

The mother was watching me with mild disapproval.

I shrugged. "Rage and fear kept me going for a long time. Sometimes it's what you need to get you moving." Glancing back at Lesil, I murmured, "She's already choking on the fear. Maybe the rage can be a lifeline. Once she's not drowning, we can give her another."

Her lips pursed. "That's not the witch's way."

"But neither of us are witches."

Turning away, I strode to the wall. "I assume I just go out the way I came in?"

She didn't answer.

I hoped it was a yes. I'd rather not walk right into a wall.

Chapter Sixteen

I made him drive.

He glared at me and started to argue.

I just threw the keys at him. He didn't catch them so they hit his chest and then the ground. I shrugged and walked around to the other side of the car, flopping in the passenger's seat. He had it shoved *way* back and I had to move it forward in order to not feel like I was sitting in the back seat.

Resting my head on the padded headrest, I started to talk.

I'd been ruminating out loud for a minute before he finally climbed in and shoved the seat back enough for his long legs.

"Anybody ever told you that you're a pain in the ass?" he asked conversationally.

"All the time." I rooted through the cloth bag Kori had shoved into my hands on the way out the door. She'd mentioned the little black pot would help with mosquitoes. My only hope was that it didn't smell like piss or something even more vile.

To my delight, it smelled rather pleasant. Herbal, certainly, but nothing unpleasant.

"We should get a map of the park," I said. "You have an idea of where all we covered yesterday?"

"Yes." He stretched out an arm.

When he started toying with my hair, I tensed up.

It didn't stop him.

Closing my eyes, I told myself to concentrate. That was what I needed to do. Concentrate.

"Good. So we mark where we covered and then find another section—"

"We need to backtrack, actually," he said, rubbing his thumb down my neck.

I batted his hand away. "Backtrack?"

"Yes. You saw the hunters. I didn't have to time to go over their back trail, but we need to. So that's where we start. We'll grab some food—and you're taking more than granola bars."

"Bitch, bitch, bitch." I'd already come to that decision, thank you very much.

"I'm serious, kitten."

"You're always serious."

His hand spread open over my neck and despite my intention to ignore it, I almost groaned at how good that felt. I was tempted to lean into—

And then I realized I *was*—

"Damn it," I snapped. "Would you stop? I thought I made it clear, I'm a little freaked out by the fact that you keep touching me even though just an hour or so ago, your Alpha was telling you that you might be killing me soon."

"Nice opening into that talk we need to have," he said, his mouth firming out into a hard, flat line. "Thanks for that."

And his hand didn't move.

"*I* made it clear—I am *not* going to kill you. Got it?" He shot me a glowering look that oddly enough didn't leave me with the urge to cringe in my seat. "Even when you do make me want to do something violent. I'm not going to hurt you. Period. Ever."

"Uh-huh."

He snapped his jaws shut with an audible crack, like he wanted to bite something. "You're so fucking difficult."

"That's funny coming from you. Really."

"Would you shut up, and listen?" he growled, the low, pulsing sound echoing through the car. "You present a problem to her if you don't find the kid. Since she *said* she'd kill you, she's going to feel like she has to. But I'll tell you this. It's *not* love that's motivating her. She doesn't give a damn about Doyle. Never has, never will."

"That's a shock. Poor kid. Does he have *anybody* who cares about him?"

A tense silence stretched out and finally, Damon sighed. "Yeah. Me."

It was the very last thing I expected to hear.

Gaping at him, I said, "What?"

"You heard me." He dragged a hand down over his face. "The boy has been living with me since he was five. He was a mess after his dad died—acting out the way a kid will. Had a tantrum and the Lady belted him in the mouth. If he wasn't a shifter, it would have killed him. He spent two days in the Lair's medical ward as it was. I offered to take him home with me to let her have some time to adjust to the loss of her brother before taking on the hardships of raising a child…and he just never went home. He's more my kid than anybody else's."

"Your kid." I slammed my head against the headrest. Or I tried to. His hand was still behind my head and kept getting in the way. "So tell me something…did she send you here to help me, watch over me, or are you helping look for the kid?"

"All of the above." He shrugged. "I'd heard you were good at this sort of shit and I wasn't having any luck on my own. So I got her to thinking we needed outside help. Then I sort of suggested to her that you'd be likely to cause trouble so maybe I should make sure you stayed on task." A smile tugged at his lips. "Probably some of my best work there. Subtle as hell, and you have to be subtle with the Lady."

"You've basically been working this from the get-go, haven't you?"

"I've been doing what I can to find the kid," he said shortly. "You've been everything from a shortcut to the biggest complication imaginable."

"Yeah?" I twitched as his fingers threaded through my hair.

"Yeah." He sighed. "At first I thought I'd fucked it up, because we were spinning our wheels, but then you started untangling all these knots, things I didn't even think to look for."

"Sure as hell doesn't seem like I've managed to untangle any knots. All I'm doing is hitting dead ends."

"The witch, Keeli. The wolf kid." Strong fingers dug into my neck, working the tense muscles there. "I don't know if I would have bothered reaching out to Banner. You did. You also reached out to your connections with the witches, so we see a pattern—non-human kids getting grabbed. Although it's weird that the Alpha's nephew would have been, too."

"I don't think he was grabbed. I think he ran." I closed my eyes. "At least that's what I thought. I'm going to assume he was better off living with you than he would be with the Queen Bitch." I smirked as I said it but he didn't say anything. "Was he happy with you?"

Damon was quiet for a long moment. "Yeah. Mostly. But word got back to her that he was getting close to his spike. She started making noises about him coming home and he hated the idea. He was terrified of her. She's his monster under the bed."

"Gee. Imagine that."

A short sigh burst out of him. "Why do you have to keep doing that? Are you *trying* to piss me off?"

"Do I have to *try*?" I groaned as his fingers hit a tight spot on my neck. "I'm almost tempted to just shut up. I'm afraid you might stop doing that."

He laughed. "Your neck is a mess."

"*I'm* a mess," I pointed out.

"You also didn't answer me."

"Shit. What do you want me to say? You work for and obey a cruel, *insane* bitch who doesn't have the soul to care for her own nephew. You're her enforcer and from what it sounds like to me, she points you in a direction and says *kill* and you do it. She's a crazy, murderous bitch and you're her *yes* boy."

I closed my eyes and wondered if maybe that wasn't a dumb thing to say, considering he already had his hand gripping my neck.

"Would you stop looking like you expect me to break your neck or slit your throat or something?" he snapped.

I clenched my right hand, frowning a little. It itched. But not much. "Well, if I really felt like you were going to do that, I'd have my sword in hand. If I'm certain I'm that close to death, I plan on going down fighting."

Silence fell.

After a few minutes, he murmured, "I guess that's a start."

A start to what?

"She'll want to kill you because she said she would. It will look better in her eyes to do what she said, despite the fact that it doesn't make any sense," he said finally. He stroked a hand down my shoulder, my arm, then rested his elbow on the console. His hand curled into a loose fist as he drummed it on the molded plastic. "Everything is about appearances, power and what pleases her. So the way to work it is to make it *unpleasant*, work *against* her power, and cast an air of impropriety— that's all it takes to make her decide it's not worth following through. She doesn't give a damn about keeping her word if it doesn't suit her. So if it's more trouble to kill you than not, then she won't lay a hand on you."

"Okay...and you're telling me this...why?"

"Several reasons." That dark, glowering look, the one that spoke of storms and anger, rolled across his face. "Pay attention, kitten. You're learning shit about the Alpha that some people have tried for years to learn."

"And you're telling me *why*?"

"Knowledge is power. Haven't you heard how important is it to know your enemy?"

"Sure." I smiled at him serenely. "So...what's your sign?"

"Cute." He folded his hand over mine and twined our fingers. "You need to know this shit."

"I never considered her my enemy. She's an obstacle at the moment," I muttered.

"She wants you dead."

"No. She'll want me dead if I don't succeed." I looked out the window and saw the sign for the small town near the entrance of the park coming up. "That doesn't make her an enemy *yet*. I know my enemies."

Brooding, I fought not to fall back into those memories.

Useless waste—

"Your grandmother."

Closing my eyes, I shook my head. "Please don't."

"Your demons," he said, shrugging. "They're not the problem right now. Neither is the Alpha. You need to focus on your allies. Who wants you alive...and I guess your family isn't among them?"

"Nope. They'd send chocolate, raw chunks of meat or fresh blood to whichever entity was to rid the world of the problem of my existence."

His hand tightened. "I think I dislike them already."

I jerked a shoulder in a shrug. It was a fact of my life. One I was used to.

"So...allies?" He stroked his thumb across my skin. Nothing so simple should feel that good. "Is safe to say that witch back in Orlando is one?"

I clenched my jaw.

"Yes. But I don't want to draw the Orlando House into this."

"You may have no choice." He ran his tongue over his teeth and then added, "Although I'm reluctant to consider it, it seems that big bastard in Wolf Haven was fond of you. Can you count on them? Goliath and..."

"Her name is TJ." I stared out the window. "She won't leave Wolf Haven. No matter what. Goliath?" I shrugged. "He might do some damage in my name, but he'll always go back to her."

"You're not making this easy," he muttered. His voice thickened with disgust as his hand shifted up and curled around my wrist, his thumb pressing in on the area near where Jude had bitten me. "The vampire is one, I'm going to assume."

"Jude may or may not be." I glanced down at my wrist, frowning at the possessive hold he had on me. "Nobody understands how his mind works."

"Did he bite you?"

"Why are you so determined to hear that answer?"

"Because believe it or not, it matters to what's going on here."

Rolling my eyes, I muttered, "Not entirely sure I'm buying that." Then I sighed. "Yes."

"How many times?"

"Once." I twisted my hand out of his grasp and glanced outside, a little surprised to see we were at the little Walgreens where we'd stopped before. He pushed the car into park, but before I could climb out he hit the locks. "Shit. What?"

"Just once?"

"Yes." I decided not to mention anything about the fact that I'd owe Jude another bite if he had to help me out of a jam. My plan was not to need him. Then it wouldn't be an issue.

"He can get into your dreams, now."

"He's always been able to force his way inside them. But he doesn't have any control over me, despite what some of the myths out there say." I smiled a little. "And that annoys the hell out of him."

Another one of the endless silences. Nobody could do eerie, unsettling silence like a shapeshifter. Nobody.

The only sound was the quiet little snick of the locks. I climbed out. I was halfway to the store when I sensed him behind me. *Keep on walking.* That was the plan.

I kept right on walking into the store.

Bottled water, energy bars—nasty things, but I figured they'd do the trick. I thought about buying some chocolate to stash in the bag, but it wouldn't hold up under the heat. Trail mix might…okay. A bag of that. I did grab a candy bar to eat on the way. Nothing bolstered the mood like chocolate.

"Done."

He wasn't behind me anymore. I'd lost him somewhere between grabbing the energy bars and finding my trail mix but I figured he'd hear me anyway. I was aware of him—*too* aware. Like a warmth hovering just above my skin and it was the craziest damn thing.

In rut—

Hell. I needed to figure out what in the world that meant. I pulled my phone out and sent Colleen a message.

Hey. What's it mean when somebody says a shifter cat is in rut?

Her response was almost immediate. And I couldn't decide if it was comical or freaked out. It was two 'O's side by side, like she was bug-eyed. I glanced around and put my back to a display of soft drinks. The last thing I wanted was for him to come up behind me, the sneak.

What does that mean? I demanded. If she'd been there, I might have shaken her. *Has he said he's in rut?*

Grumbling under my breath, I tapped back, *Would you just answer the damn question? No. He hasn't said a damn thing and this isn't about anything he has said. I heard somebody else say it while I was working the case.*

And that was absolutely not a lie.

Oh. Good. That's good. Rut's crazy. It's basically their emotional commitment. It sounds like going into heat, but it's more than that. It's an emotional connection, it's physical...and they have to want it, too. It's like Mother Nature gives them a choice in the matter. Not fair, if you ask me. Do we ever get a choice who we fall for? But I've heard it's supposed to be really intense.

My head felt a little weird. Okay. A lot weird. Swallowing, I tapped back, *Thanks.*

She sent me back a smiley. *Hey, don't let the sexy asshole bite you. I think that's kind of their sign they've accepted it. And if you let him...well, you're telling him you've accepted it.*

I was still trying to wrap my mind around that when two things happened.

I sensed a shift in that weird energy that was Damon's presence.

And my instincts started to scream a red alert.

Ducking around the display, I moved. My hand itched. I wasn't scared. I was furious—didn't even know why.

And then Damon was there.

"Do that disappearing act," he growled in my ear.

I shook my head, staring toward the front of the store. "No."

"Do it," he ordered. "*Now*"

"Heads up, genius. In a store. Security cameras and scanners. That's one of the few things I do that can save my ass from a major jam and I prefer not to let that secret get out to the masses. I said *no*." I shot him a dark glare over my shoulder and then went back to staring at the door as my heart pumped harder and harder.

When they came through the door, I wasn't even that surprised.

"Kit, I don't want them seeing you!"

I sighed and turned around. "*You* are more likely to make them notice me than I am," I pointed out. Without looking, I snagged the basket and headed down the aisle. "Come on."

He was still snarling at my back, all but stepping on my heels.

"You can make yourself seem more human than this," I said quietly. "If you don't want us catching attention...*blend.*"

"I don't give a flying fuck if they notice me."

"Yeah, well, I'm standing two feet away." Reaching inside my vest, I tugged out a black bandana and quickly tied it over my hair. We passed a display of reading glasses and I snagged a pair, tugging off the tags and sliding them on. Immediately, my vision went blurry but I could handle that. Inside another pocket, I had a rolled up skull cap. I pulled it out and shoved it at Damon. "Take it. And tone it down."

Bit by bit, the heated wave of his energy melted away until I couldn't feel any of it.

The warning sirens in my brain were still going off, though.

"You can work around the front of the store," he said softly. "Get outside, wait in the car. They are moving over to the refrigerator section—you'll have a few minutes."

"Bad idea. They've got dogs. The dogs smelled me yesterday and will probably be outside—they'd catch my scent in a second." I saw the aisle I needed and smiled. Perfect. I pointed. "You. Right there."

He stopped and looked around and then gave me a pained glance. "You have got to be shitting me."

"No." With a pleased smile, I moved further away. He could study the tampons and pads, and the panicked, glazed look in his eyes was ideal. Me? I parked myself right in front of the remedies for yeast infections, about ten feet away. As I did so, I casually slipped out of my vest, untucked my shirt. I held the vest over my arm. I couldn't get to my weapons as easily, but I wasn't going to need them.

"This is stupid," Damon muttered, his voice drifting to me across the distance between us.

I snickered, shooting a look at him.

He was crouched on the floor, and if I wasn't mistaken, there was a dull red flush on his golden skin. Oh, yes. Perfect, indeed. He had a hand on the back of his neck and he looked about as self-conscious as I thought he could ever look.

An employee came down the aisle. Just as she was going to pass me up, my ears caught something—Damon had tensed as well. I caught the employee's attention and spoke, making my voice about as high-pitched as I could without sounding like I trying to alter my voice as I said, "Um, can you help me a little?"

The lady paused. Her nametag read, *Marie, Pharmacy Tech.*

A blush settled over her cheeks as she glanced at the box I held.

Monistat 7.

"Um, you might be better off—"

The group of men trailed by. I felt the gaze of one them cut my way. Linger on Damon, then brush to me. I stood with my back them—they wouldn't see much, just my height, body type. "Will a generic help with a yeast infection as good as this will? Cuz this thing is *killing* me…I haven't been able to have sex in like a week and I'm *dying*…"

Poor Marie went red.

The men disappeared.

Two minutes later, as Damon came prowling my way, I smiled at him. "Did you find what you needed? I can always ask Marie to offer some advice."

The storm clouds in his eyes glittered. If I wasn't mistaken, something that *might* have been a smile almost appeared on his face. Almost. It was gone so quick, I couldn't quite tell.

"You're lucky that worked." His voice was flat.

Rolling my eyes, I dropped the box Marie had all but shoved into my hands back on the shelf. "Pal, that wasn't luck. Regardless of your race, men tend to still be *men* and you all freak out at certain things. And I'm damn good at not getting noticed."

My hand was still itching. Even though I couldn't see them, I knew they were still in the store. "They aren't gone yet," I murmured.

"No. They are up front now—at the cashier. They should be out of here in a few minutes," he drawled. He moved around me, curling one hand around my wrist and commandeering the cart with the other hand. "Come on. I'd rather not continue to lurk in the feminine hygiene area."

"But you do it so very well…"

We didn't leave for twenty more minutes.

I think we had every employee watching us for signs we were shoplifting by the time we headed out. I made sure to pay for the reading glasses I'd used, even though I dumped them in the trash on my way out.

While we killed time in the store, Damon added more to the cart—protein shakes. About twenty of them. I eyed them narrowly. "Those are going to fun to haul around with the water."

"I'm hauling them. You're drinking them."

"Wow. All twenty of them?"

He didn't respond as he added a couple of boxes of those meal bars designed to help with a weight loss program to the cart. "Are you trying to tell me I need some help to maintain my girlish figure?"

"They've got calories and protein and they'll serve well enough if you start to crash. Hopefully you won't have to hide the way you did yesterday, but if you do…" He shrugged.

"If I had my damned bow, I wouldn't have been hiding at all," I muttered, more to myself than anybody else. I would have taken those men out, one by one. Just for the sheer fun of it.

Hunting—

Rage choked me and I had to swallow it back down as the itching returned to my palm and I could hear the sweet, sweet melody of the sword's call at the back of my mind. *I am here, I am here—*

Yes. She was there, and I wanted her so badly—

As we stepped out of the store, I pulled my sunglasses out of my vest and slid them on, following Damon across the parking lot.

"Just how good are you with the bow?" he asked.

I stared at his back. "Is that a rhetorical question?"

"No. It's the question kind of question…as in, I ask it and I want you to answer." He popped open the trunk and gave me a narrow look.

Rolling my eyes, I snagged a couple of the bags and dumped them into the trunk of my car. "I'm good."

"How good? As much as you are with your sword?"

A faint smile curved my lips. "You know, you've never really seen me with my sword, so you don't really know if I'm any good or not."

He shrugged, tossing a couple of cases of water into the trunk like he was throwing around pillows. "I watched you practice."

"Practice is easy. Almost anybody can learn to hold a sword if they put their mind to it."

"So are you telling me you're no good with it?" He started breaking into the supplies. "Grab the backpacks."

I hauled them out of the trunk and dumped them in front of him. "No. I'm damn good with it."

"Yes. I imagine you are. Besides, you've managed to get it in between you and me a few times. That's not something an amateur would be able to do. So…back to the main question. How good are you with a bow?"

"Better than I am with my sword." I shrugged and reached out to the touch the blade in question. "The sword…she's mine. She's part of me." *She came to me*— I wasn't going to tell him that, but she was mine. "I'm a talented swordswoman, and I'll get better. But I've got a gift for the bow. Always did. Swordplay, I learned through trial and error, sweat, blood…"

Broken bones, pain—I paused, swallowing as I shoved all of that back in the tight box where I'd fought to keep those memories confined. They didn't belong out here, in the light of day, in the present. I'd left that horror behind. I wanted it lost, in the depths of memory, not out here taunting me. "But I was always good with my bow. Much to the disgust of my aunts, I was actually one of the best they'd ever worked with."

A hand touched my cheek.

As he guided my face around to his, I blanked my expression.

He said nothing. The pad of his thumb stroked over my lip.

I felt naked standing there. Stripped bare.

And I was having a very hard time thinking of him as the asshole I needed him to be.

But I needed my head clear.

Pressing my hand to his chest, I backed away. "We're wasting daylight," I murmured.

"Yeah." Tugging the bandana off my head, he pushed his fingers through my hair. "We've got one more stop to make, but it should be quick."

Chapter Seventeen

Bait and Camping Gear.

That was all the sign said.

Arching a brow at him, I asked, "Are we going fishing?"

"Sure. I'll catch it. You clean it."

Wrinkling my nose at him, I said, "You wish. I only clean what I catch."

That wicked grin curved his lips again as he parked in front of the long, low building.

"Why are we here?"

As he climbed out, he looked at me over the hood of the car. "Can you shoot any bow? Or is it something like your sword?"

"I can use any damn sword I want," I said dryly. "Needs to be suited to my body type, but just because I *prefer* my sword that doesn't mean she's the only one I can use."

"I'll take that as a yes." He headed toward the building. When I didn't fall into step behind him, he paused and looked back at me. "Either you come in or I pick it out on my own."

No. I don't think so.

I didn't see a single bow in sight.

Staring at him, I crossed my arms over my chest. "Wow. Quite a selection."

"Just wait a minute, baby girl." He laid his hand on the small of my back and guided me to the far end of the store where a skinny guy with skin the color of dark chocolate, worn as faded leather, and creased from years under the sun sat behind the counter.

The guy looked up at us and smiled.

"My boy down at the cash register will check you out, son."

Damon didn't move.

"We are looking for some extra supplies. Of the special variety."

"Are you now?" He just stared at us.

"Yes. Looking for a bow."

The man shook his head. "We just have bait and camping gear here, son."

Damon arched a brow. "I heard otherwise. And we're in a hurry. If you let us see what you have, I'll pay double."

"Oh, really…"

And that was all it took.

As he led us into a narrow back room, the man said, "You need to be aware it's illegal to hunt in the park. If you get caught, I didn't sell you anything. If you say otherwise, you won't ever buy anything from me again, son."

"Not a problem."

Something a lot of people don't know about the aneira. Weapons sing to us. They whisper. They talk. Even modern weapons do it, although it's muted, almost like a radio station that's gone all static-filled. Most of the weapons in there spoke to me in that muffled sort of voice, although there was a compound bow that wasn't bad.

But there was something else—

I followed the sound of it while Damon paced along at my back.

"So, son, what are you looking for? Big guy like you might like this one…" He touched a big piece of work. I recognized it. Overpriced, but the manufacturer made them well. However, I wouldn't be able to draw the damn thing. Its main feature was that it was made for big guys. I wasn't big.

I kept walking and paused by the one bow that did seem to whisper to me. It wasn't the one singing—I still couldn't see, but this one…I touched a hand to him.

"That's an awfully strong bow for a girl your size, sweetheart," the man said, glancing at me dismissively.

"Really?" I picked it up.

Made by Athens. I hadn't used them before. But when I touched the bow, his whisper grew to a steady stream, one I decided I liked, even as the song in the back of my head grew louder. Smiling, I drew back on the bow. "I like him," I murmured.

"We'll take it," Damon said.

I released and lowered the bow, held onto it as I kept walking. There was a cabinet the end. The singing came from there. "What's in here?"

"Ah…"

Damon said quietly, "Remember I pay double."

"Handmade. Traditional bows. The compound would suit you fine and it's a lot cheaper, especially since you have to pay double. Despite what people think, if you know how to shoot, the compound is no more or less accurate than a recurve bow." The man was standing at my elbow now, although he was actually talking to *me* now, instead of Damon.

"I know." I smiled. I had to see what was in that cabinet. Had to.

"The cheapest bow in there is fifteen hundred dollars. That means it will cost you three thousand. You got that on you?" he asked, his voice edging into belligerence.

I looked at Damon, deflating a little. I didn't. But I had to have what was singing to me…singing so sweetly, I almost wanted to cry.

"I got it," he said.

I couldn't stop the smile that spread over my face.

When he opened the cabinet, I saw her.

Oh, sweetheart…come to mama…

"Oh." Blindly, I shoved the compound at Damon and greedily reached for her. She was…oh. "She's lovely."

Long and elegant, carved by hand. I touched her and listened to her song for a moment. I half-expected to hear the tribal flutes and drums of Native America, but that wasn't what I heard. It was tribal, all right, but this sounded of Africa.

"She wasn't made by Native Americans."

"No." That was all he said.

It didn't matter. I didn't need to know the story behind her. She was mine. "How much?"

"Two thousand dollars."

I grimaced. Damn, this was getting to be a costly shopping trip. This beauty wasn't going into the park with me. I wanted to get to know her better before I did anything with her. Wooden, carved with pride, by knowing hands...I could feel it.

Stroking a finger down the carved surface, listening to the beat of her song, I smiled for a moment, just enjoying the music of her. Finally, I pulled myself away and then turned to Damon. "I could use both," I said quietly. "We can take it out of my fee."

"I got it."

By the time we were done, the total was almost six thousand, including the arrows. Fiberglass for the compound, but the traditional bow had wooden arrows to go with her as well. They were almost as pretty to hold as she was. I thought I might try my hand at carving my own sometime.

The man tried to charge a few hundred for sales tax, but Damon stared him down. "You and I both know you're not reporting these sales to the IRS, so why bother?"

A beatific smile curved the man's weathered face. "True, true...you sure the steel tips will work for you? I've got others."

"Others?" I asked absently, still stroking the bow. Next to my blade, I'd never had a weapon talk to me so sweetly. Never.

"Silver tipped. Hollow and solid. Iron. Copper. In case something other than steel is your preference."

He said it casually, so very casually.

But there was no way on earth those words had a casual meaning.

Next to me, I felt Damon tense. Blood crashed in my ears. Roared. Rage thundered and I tasted the fury as it climbed up my throat. *Silver—silver for shifters. Iron—iron hurts witches, weakens them and affects their ability to cast magic, heal themselves...copper? What is affected by copper?* And I couldn't ignore the very simple weapon of a wooden arrow—wood through the heart of a vampire.

"No." I gave him a smile. "We're good with the steel. I just want to get in some target practice."

I prayed I wouldn't have to drag Damon out of there.

I stashed my lovely new toy away even though what I wanted to do was use her for the very first time on the man with his kind smile, liquid eyes...and black heart.

He knew what he'd been offering.

If he'd known what Damon was, he wouldn't have made that offer.

Good thing Damon had throttled back in the store and hadn't let it loose yet, but damn.

I could feel the intensity of it lurking, though. He was furious and I was almost afraid of what was going to come boiling out of him. After I'd hid the bow, I left the other one in the trunk in plain sight and shut the trunk. Not meeting his eyes, I stared down the road. "Who drives?" I asked, keeping my voice level.

Careful, careful…

"I will."

I nodded and started for the passenger side, but he stopped me, caging me in at the trunk, one arm on either side. "You're afraid," he whispered, ducking his head and burying it against my neck.

I shivered a little and then my mind went blank as I felt the scrape of his teeth against my neck.

Colleen's message rushed through my mind.

Hey, don't let the sexy asshole bite you. I think that's kind of their sign they've accepted it.

Hitching up my shoulder, I shrank away from him a little. "I'm not…shit. Look, we don't have time for this. You feel like a time bomb in my head and I understand why, but it's still an unpleasant feeling."

"Kit." Big hands cupped my face. "You ever going to get the fact that I don't want to hurt you?"

I stared up at him. "I'm processing it. Doesn't mean I entirely believe it. And right now, it doesn't even matter. There's a job to do."

A muscle pulsed in his jaw. He nodded slowly. Then he reached up and tugged my sunglasses off.

When he lowered his head, I felt my heart practically jump up into my throat, but it wasn't fear this time.

His mouth slanted over mine and I groaned, opening for him even as sanity tried to rear its ugly, stupid head. Slow, easy…like he was trying to coax me into believing every word he said. And the crazy thing was…I was almost ready to do just that. His tongue stroked over my lips, teased its way into my mouth. Over and over, such a gentle, easy seduction, belying the anger I could still feel beating inside him.

When he broke away—too soon, way too soon—my heart raced, my body ached and throbbed and screamed for more. "I can be madder than hell and still control myself. Any time I've ever done anything, it was for a reason. Maybe it was a stupid reason, and I'm sorrier than you're ever going to know, but I am *not* going to hurt you," he whispered against my lips.

As he walked away, I let myself lean against the car while I tried to will some strength into my legs, some sanity into my brain.

This had become a hell of a lot more than just a job.

Getting the bow into the park wasn't hard. I just faded out and walked right past the park rangers with it.

Now, two hours later, I had the bow in one hand and I was ready for a target, any target, just to alleviate some of the frustration.

"What was the deal with you and that bow earlier?"

I didn't pretend not to understand what he was talking about. There wasn't much point.

It was hot, I was sweaty, cranky already and more than a little freaked out. So far, we'd seen more gators than I'd really rather *ever* see in my life.

Gators scare me. I can't help it.

There were also snakes and while they didn't scare me so much, I wasn't overly pleased to know they were slithering around out there. I could *hear* them. The same way I heard the slow, lumbering crawl of the gators...sometimes I wish I had the hearing of humans. Would make this easier.

Stroking a thumb down the fiberglass of the compound bow I'd brought with me, I debated on what to tell him.

"Well?" he asked, shooting a look at me.

"What kind of shifter are you?"

He stopped in the middle of the path and turned, staring at me. "Why?"

I shrugged. "You're asking something that has to do with what *I* am. I figure it's fair play."

"I'm just asking what the deal is with the bow." The black slashes of his brows dropped low over his storm-cloud eyes.

"Yes...and the deal has to do with what I am." The compound bow murmured in the back of my mind, a soft pleasant little stream of nonsense that I couldn't pick apart, but it was nice. I liked it. Background music, I decided. "What you change into is what you are. Sooo..."

He continued to stand there, hands planted on his hips as he studied me. Sweat had dampened the collar of the olive green shirt he wore, but while I suspected I look like I'd been ridden hard and put away wet, he looked like he had just been out for a jog around the block. At dawn. "I might tell you," he finally said. "But you have to answer a question first."

I rolled my eyes and went to edge around him. "Sheesh. Forget I asked."

"No. I want the answer." He blocked my path simply by placing his body in front of me. Too big. Too...*there*. And he wasn't holding back that wild energy of his anymore, either. It was almost as hot as the sun beating down on my head, but its heat was different. I could feel it licking at me from under my skin and it drove me nuts. "It's an easy enough question. I just want to know whether or not your word is important to you."

"What?"

"Your word. Does it matter?"

"Oh, for crying out loud." I elbowed him in the gut, determined to get past him this time. I managed by wedging between him and a tree, scraping my arm against it in the process. The endless tangle of the Everglades spread out in front of me and my gut crawled as I studied the terrain. Just off to the left, I saw the glint of water...and a long, reptilian form. Another gator.

"So you're a liar, then?"

I spun on my heel.

"No," I snapped. I don't lie. Even though the aneira had never bothered to teach me many of their more honored traditions, it seemed as though some of those traditions had come to me simply through my blood.

My heart is strong. My blood is noble—Once upon a time, honor had been everything to the aneira, or so the legends said.

I didn't lie.

And when I gave my word, I felt honor-bound to keep it. If I thought I couldn't keep a promise, I simply didn't make it.

In the quiet, white-hot heat of the day, I glared at him. "Are you happy?" As I went to turn, I shot another look to the water and suppressed a shudder. The gator was still there. If it moved, I'd hear it, but the fear was still twisting inside me and shutting it off would be about as easy as stopping the flow of the St. Johns River.

A big arm came around my waist. "The gators aren't going to bother you." His hand spread wide over my belly. "I'll tell you what I am, but you can't tell anybody...not until I say it's okay. Nobody in the clan knows what I really am. They made an assumption when I came to them and I let them think it."

"Why do that?"

"Because I'm one of just a few..." He turned his face into my hair and I had the weirdest sensation he was breathing it in. "I was orphaned. Like Doyle. When I was a kid. I'm hunting down the fuck who killed my parents, and one day I'll end that bastard's miserable existence. But until then, nobody can know. If I tell you, I have to trust you won't share it with anybody."

"Why would you tell me?"

"Why wouldn't I?"

The hard, heavy thud of my heart against my ribs left me breathless and it was a few seconds before I could breathe. "The thing with the bow isn't quite that personal, Damon. Not much of a trade. Look... it's just a..."

"Leopard," he murmured against my neck before I could say another word. "Clouded leopard out of Borneo. There is only a handful of my kind left. My father came from Borneo and I took after him. My mother was human, lived in New Zealand. Everybody assumed I came from one of the Himalayan packs. A lot of them interbreed with humans and when they made the assumption, I let them...it suited my purposes."

Leopard. As the puzzle of that settled into my brain, my lids drifted down. "Didn't I just tell that you didn't have to tell me?" It was a heavy weight. He'd kept it secret for a reason, and whatever that reason was, I wasn't sure I wanted to carry the burden.

"I wanted to. I want you to know what I am. Now...the bow."

"It sings."

Off in the distance, I heard the slight shift as the gator moved around. He had noticed us, I thought. Shivering a bit, I took a breath and blew it out. "Weapons...we hear them. The modern weapons are just static and noise mostly, although this bow, there's craftsmanship in him. Somebody worked on him—cared," I murmured, stroking the compound bow and smiling a little as I sensed a small pause, almost like pleasure, in its music at the back of my mind. "Every weapon I own, I picked because it spoke to me in some way. I could hear something singing to me the minute we went through the door in the back room. And the minute he opened that cabinet and I saw her…"

"Her. You talk about them as though they live."

"For me, they do." Rustling in the grass drew my attention and I looked over. The spot on the bank where the gator had been lying was empty. "Now…you can stand here and chat all you want, but I want to move."

He laughed a little. "Okay, baby girl. But you ought to know…I could have that gator for lunch if I wanted."

"I'm not worried about *you*."

An hour later, we got into a fight.

He insisted we head to the east.

But something tugged me west.

"I can fucking smell their back trail," he growled. "If your ears were any better, you could even hear their damn dogs."

"My ears are just fine." I sneered at him. "I *can* hear them."

But that wasn't where I needed to go. Gripping my bow, I pointed to the west. "You go on wherever in the hell you *want*. I'm going this way."

West was wet. West had next to no path and I could also hear the slither of snakes and the rustle of gators.

As much as I'd like to pretend it didn't matter…it did.

I didn't *want* to go that way.

But I had to.

Something pulled me—

I couldn't even define what it was. The cloying stink of wet earth, water, smells I just wasn't used to flooding my head, but I wasn't going east.

While he stood there glaring at me, I started through the undergrowth. A snake slithered over the toe of my boot. I managed to keep my hiss behind my teeth. Barely. Grass snake. Harmless. Fast. Still, a snake and not anything I wanted crawling across my damn boot.

A hand closed over my elbow and jerked me to a halt before I took another step.

"Why?"

Still staring at the tail I could make out in the grass, I thought absently, *Because why* would *I want a snake on my boots*…?

"Damn it, Kit…"

I lifted my head and stared into Damon's eyes. Abruptly, I lifted my hand, touched his cheek. "You've got the most amazing eyes," I murmured. A split second later, I realized what I'd done and went to jerk away while blood rushed up to stain my cheeks red.

He covered my hand with his, lowering his head and pressing his brow to mine.

"I'd ask if that was your way of changing the subject, but considering you look like you just bit a lemon, I don't think you mean to say that."

"Ah…"

He nipped my lower lip. "Why this way, baby girl? Just answer me."

Just answer. He made it sound so easy. But it wasn't. I eased away and stared out into the distance. "Something's calling me. I have to go this way."

It was getting late.

The sun still blistered the sky.

We'd gone through half the supplies in our packs.

I was holding up a hell of a lot better than I had last time, but we hadn't found anything.

I could still feel that odd tugging, drawing on me like a thread had been wrapped around my insides and it twanged every time I tried to stray from this path.

But it was getting late and we weren't exactly equipped to camp in the Everglades.

"How long have we been out here?" I asked as Damon came striding back through the undergrowth after answering the call of nature. Men had it so easy. I lived in fear of a snake biting me in areas no snake should ever see.

"Six hours." He glanced at the sun. "We have maybe an hour before we have to head back, if you're up to walking. I can get you there faster if you need me to carry you."

"I'm good. Today was easier."

A grin split his face. "You hiked all damn day. Yesterday you sat in a tree."

"Yeah. Unable to move, balancing in ways I'm not meant to balance." An hour. Not much time. Brooding, I started to walk.

I hadn't taken two steps when I was jerked up and whirled around. My head was still spinning, or at least it felt that way, because what I saw in front of me just didn't make sense for a minute.

"What…" I licked my lips and shook my head. "What the hell is that?"

"We triggered something," he whispered against my cheek. "I saw it just as you hit it. I'm sorry, kitten."

Heart still racing, I stared down into the gaping, dark hole and felt my mind spinning away into the darkness of memories. Dark, awful memories.

"Let me out…"

Even though I knew I couldn't climb the slick rock walls, it didn't stop me from trying. Pain sang through my back from the latest whipping and every inch of me hurt, but that didn't stop me, either. I had to get out of that pit. I had to. "Let me out!"

Rana stood over my head, staring down at me with eyes so like my own. Her face wasn't creased with that smile that Grandmother so often wore. No, I couldn't read anything on Rana's face and sometimes, that made her scarier.

"You will stay here until our return," Rana said. She glanced at the guards at her sides and then back at me. "The Dominari is not for weaklings or halfbreeds, Kitasa. You shouldn't have asked."

I didn't hear her words. Didn't notice the guards.

I only saw the walls of the pit as I struggled to climb out. "Let me out!" I screamed, trying to scramble my way up.

My nails, already ragged, broke. I tried to climb until my fingers bled and my arms ached.

It was hours before I admitted the futility of it. My throat ached from my screams.

Trapped. Trapped in a dark, hellish hole that saw no light and no sun... Trapped until they returned?

"Breathe..."

Hard hands, almost brutal in their strength, gripped my head and I found myself nose to nose with Damon as he shouted in my face. "Breathe, Kit!"

I sucked in a desperate breath and gasped, "Why are you shouting at me?"

"Shit." He closed his eyes and snatched me against him. "You...shit. Gimme a minute."

I was shaking. My clothes were sweating, sticking to me, and his body was as hot as a furnace, but I was cold.

"What happened?" he whispered against my ear. "What happened?"

"A pit." I had to force the words through chattering teeth. "They put me in one...once. When I was fifteen. I just—sorry. Bad memory. Okay in a minute."

The hot mantle of his fury spread around me but for once, it didn't scare me. I so desperately needed the warmth. "Shhhh," he murmured as I cuddled closer. If it had been possible to disappear inside of him, I might have done it. Might have tried. Twisting my hands in the fabric of his shirt, I breathed in the hot, musky scent of him, focused on everything around me—everything that didn't smell of my own blood and waste, the weirdly flat scent of cold stone. The brackish scent of water, the hot humid day, even the disturbing scent of reptile that lingered all around. Anything was better than that awful memory.

"I'm okay," I whispered after a long moment. "I'm okay."

He continued to hold me. "I'm not."

A weak laugh escaped me. "But we can't stay like this if we want to figure this out."

"We need to call it a day."

I shook my head. "No."

Oh, hell no.

Because oddly enough, as the rush of fear and panic faded, I realized...that tugging had grown stronger.

"What do you smell, Damon?" I eased back and studied his face. "There's something here. Or close. Has to be. What do you smell?"

"Humans." His nostrils flared. "A lot of them. I know the place. We'll come back."

Shaking my head, I said, "No. We have to find whatever they didn't want people finding."

Now.

Chapter Eighteen

Every step made the urgency grow stronger.

Every single step.

And after another ten minutes, something about Damon's demeanor changed. It was subtle at first. I barely noticed because I was so busy dealing with the mad itching that had settled in my palm. This wasn't the place for my blade, I suspected, but she was calling me…singing to me and she *wanted* me.

But he'd gone from a lazy predator on the prowl to a focused hunter. As he turned to gaze off to one side, I noticed the light reflecting off his eyes—not normal. His nostrils flared and I could all but see him pausing as he rolled those tastes around in his mouth.

A few minutes later, he picked up the pace and I had to jog to keep up. He was still walking, but those legs of his covered a lot of ground and fast. And each pace was a tug inside me.

Closer. Closer. Closer.

Glancing up, I checked the sun.

And that was when I saw it—

Shit—

I drew an arrow, fired.

As Damon spun around, the arrow buried itself in the camera.

"We're being watched," I said flatly.

A short, terse nod and he was moving again.

I was in an all-out run now, fear crowding the back of my throat as memories of that pit danced in the back of my mind.

A huge, fallen tree blocked the path. Up ahead, Damon turned to glance back at me as I leaped on top. He'd taken it and landed with room to spare. While I didn't have to clamber up and over, I couldn't do it with the grace he managed. As I went to hop down, he shouted.

I slipped—

Clambering for a hold, I shifted my weight backward over the fallen giant. I didn't know what it was—

Distantly, I heard something crash.

But that wasn't what worried me just then. I was sprawled on my back, in an awkward-ass position. And about six feet way was one giant snake. Swallowing, I tensed. It watched me, eyes glittering as its tongue tasted my air.

"Kit."

I didn't say anything.

Flexing my hand, I let the sword come. She was happy now, and I was pretty damned pleased, too.

"Kit, be still. Just—"

The python moved.

I rolled away, coiling my body in one of those brutal moves my aunts had hammered into me for years. As I landed on my feet, I brought the blade down. I missed the first time and the snake came at me again.

A thunderous roar cracked through the air.

I struck again and this time—the blade tasted blood. She carved through thick skin, bone and muscle and I was all but sobbing as I went to my knees.

Giant clawed hands hauled me into the air.

I shrieked and swung out. The blade cut into furred skin. A growl echoed all around and I cut again before one of those big hands caught my sword arm. "Shhh. It's me, baby girl. It's me."

The voice was alien.

But I recognized the words.

Damon.

"Shit. Oh, shit." Shoving against the furred wall of his chest, I struggled. "Put me down."

He didn't. I kicked him. He let me.

Then I started to shake. "This job fucking *sucks*. I think I hate you sometimes."

"I know." When he pulled me close this time, I let him.

One of those giant hands stroked the back of my head as he rumbled against my ear, "I kind of hate me right now, too, kitten."

After the snake, I needed a drink of whiskey—preferably the whole bottle— before I could keep going, but it was a luxury we didn't have. So I gathered up my bow and cleaned my blade. This time, instead of sending her back, I just drew the spare sheath I carried out of my pack and settled her into place at my hip.

I was happier with her there.

She was, too.

When I went to climb over the log, trying hard not to look at the snake's beheaded body, Damon lifted me, cradling me like a doll. "There's a trap—one of the old fashioned kinds, made to take a leg right off," he said softly. "I saw it when I looked back at you."

I closed my eyes. "Lovely."

"Yeah. Humans...the people who did this have their stink all over the place. I think they had their dogs drag their clothes everywhere or something because it's everywhere. Only way to explain why it covers so much. I even smell it up in the trees."

He sat me down a few feet away and took a minute to do a long, thorough study. "Something's not right about this. They're too prepared. Somebody gave them an idea what to expect, in case people like us came looking for them."

"So they have help."

"Yes."

I glanced at him, massive-bodied, covered in golden fur with dark gray spots. Absently, I lifted a hand and placed it on his torso. He stiffened and looked at me. "Walking around like this is going to attract a lot of attention," I said, ignoring the painful crawl of blood up my face.

He was nearly two feet taller than me in that form...and utterly naked, save for the fur. Fur didn't count. The odd meld of leopard and man stared down at me. "We're not walking through a city street, kitten," he said, his voice a deep, bass rumble. Then he tipped back his head and breathed in the air. "And you're the closest thing to human around for miles."

I made a face. "I'm not human."

"I said closest." One of those clawed hands covered mine. "If it scares you, I'll shift back."

"I just sliced and diced a Burmese python while you were busy growling at the universe, you overgrown housecat." I absolutely wouldn't say I was afraid of him. It was unsettling as hell, but I was almost ready to believe he wasn't big on the idea of hurting me. "I think I can handle you."

The look on his face might have been amusement. But it was hard to read him in this form.

"I can't wait until you're brave enough to try."

I skimmed a look over him and then started down the trail. "Not like that, pal."

Needling him settled my nerves. A lot.

Now...if we could just get through this without any snakes. Gators. Anything like that. Give me crazy humans, bloodthirsty rats, even arrogant vampires—

"*You only had to ask—*"

"Shit."

Jude's voice was a bare echo in the back of my mind, one that was weak, spread thin by the miles.

I'd had a few days reprieve, one I'd enjoyed too much. Why in the hell did I have to go and think about him?

"*Perhaps you missed me...even if you will not admit it, dearest Kit.*"

Unable to focus on everything around me and still talk to him, I stopped once more.

"Kit?"

I looked at Damon and shook my head, holding up a hand. "*I'm not your dearest anything, Jude and I'm...having problems. Go away.*"

"*Are you ready for my offer of assistance? You're so far away it will take some time to get to you.*"

"No—"

Damon's eyes narrowed.

Error—error—

Swearing mentally, I covered my face and turned the conversation inward. "*No. I don't need assistance. I'm handling this fine on my own.*"

"*Ah...but you're not. Where is the cat, Kit?*"

Something lurked under his voice and I felt a presence on my mind. A weight. Pushing. Prodding. *"That doesn't concern you. Leave me alone, Jude. I'll let you know if I need you."*

"Oh, you'll need me, dearest Kit...and the cat will not be able to help you. I will. Don't wait too long."

His presence didn't fade.

It was just gone and I groaned, dropping my hands.

Damon was staring at me.

I waited. He had something to say, I knew it.

But he didn't say a damn thing, just turned and started to walk, pausing only long enough to grab his pack. The shreds of his clothes, he ignored. I didn't. There were too many witches around who do weird things with magic and all it would take was a shred of clothing, a single hair. I shoved the ruined clothes into my pack, aware of the fact that he was watching, waiting in silence.

Once I was standing, he started to walk. A slower pace this time, more careful.

The sun was getting closer and closer to the horizon. But I didn't bother to mention it.

He already knew.

Moving slower meant we could see the few remaining traps easier.

There was another pit.

One more that would take a leg off. The one after that was the worst, though. And we caught it because there was just next to *no* scent there. Nothing. The scent that was there was faint, so faint we barely even caught it.

"Nobody walks around this spot," he said. "Right here. Easiest path over and everybody goes around. Why is that?"

I stared at the mostly cleared path that separated us from the area ahead. *That* was where we needed to be, I knew it. It was practically shining like a beacon. It called to me and even *I* could smell something up there...something not human. And voices...was it me, or did I hear voices?

"They want us walking there so they can blow us up?" I offered.

He shot me a narrow look. Then he looked around. "Stay there. Don't move. Got it?"

I lifted my hands and gave him an agreeable smile.

He didn't look overly convinced, but he disappeared into the growth and I stood there, sword in one hand, bow in the other.

They wouldn't have ...well, seriously. Would they have planted a landmine sort of thing there? Really?

I pondered that idea for the next ten minutes, scratching absently at a mosquito bite. The medicine Kori had given me had *really* worked. Needed to put it back on. But before I could, I felt the warm brush against my senses that meant Damon was coming back and then he was there.

"Move."

I glanced over my shoulder and then gaped.

He was hauling the dead body of the python. "What are you doing?" I asked.

"It's heavy," he said, shrugging. "If it's rigged, it's going to need something more than a rock and I'd rather not toss something that will turn into shrapnel on us."

He looked around and then nodded. "Behind the tree. Check it."

I groaned and then looked at the tree in question, checking it *very* well. A couple of small things skittered away. The biggest was another grass snake. Not a problem. It didn't even crawl over the toe of my boot.

"...careful..."

I tensed.

"Did you hear that?" I whispered.

"Yes." He looked at me again. "Get behind the fucking tree, Kit. If they are watching, we need to move."

I moved.

I heard a thud—

Saw the blur of his body as he came at me.

And smoke.

Chapter Nineteen

Wails rose in the air, flooded it as surely as the smoke and debris.

Tortured and pitiful, broken and sad.

"No, no, no, no!"

They really had used a landmine.

What in the *hell*—?

And those voices. I really did hear voices.

As we eased closer, I gripped my sword.

Three voices. I could pick apart three distinct voices.

"They're gone…they're gone…"

I saw the lip of the pit and my mind tried to fade away on me but I battled it back.

Damon's hand grabbed the back of my neck, squeezed. "Don't," he said. Even though his voice was gentle, there was a thread of command in it. "You act like you got balls of steel, now is the time to show it."

"If you don't quit bossing me around, I'm going to *show* my balls of steel…and cut yours off," I muttered, shoving back another round of the shakes. Then I glanced down and smirked. "They're rather exposed."

One of those weird expressions—was it a smile?—came and went. "That's my girl. Come on."

He went first, checking every step of the way.

Then he knelt at the lip of the pit. I moved to stand at his side, resting a hand on his shoulder and clinging to sanity by the threads.

Three terrified faces stared up at us.

Two girls and one boy who was painfully close to a man.

Blond, yes. Blue-green eyes like Doyle had.

But the face…a familiar face.

Sanity tried to twist away again. Time shifted—reversed. That face, staring down *at* me while I clambered up a rope. Me kneeling on the ground, all but ready to kiss the soft grass, so grateful to be out of the pit.

Then, cold water—cruel hands.

Rathias—a third cousin. One of the crueler ones.

She said to let you out tonight…you're out, cousin. Now you can say thank you-

A sharp wail split through the memories crowded into my mind and I shoved them back, breathing shallowly as I stared at the girl instead. Girl. This one was a witch. Red-haired, green-eyed, skinny and frail. She looked like she didn't stand a chance against the muscle the shifters could weld.

The shifters…

Against my will, I felt myself looking back at the boy. The blond hair.

The eyes.

Through a throat gone tight, I whispered, "Is that Doyle?"

"Yeah."

I stumbled away and went to my knees.

Rathi—

"Kit, what the fuck is the matter?"

I wanted to run. Everything in me screamed it.

Behind me, I heard long, low, furious curses.

Swallowing, I slipped out of my backpack and unzipped it. Coiled in the bottom was a rope. We hadn't planned on needing it, but then again, we hadn't planned on coming across snakes, steel traps or landmines.

And I hadn't planned on finding a kid with a face that looked like the hell of my past either.

"Why doesn't he look like the picture?" I asked quietly.

"The spike. Hitting him hard." Power ripped, rippled and I found myself staring into Damon's face—that familiar face. "What's wrong, kitten?"

No. Mutely, I shook my head and I passed the rope over.

Not now.

Probably not ever.

I couldn't do this now.

"No time, remember?"

They were all weak.

Malnourished.

Doyle was the worst.

He watched me like…well, a predator who'd sighted its prey. Even after Damon had forced three bottles of water and several of the protein shakes on him, the kid still had a half-wild look in his eyes.

A few times, he made a move toward me and each time, Damon stepped between us.

The girls crowded around me and I let them.

The little witch broke down sobbing, wrapping her arms around my neck. "He's spiking and he's trying so hard, but…"

I heard the unspoken words. Hell, I could see it.

Doyle was teetering on the brink. "It's okay," I told her. "But we can't stay here."

We started out, me herding the girls along in front, even though every instinct demanded I *not* leave the hungry, predatory kid at my back.

Several times, I heard a growl. Snarls.

Once, there was a weird, rushing sound and I looked back, saw Damon holding the boy in a bear hug. He stared at me. "Go," he said flatly. "We'll be along."

I grimaced and kept moving.

If I thought that first day in the park was hell, no. This.…*this* was hell.

It was nightfall before we reached our car. There were more traps set, but we evaded them with ease, thanks in part to the little witch. Her name was Erin and she told me she'd been out on two hunts already. She said this in a broken, awful little whisper.

I wanted to cuddle her and hold her and promise nothing else would ever happen to her.

But I didn't make promises I couldn't keep.

Park rangers were up ahead. Shit.

My bow. My sword. I had them clutched in my hands and I stopped, shooting Damon a look and then I groaned as I saw his utter lack of clothing. He calmly dropped his pack and pulled out some clothes. He'd lost his shoes—did he have shoes?

"Kit. Do it…and don't argue," he told me.

I sighed. There was no point in arguing with this. I'd rather not let the rangers see the weapons, although how he was going to explain the kids…

Erin's eyes rounded in surprise as she watched me fade away. The girl shifter barely seemed to notice. I think she was in shock. Doyle, though…he still watched me. Even though he couldn't see me. The utter hunger in his eyes froze me.

Damon managed to get dressed before anybody saw the small group and I stayed at their back as he headed over to the car. All that weird power mantled down, too. *Good job*, I thought absently, still keeping Doyle in my sight. He was tracking my scent, the sound of my heart. Scaring the hell out of me.

"Hey there," Damon said. "Sorry, guys. Brought my stepson and his friends out here and they wanted to go out for a while on their own. I was stupid enough to let them and they got lost. Took me a few hours to find them—I was about to call you all when I finally caught up with them an hour ago."

Good way to play it…

It took another twenty minutes to get out of there before the park rangers were convinced everything was all good and nice and normal.

They did ask about his shoes. He confessed he was a shifter and that he'd ended up shifting to track them down. He'd lost his shoes somewhere, but he'd been so worried about the kids, he hadn't realized it until later.

The rangers' reactions were mixed. Two were okay with it. One stared at him with disgust—that wasn't an unusual response for humans.

Finally, they nodded and let them pack up their gear. It was awkward, scrambling into the back. Damon's order had come through clear—*All you girls into the back. Me and the boy are up front.* I worked the keys out of my pocket and dropped them into the seat, hoping the rangers didn't notice.

Once we were on the road, they headed out.

A few minutes later, I let myself fade back in. Immediately, I wanted to hide again because as I shifted in the seat, I saw Doyle turn around, staring at me.

Wide, hungry eyes. His nostrils flared and his lips parted as he breathed the air in.

Damon hit the windows and a blast of cool night flooded the car.

"Doyle, turn around."

The kid didn't.

"Doyle," Damon said quietly. "If you don't turn around and look away from her right now, I'm going to get pissed. Please don't force my hand on this."

A hungry, miserable little whine escaped the kid.

But he turned away.

I continued to watch him the entire way.

It was the longest damn drive of my life.

So miserably, achingly long that I couldn't even breathe a sigh of relief at finishing the damn job.

"You'll stay here for now," the mother said as she stared at the abused teens being tended to by the healers.

"Is...is that wise?" I swallowed, thinking of the intensity on Doyle's face.

That kid, around all these women? Many of them pacifists?

"Yes. This was an organized thing, Kitasa and you know it. Nowhere around here will you find a place with the protection I can offer you."

Reluctantly, I had to admit she was right. But this boy...

I flicked him a look. One of the few men in the house was tending him and the boy was back to watching me. Damon was between us—I don't think he'd given up that position once since we'd found the kid and I was painfully aware of the fact that I was relying on this guy to protect me...from a *kid*.

If Doyle lost it and came for me, I'd kill him. If he went after any of these witches, I'd kill him or Kori would.

She could do it easily in his current state. And I probably could. I *thought* I probably could. He was still weak. He was malnourished and more, the spike was making him uncontrollable. I could see it in the fluctuations of his energy.

But I didn't want to kill a kid.

Especially not one who meant something to Damon. But I'd be damned if I took the hurt I suspected *this* boy could bring.

"He doesn't mean harm," the mother said tiredly. "He..."

Eyes cut our way.

She gestured to the wall and I followed her through, trusting Damon and Kori to control whatever happened in the hall for a few minutes.

"He had to control everything for nearly two weeks," she said, staring at the mirror as though she could see everything happening in the room. "Some part of him was in control enough to realize that the two girls, the witch and the werewolf, weren't strong. He wouldn't prey on the weak. It shows some sign of the kind of man he'll be." A nervous smile curled her lips. "Think of it as a compliment. He sees an equal in you. He doesn't see somebody he would be abusing, but an equal."

"Yay, me."

She stroked my arm. "A day or two. Some food. Let him realize he's safe and he'll settle. There's a good heart in him, he just..." Es shook her head. "It was horrid, what happened. At one point, they had seven people in that hole. Seven. And he watched as one by one they were dragged away."

"I'm going to kill them," I said quietly.

Her hand fell away. "It's not our way." Her nearly colorless eyes flickered. "Anger. Rage. But…" She slanted a look at me and nodded. "It's a cancer that does this. A cancer must be cut out or it can spread."

Cutting it out sounded pretty damn good by me.

As she turned to the mirror, I went to follow but she looked back. "Perhaps you should go elsewhere…the library. The kitchen. Even just a soak in the tub, Kitasa. The more you're around him, the harder it's going to be for him to break this obsession. Let my witch heal him. We'll feed him."

I thought it through, then nodded. Yeah. Good idea.

I didn't need to be around him just then anyway.

"Let Damon know."

I wanted food.

But she'd said a soak…

The room where I'd slept here the night I'd burnt was my hand wasn't where I was led this time.

There was a larger room.

Lovely, done in shades of red and brown and when I opened the sliding doors, I had to catch my breath. A huge tub dominated the room. A soak. Yes. I'd soak. I'd soak until I turned into a prune.

While I was running the water, there was a knock at the door.

I opened it to discover Jo. She smiled at me absently, like her mind was in another world. She pushed a tray of food into my hands and then drifted—literally—down the hall.

I eyed the cup of coffee narrowly. Coffee. Caffeine, did I really want that? Except I rarely said no to coffee. It was like saying no to chocolate or a pretty new blade. I took a sip and grimaced at the motor oil taste of it. Who in the world brewed it here?

Juggling the tray one-handed, I kicked the door closed and carried the food over to the tub. It had a wide lip and I put the tray down as I got undressed. Time for something totally slothful, I decided. I was going to eat and take a damn bath at the same time. Steam was curling up in little wisps over the tub and when I checked the water, it almost boiled me. Perfect.

Near the foot of the tub, I saw a couple of jars of bath salts. While I nibbled on a slice of cheese, I checked them. One smelled of apples. No. One was like rainwater. Not bad, but not right, either. Another was some sort of mint and that was way too strong for me. The last one was subtle, just barely scented of vanilla. Perfect. I added a little and climbed in, making sure the tray wasn't going to fall over.

Coffee in one hand, I hissed at the heat of the water and decided that this could very well be heaven. Or about as close to it as I was going to get on this planet. And

I was going to damn well enjoy it for a few minutes before I stumbled into bed. Exhaustion preyed heavily on my mind and I needed sleep in the worst way.

Sleep. So I could deal with getting Doyle back home and safe…

And then come back down here and tear this place apart until I found every last soul behind—

Sleep grabbed me.

I never remembered it.

One minute I was munching on the cheese and fruit, nibbling at a sandwich and wondering if the coffee was going to keep me awake. And then I sat the coffee down to reach for…something.

And I was just under.

Asleep in the bathtub. Yes, home accidents can even happen to the NH population.

"You look exhausted…"

At the sound of Jude's voice, I slapped an arm over my chest and huddled in the bathwater as I searched the dim room for him.

He was a mist at first and it seemed like he formed out of the steam that danced above my bath, solidifying by my feet and staring down at me with that slight smile of his. That one that made me think of superior gods looking down on their creations with indulgent if puzzled amusement and thinking…*whatever is that silly thing doing now?*…right before they swatted the fools back into the stone age.

Glaring at him, I said flatly, "Get out."

"Oh, come now, darling Kit…you don't really want me to leave you alone while you're asleep in the bathtub," he drawled, kneeling down.

I glared at him.

"You look so happy to see me," he teased. "As always. Judging by your light mood, does that mean you've completed your job and you'll return home?"

"Job's not done."

He cocked his head. "You still haven't found the boy?"

"Oh, we found him." But I wasn't done. I was done when I found the fuckers behind this and ended them. "Now go away."

"Really, Kit. All I want to do is talk…"

"Yeah, well, find somebody else." I gave him a sour look as I drew my legs up to my chest and glared at him. Blond hair framed his face and for all the world, he looked like an angel. A deadly one.

"But I like talking to you." He smiled again and trailed a hand through the water. "I like watching over you. I like being near you."

I snorted.

His brows dropped low over his eyes. "It's the truth. You…the energy in you is pleasant. I could feel it without even having fed from you, but ever since I have?" A ruby red gleam settled in the back of his gaze and my heart jittered in my throat. "It's a pleasure like no other, Kit, and I can't wait to have it again. It's unparalleled. I suspected it would be wonderful. I underestimated."

Was this the way a mouse felt when it was thrown into a cage with a snake, I wondered? Even in the dream, I was feeling freaked out. Very freaked out.

"I want to be alone," I said flatly. *I want you the hell away from me.* "I'm tired."

"All the more reason I should be here." A slow smile curved his lips. "At least if I'm here, I can make you wake if you start to slip under."

Then he narrowed his eyes and murmured, "Or worse…I knew this was going to happen. You can't trust the cats, Kit."

"Just get ou—"

Cooler air danced on my flesh.

"Wake up, Kit. He's coming. You have to wake up," Jude said. I saw him staring past me. "Wake up!"

I sneered at him even as my mind started to move in that direction. But something wouldn't let me—

Something grabbed me. Shoved me under.

Voices yelling. Jude's, a roar in my mind.

"The fucking cat—he's trying to kill you—the bitch had her job done. Stop fighting me—"

Other voices, over the rush of water in my ears.

But I couldn't breathe. Couldn't—

"Let me in," Jude demanded.

Couldn't breathe…couldn't…couldn't…

"You stubborn little bitch! Breathe!"

Something pushed down on my chest and I thought my ribs were going to crack under the pressure.

Choking.

I was choking.

A sensation that was all too familiar.

Hard hands shoved me, rolled me over as I emptied my gut, my lungs of the water, of every bit of food I'd put in my belly.

Even when I'd purged myself, I couldn't stop retching. Couldn't stop coughing. My heart thundered in my ears and I was cold. So fucking cold. Shivers wracked me and fear pummeled me. Part of me kept thinking…*what…what…what…*

But my brain wouldn't let me even complete the thought because if I *did*, I might have to answer the damn question.

An eternity might have passed before I managed to get past that *what…what… what…* stage.

"Kit…"

Damon's voice…

I shoved away from him as terror took back over.

Jude's voice was a whisper in the back of my mind. An insidious, ugly little whisper. *"He tried to kill you, Kit. Let me in. I can help, but not if I can't get to you in time…"*

Shivering, cold, I scrambled to my feet and stumbled out into the bedroom. Grabbing the blanket, I wrapped it around me before I let myself turn around. It was something of a shock to realize there were a half-dozen people in there. Damon, Kori, Es, Jo, Tate, and a witch I didn't know.

"What...?" I cleared my throat and tried again. "What in the hell is going on?"

"That fucking leech was in your head again, wasn't he?"

I was shaking so bad, I could barely speak. Couldn't think. Blood roared in my head and I could still feel the weight of *him* inside me—"*Get away from all of them. They'll harm you, Kit. Come to me. I'll take care of you.*"

"Kitasa..."

I flinched at the sound of my name. Es touched my arm. Instinct grabbed me— *get away, get away—*

"No, Kitasa...I won't hurt you," she murmured. Her hand touched my temple. "You know this. He's in your mind. You have to let me help you get him out."

The battering in my head increased.

Get away—get away—I bolted.

Or at least, I tried.

Powerful arms grabbed me from behind.

He's going to kill me—

"No, dearest. He means you no harm...be at peace..."

Panic crowded my mind and the only thing I knew was that I had to *run*—

Bright, blinding light exploded behind my eyes.

Chapter Twenty

"Shhh."

Vaguely I grew aware that the room was moving. Swaying back and forth, like a ship tossed on the waves.

Or maybe I was the one swaying.

The dull ache inside my head subsided enough for me to make a judgment call. Yep. It was definitely me. And that pitiful moaning sound? That was me, too. Kit Colbana. Descendent of the legendary Amazon race. Nearly drowns herself in her own bath. I *think*. And moaning like a pitiful little baby.

"Shhh, it's okay, baby girl. It's okay."

Damon. Damon's voice. His chest under my cheek. Moving rapidly. I could feel the bang of his heart against my cheek and he had a hand in my hair, kneading, flexing—agitated.

Judging by the rough growl of his voice, I suspected *very* agitated.

As another one of those little whines rose in my throat, I swallowed it down.

Go, me.

I managed to stop whimpering.

"Kit?"

He eased back enough to look down at me and I found myself staring into glowing, shifting eyes. Yeah. I'd say he was in an agitated state.

"I…I think I'm okay," I whispered, jerking my eyes away. Fear danced on the back of my tongue, but I was going to deal with that, too. I didn't know what happened. Needed to understand that before I had another break with reality.

Es was still in the room. So was Kori. At some point, Jo, Tate and the other one had left. My hair was drying and my skin felt tight and itchy. How much time had passed?

Licking my lips, I darted a look at the mother. The calm look on her face should have been reassuring, but in that moment, nothing could reassure me. The bones in my legs felt like they had dissolved, but I needed to *move*. I eased away from Damon and some part of my brain told me he wasn't going to let me.

He's going to kill me—

I twitched under the memory. It didn't feel right. Even now. But the terror. Shit, that terror.

His arms fell away and when I had a hard time standing, he eased me upright and his hands didn't move until I was steady. Shame crawled up my throat, a nasty, awful thing that just wouldn't go away. Scratching at my arm, I looked at Es, at Kori, glanced at him from the corner of my eye. "What happened?"

Es and Kori shared a look, but then they looked at Damon.

I followed their glance, because it seemed if I wanted answers, he was the one who had them.

"You were under the water," he said flatly. He had moved to stand over the fireplace, staring down into it. The dancing flames cast him into light and shadow as he stood there, eerily reflecting off eyes that had yet to return to normal. Lids drooped low, shielding his gaze from me. He rolled his neck, his shoulders—it was like he had too much energy trapped inside him and I realized something. All of that power he normally had dancing above him, he had it locked down. I couldn't see any of it.

I flexed my wrist, absently.

He looked at me. "Your sword is on the bed. You were thrashing around and it was…"

Instead of finishing, he just shrugged.

I nodded. "The water. What happened? You said…"

"I walked in." He turned away from me. "Es was getting Doyle settled down. Said he might do better with no outside stimulation and she had a room where she sometimes puts…damaged people. She could keep him safe there. Unchained, unrestrained, and safe. He wouldn't hurt anybody else, and he wouldn't have to be chained up either. The way he was going…fuck. Anyway, once we had him in there, I came up here. It's night. I worried. The leech…"

Jude—

Immediately, my brain screeched to a blank stop and my heart started to race. Panic, thick and hot, churned inside me. I could hear Es, but only vaguely. The heat in my palm was too much and then she was there. My blade. Damn it, I could fight this time.

Fight what—somebody who is trying to sneak into your mind?

"Kit, calm down!"

I swung out and felt the blade connect. Somebody—a woman—shouted. Something hot glanced off my hip.

A thunderous snarl echoed through the room.

None of it mattered.

Had to fight.

Had to get away—

"Kit…"

I struck out again. Blood. I smelled blood.

"Kit."

Hands caught my face.

Wet hands.

The smell of blood—thick with magic, *alive* with it—flooded my senses and somehow snapped me back to myself.

Dazed, I struggled to think past the panic.

"Damon, you need to let me calm her down."

"Es, the next one of you to try and throw magic at her is going to be digging my claws out of their gut, you understand me?"

Damon. Damon's voice.

I blinked and blinked, struggling to focus my eyes. Red. That was all I could see. A wash of it—

"Kit." Something under that red moved…

Oh, hell.

It wasn't red.

It was *blood.*

His neck. His chest. Healing, slowly, but covered in blood…because I had sliced into him.

"Damon?"

A harsh groan escaped him and then his lips touched my brow. "Yeah. It's me, baby girl. You're okay. You hear me? You're okay. Nothing hurts you when I'm here, got it?"

A hysterical laugh bubbled up out of me. Okay? I'd just damn near lost my mind and torn into somebody who could kill me as easily I could breathe. And he's telling me that I'm *okay?*

No. I really, really wasn't.

Damon kicked Kori out.

She went, bleeding and grudgingly. I didn't know what had happened and just then, I didn't care.

The mother wouldn't leave. She brought me a cup of tea. "Drink it. Please. It's just a special mix of mine—no magic—" She gave Damon a narrow look. "But it will calm your nerves."

I didn't think *that* was possible. I could smell chamomile, strawberry leaves and other familiar things in it, plus other herbs that I couldn't identify, but nothing would calm me down tonight. To make her quit hovering, though, I took a sip. "Somebody needs to explain what happened," I said after I tried the tea.

"As your cat said…he found you in the water."

I swallowed and looked at Damon. He was holding me in his lap. His blood was drying on him, on me, but just then, there was nothing either of us could do about it. I had to know what was going on before I went insane. "Did I…?" I licked my lips. "I fell asleep. I remember being tired. I must have fallen asleep."

Damon stroked a hand up my back. "I came in. You were under the water. Your eyes were open. I tried to pull you up and you fought me, Kit. You didn't *let* me pull you up and you felt a hell of a lot stronger than I think you are."

Shuddering, I shook my head.

He rubbed the back of my neck, staring at the wall in front of us. "I yelled for Es —I…" He paused, clenched his jaw. "She was in here almost right away and I was still trying to pull you out of the water. She hit the drain and said something…"

"I could feel an unnatural pull on your mind," Es said quietly.

Damon shrugged. "She did something. I can feel magic, but I don't understand it. I was able to get you out—you weren't breathing. Starting pushing on your chest and then you started coughing up the water."

Closing my eyes, I buried my face against his chest, wishing I could just…*stay* there. Blood and all. Right here, I almost felt safe, as long as I didn't have to think.

But Damon's stock in trade was being an asshole and he wasn't going to let me hide, it seemed. "It was him, wasn't it?"

I cringed.

"Kit. We can't fix this until we know what happened," he whispered against my temple. Gentle, soothing strokes up and down my back.

Tears leaked out of my eyes.

"I fell asleep. And he was there. I told him to get out and he was just being... himself." The panic tried to crowd in.

"Stop." Damon gripped my shoulder. "Listen. Fight it back, you stubborn little bitch, you hear me?"

I saw his eyes—green eyes, that smile. *Wake up*...hands shoving me down.

"Kit. Where's your fucking sword?"

My palm itched. I popped my wrist.

"That's it," Damon whispered. "Call her."

I groaned and listened to the whispering of the blade at the back of my mind. Just that was enough to ground me. Gave me the strength to think past the fear. "I...I think I'm okay."

"Hold your sword, Kit," Damon said quietly. "You're steadier when you have it."

I closed my eyes. There had been a time in my life when I had gone to sleep cradling her next to me. Times when I couldn't sleep without her, when I wouldn't eat, wouldn't leave the house for anything unless I had that damn blade. I didn't want to go back to being that scared again.

"I want her sheathed," I whispered.

Distantly, I heard the soft brush of fabric. The creak of leather. And then Damon said, "Thanks." Then he pushed the sheathed blade into my hands. "She's here. Now get this done. Hiding won't make it easier."

Hiding might not. But running could, I thought absently. Gripping the leather, I swallowed back the panic and made myself talk.

"He was in my dreams, talked about my..." I swallowed back the bitter taste of fear. "Talked about my energy, how it made him feel alive. Then he said how much better it was since he'd fed from me. It freaked me out. I told him to leave. I remember that. Then there was...something. I don't know if somebody else was in the room, or if he wanted me to think somebody was. I don't know what happened. He told me to wake up, and I *wanted* to, just to get away from him, but I couldn't. Then...something shoved me under."

I gripped the sword to me and closed my eyes.

"He told me you were killing me, Damon. I'd done the job and the Alpha was done with me so you were going to kill me."

I finished the tea.

I can't much say it calmed my nerves, but I finished it.

Es took the cup and continued to stand there, studying me critically.

"What?" I asked wearily. I needed to get the blood off of me. I needed to sleep, but I was terrified. I needed...shit. I didn't know what I needed.

"You said he mentioned your energy."

I gave a short, jerky nod.

A troubled look into her eyes. "And he's fed from you."

"Yes."

"How many times?"

"Just the once," I said quietly. *Never again—I'll die before I let him feed from me again.* I'd rather *be* dead than let him deepen this...whatever. Maybe Damon had been right, after all, and death was better than fucking with a vampire.

Es rubbed her brow. "Not all vampires are like Jude, child. Some are just more...apt, we'll say, to feeding from a psychic vein. It appears that's what Jude was doing and he's found a vein he very much likes in you. The blood feed deepened his connection to you. And it likely gave him a taste for more." She lifted her head and the pale gray of her eyes glinted with warning. "He'll try again," she said, her voice blunt.

"I know that." And that's when my chaotic, jumping brain finally settled and I knew what I needed to do. I needed to figure out how to kill Jude. Tall order. I wondered if I could get my hands on a small range missile. It could maybe do the job.

"Why did you let him bite you, Kit?"

I glared at her. "At the time, I didn't think I had much of a choice."

"Well, that's understandable." A faint smile curled her lips. "Life happens that way at times, doesn't it? But you have options now. Choices. But the fact is...he bit you and there's a bond. Jude is old. He's not ancient, but he's got some years on him, so he's strong. He's also ruthless and something of a...well." She pursed her lips and then said, "To be blunt, he's a dick."

I stared at her and then nodded. "I can agree with that."

"He occasionally has his moments where he isn't a total bastard, but even those moments are usually fueled by some innate drive to manipulate. He is always scheming." She studied my face. "I heard he aided you once. Years ago. Even then, he was likely scheming. Don't believe he has any innate sense of decency. Many vampires do. Jude does not."

"We just established he's a dick, right?"

Es chuckled. "Indeed we did." She reached out and caught my wrist.

I tensed as she traced over the path where he had bitten me. I couldn't *see* where he had bitten me and there was no way anything lingered.

"It leaves a mark." She looked up at me. "A healer can see it. It will fade in time, but the mark is there. Just as the bond is there. Bonds are odd things, though. If a stronger bond is set in place...or if a new bond is formed, he won't have the ability to call you."

I jerked my wrist back. "Meaning...what? I should find a local vamp to bite me?"

"It's an option." She smiled. "Kori's lover is a vampire, and a lovely lady. A kind one. Plus, she's a friend of the house, meaning she would have our protection should Jude decide to get...pissy. I'd rather enjoy that," she said. The grin on her face took on a devious slant. "I'd enjoy it quite a lot, actually."

I just stared at her.

"Not all vampires are of Jude's ilk, Kit. As I said. It's an option."

"Not a good one," Damon growled.

He had taken up residence over by the fire again.

I shot him a nervous glance.

Es made an odd little humming noise under her breath. "Well, there are other options, other bonds. Stronger ones."

"Quiet, witch." He bit each word off like he'd rather be biting *into* something.

Sighing, Es said, "Another option—I can offer you a spell. A charm of sorts, like what I did earlier that knocked him out of your mind. It will only last while you are in my home and I'll have to do it again every day at sunset. It will work. But it's only a short-term option. If that's what you choose to do, the best choice might be for you to buy a plane ticket and then lose yourself somewhere very, very far away from here, Kit. If you stay away from him for a few months, the bond will fade and then he won't be able to call you like this again. I'd recommend you have the local house spell your home against him and you should keep your distance from him in the future."

"I'm not running." Even as I said it, I wanted to kick myself. I'd run before and done very well with it. What was wrong with me? "I'm not running away from that bastard."

A soft smile curved her lips. "Then you need to think through the other options." She brushed my hair back. "You could try approaching the Assembly. He did bite you without explaining all that would happen as a result and that is an ethical violation. But I wouldn't recommend that."

"Bad idea." I shook my head. "Makes me look weak in their eyes and I'd rather not look any weaker than I already do."

"Kitasa..." She chuckled as she turned away. "The Assembly hardly sees you as weak. Not as physically strong as some, but you're impossibly clever, incredibly quick and you managed on your own in this world. It's a singular sort of strength, but strength nonetheless. You should rest. You can think this through in the morning."

Chapter Twenty One

I stood in the bathroom, staring at the shower.

I needed to get in there and get clean.

I couldn't even manage to let go of the blanket wrapped around me, though.

I am aneira. My heart is strong. My aim is true. And I'm now scared of water.

There was a knock at the door.

The sound of it made me flinch.

When I didn't answer, Damon just came inside. One look at me made him sigh and he tugged the blanket out of my death grip. He didn't take it away, just held it steady, ready to lower it. "It won't get better if you don't face it," he said quietly. "Sooner is better."

"I just drowned, what, a couple hours ago?" I said. I sounded like a bitch. I didn't care. "I think I can have a day or two to freak about it. It's totally understandable that I have a few reservations about water right now. I should be *allowed* to freak out a little."

"You can freak about it for the next hundred years." He looked down at me and brushed my hair back from my face. I could see the blood on his hand. "I'm going to. I know that."

"Why are we all bloody?" I spread my hand over his chest. There weren't any wounds left, but earlier, his chest had looked like somebody had tried to carve him up like a Thanksgiving turkey.

He grimaced. "Well, I got to see firsthand how good you are with your sword. And you're good. Very good."

I closed my eyes. "I did this."

"You were panicking—thinking about that fucking leech."

Fear tried to crowd in again, but I gamely shoved it back. I couldn't panic every time I thought of him. Especially not since I was still thinking about *killing* him.

"I'm sorry."

"No reason." He laid a hand on my throat and then grinned at me. "Maybe we can call it even now. I think, inch for inch, you did a lot more damage in the long run. You definitely got a pound of flesh and quart of blood."

I surprised myself by laughing. "Hey, I can't heal in the blink of an eye." Staring past him to the shower, I swallowed. "Will...will you get in there with me? Please?"

The glow in his eyes flashed. A growl broke free—for just a second and then it was gone. He gave me a single, short nod then he caught my wrist, guided it up to the blanket. "Hold it a minute, kitten."

The sound of the water coming on shouldn't make me quake. It did.

I thought, oddly, of my grandmother.

Closing my eyes, I thought, *She didn't break me, damn it. I won't let him do it, either*.

Distantly, I heard the quiet whisper of him stripping off his jeans. "These things are wasted," he muttered. The thud of them hitting the ground. Think about mundane things. Maybe even not mundane—I popped open one eye and stared at him.

Wow.

Very, very, wow.

Not mundane at all.

Blood streaked his chest, his arms. The lines of his tattoo shone through the dry red. I laid a hand on it. "How were you able to get this done?" I asked softly.

"Before I spiked. Healing is still close to human rate then." He studied me. "You ready?" he asked, his voice quiet, soft. Gentle, I decided.

The world's biggest asshole was gentling me into the shower.

And I wasn't going to start crying again.

With a jerky nod, I let go of the blanket. My legs didn't want to work. Nothing did. But I finally managed to climb in. I tensed at the feel of the water. Panic—

"It's okay, Kit," Damon murmured against my neck. "Nothing hurts you when I'm here. You got me?"

I made myself move deeper under the spray, watching as the water struck us both. It ran red as it washed away the blood. Heat curled around us, wrapping around us just as surely as his arms did. He pulled me against him and I went, sinking against his chest. I could lean on him, I realized. I really could. And it wasn't so bad to do it.

"Why did you tell her to be quiet?"

Damon stroked my back. "You've had enough thrown at you tonight, baby girl. Haven't you?"

Yes. I was pretty sure I'd had enough thrown at me for the next two hundred years. But I wasn't going to sleep any better until I had a handle on all of this. I *needed* a better handle on all of this. It was driving me crazy.

"What in the hell does in rut mean?"

He growled and then the hand he'd be stroking up and down my back dropped down to my hip and he pulled me flush against him. Thick and hot, he throbbed against me. "Hell, little girl, what do you *think* it means?"

I snorted. "From what I've heard, it means more than you need to get laid."

"Shit." He boosted me up until we were on eye level. "You really don't have any clue what it means," he muttered, staring at me, eye to eye, mouth to mouth. Against my chest, I could feel the racing of his heart and it met my own, beat for beat. "And trust me...right now, you're wet, you're naked, and I want you like I want my next breath, like I want my next shift. But you were just jacked over in the worst way and we don't need to have this talk while you're vulnerable."

I wrapped my legs around him. "Then we don't talk."

"Kit..."

Twining my arms around his neck, I pulled him close. "Don't talk. We can talk tomorrow. But right now...I need not to think."

I could feel him between my legs. So close. So temptingly close.

"Baby girl..." he groaned. His head fell back and I saw the muscles of his body flex. Bulge. A shudder wracked him. "You're certain, damn it?"

"Yes." I leaned in, licked the water from his chest, tasted the lingering salt of his blood. I nipped him and he shuddered again, snarling so loud the sound of it bounced off the walls.

"Don't." He fisted a hand in my hair, pulled me back. "Don't kiss me. Don't bite me. Just..."

He pressed against me. "Don't bite. Don't let me bite you." As he started to push inside, his eyes locked on my face. I stared at him. This was happening. Had it just been a week ago that this guy had strolled into my office and I'd kicked myself for not staying at home to work on my taxes?

And now...

Held up by his forearm under my hips, locked in place by his hand tangled in my hair, I shuddered as he slowly, oh, so damned slowly sank inside me. I arched against him and twisted, trying to work him deeper, but he growled. "Be still. Just be still."

Be still—how in the hell could I be still? I raked my nails down his shoulders and twisted again, tightening my legs around his hips. He snarled again and the sound of it arrowed straight through me, centering low in my core. "Baby girl..." He did that odd little thing where he snapped at the air with his teeth.

I smiled at him and moved just the same way. Again. Again—

He slammed into me and I screamed.

Hot, blinding pleasure shattered me as I clung to him, scrambling, trying to get closer, but that iron fist in my hair wouldn't let me. He surged inside me and the pleasure, so harsh and deep, washed over me. It exploded and left me empty and still he moved.

Suddenly he tensed. And then, he let go of my hair. I felt him swell inside me and he started to lower his head. Then he stopped. "No..." he muttered. "No." He growled and then lifted his hand. The scent of fresh blood tinged the air and he sank his teeth into his own wrist as he climaxed.

"Are you okay?"

He stroked a sponge over my back.

Drowsily, I muttered, "Thoughtlessness achieved. You're a good thought destroyer."

He chuckled. "I'll put that down on my resume when I'm out looking for work."

"Uh-huh."

The hot water still beat down on us. "We're not being very conscientious. We're using up all her hot water."

"We'll be out in a minute," he murmured. He slicked some shampoo through my hair.

"You can also put down *excels at washing hair*."

He tugged on my short, soapy hair. "Ha, ha. You should know this is a singular honor. Other than mine, I don't think I've ever washed anybody's hair."

"You must just be a natural." The heat had worked its magic. Although it was possible it was the sex. I couldn't think worth anything. When Damon turned off the water, I shivered a little, crowding against him. His arms came around me, easing me close for a minute as he brushed his lips across my neck.

"Let's dry you off," he whispered.

I nodded and climbed out, but when I went to grab a towel, he beat me to the task, stroking me down with a fat, fluffy one that felt warm and soft against my skin. Dazed, I stood there as he finished the job and wrapped me in yet another towel, a dry one. "Wait."

Wait, the man says, I thought. All I wanted to do was sleep. Absently, I scratched at my arm. Needed lotion—

He appeared back in the door and I frowned when I saw my bottle of lotion in his hand. "You're always slicking this on after a shower," he said, his eyes lingering on my hand for a minute, watching where I'd been scratching. There were questions in the backs of his eyes. I could all but see them, if I'd just let myself look.

But I'd had enough. Seen enough. Handled enough. I just couldn't take any more.

How in the world would I explain the neurosis, anyway? After years of being filthy and grubby and dirty, I had an almost obsessive need to be clean? The first few years, once I'd finally stopped running, I'd sometimes showered three or four times a day. When I had money, I'd glutted on things like nice soaps and lotions or shampoos, all because it was exactly what I'd never had.

And still, I couldn't forget the awful, terrible way I'd always felt when my grandmother stared at me. Dirty. Useless. Skin crawling with vermin because she wouldn't even let me clean myself decently.

No. I wasn't going to try to explain any of that.

Much easier just to stand there and let him slick the lotion on me...what woman wouldn't enjoy that?

"You going to add masseuse to your list of skills?" I teased him, swallowing around the ache in my throat.

"Only if you're hiring, baby girl."

I reached for the lotion, but he held it away, eying me with a glittering, watchful look in those dark eyes.

It wasn't exactly a chore, standing there as he rubbed me down, strong hands gliding across my skin, rubbing lotion in and stroking over my belly, my hips, lingering over my breasts, my legs. But never long enough in any of those places. Even when I might have *tried*.

"You need sleep," he muttered against my neck. "And I need to get my head on straight."

Why should *he* have that luxury? I wondered.

But we ended up in the bed, his long body tucked around mine.

Sleep. Yes.

Sleep sounded nice...

My lids drifted down. His hand rested on my chest, between my breasts with his palm just above my heart. I could even feel the slow beat of it against his hand. Sleep, I told myself. I needed it. Had needed it earlier, but then Jude—

I tensed.

Terror trickled inside and like the mythical hydra, the damn thing multiplied every time I tried to cut it down.

Sleep—can't sleep—what if he comes—

"Kit."

Damon's voice was a harsh, brutal slap against my senses even if his hand was a gentle stroke down my side.

Gasping in a desperate breath of air, I said, "I'm here. I'm fine. I'm here—"

"Go to sleep. Stop thinking. Just sleep."

"But…" I squeezed my eyes shut. *I can't I can't I can't!* "What if I sleep and he does it again?"

"If he tries to come in on you again, I'll know." He flexed his hand on my chest. "Your heart rate changes. Your breathing does. Even the feel of your body changes. I'm right here, and I'll know. I'll get every damn witch in here if I have to drag them in kicking and screaming. Sleep, Kit. You need it…and I'll be right here, I swear it." He pulled me closer and nuzzled my brow. "Just sleep. I'll be here with you…"

There were no dreams.

At least not of Jude.

I dreamt of the park.

Of endless trails, of traps unseen. Of children who screamed for rescue and pits that went so deep, nobody could see the bottom. And all the while, people begged for help and Damon stood by watching. Watching *me*. Not them. *Me*.

After I'd stumbled across yet another hole, I turned and stared at him. This last one…it hadn't been empty. There were bones in it. As they shone up at me, bleached white by the sun, I glared at Damon. "This isn't *done*," I told him. "We have to stop this. We have to."

Wide shoulders moved in a lazy shrug. "Is that what we're doing?"

"Just don't get in my way," I warned him.

A familiar grin tugged at his lips. "Baby girl, the only time I've been in your way is when you put me there."

He was gone before I could figure out what that could mean. Gone before I could ask a question. Gone…but there was a giant cat stalking along at my back. His tawny pelt smooth as silk, the sooty gray marks rippling over his muscled frame.

"Damon?"

The great cat's head swung up to look at me and he watched me with Damon's eyes.

"How do we stop this?"

He sat down and started to lick one paw.

Fucking cats.

Frustration chewed at me as I headed off through the undergrowth. His voice followed me. "I was just here for the kid, baby girl. That's all My Lady wanted. The rest is up to you and I don't think you can handle it. Nobody thinks you can."

I flipped him off.

His laugh chased me.

Nobody thought I could handle anything.

Maybe they were right, but it wasn't going to stop me.

I tripped over the massive body of a beheaded snake and found myself in a pit. Surrounded by bones. I started to scream, but all that came out of my mouth was the sound of a phone ringing—

I jerked upright in the bed at the second ring.

Damon stroked a hand down my belly. "Sorry. I should have turned the damn thing off."

Laying my hand over my heart, I tried to make myself breathe. "Yeah. Like she'd really appreciate that."

He watched me. A brooding look entered his eyes as the phone rang a third time.

"You have to answer that," I said quietly.

A muscle twitched in his jaw. "I don't *have* to do anything," he said flatly.

After the fourth ring, it went silent.

"Why did you do that?" I asked, dragging a blanket up and trying to ignore the way my heart continued to jitter around inside my chest like a hummingbird on Torque. I hadn't ever touched that drug—it was speed for shifters and would probably kill me, but I imagined it would jack up my heart like this.

"Because once I talk to her, I'm going to have to answer questions, probably gather up Doyle and head back. I'm not ready to do that yet. As long as I don't talk to her, it's not an issue." Wide shoulders moved and I found myself distracted by the way the tattoo played across his skin. The stark, unyielding lines of it mesmerized me and I found myself wanting to crawl on top of him and learn it with my eyes, my hands, my...

Shit. Now *really* wasn't the time.

I swallowed and jerked my eyes away from him, staring at the wall in front of me. "You can't avoid it forever. You know that."

"Yeah. I'll have to take the next call, but..." his voice trailed off and he sighed, lowering his head and staring at the floor while he rubbed the back of his neck.

He looked tired. It was an odd thing, I thought, seeing him look tired. "Did you sleep?"

Gray eyes flicked my way. "Yeah. Not a lot, but I don't need much anyway." He shifted on the bed, moving until he was kneeling over my thighs, hands braced on either side of my hips. "You had some crazy dreams. And you talk in your sleep. Muttering about snakes and trees and bones."

"I was dreaming about those kids. Whoever is behind this..." I nibbled on my lip and toyed with the sheet. "This isn't done for me. I can't...I can't walk away from it."

His eyes studied my face. "She'll call me back. I'll have to go…for now. I don't want you diving into this without me."

I didn't answer him. There was just no way I could.

"Kit…" he growled.

"Don't," I said softly. "You're going to try to make me say something I can't say, snarl at me, try to intimidate me into something that just isn't in me to give. I won't do it, Damon. I won't."

Threading his fingers into my hair, he tugged me close, pressed his brow to mine. "Foolish little girl…I still think you're a foolish girl. Why in the hell am I here with you?"

"Nobody is making you stay."

"Yeah, somebody is. You are. I just fucking *can't*." He growled the words against my lips and nipped me lightly.

It turned into a deeper kiss that left my blood humming, but before I could do anything about it, he rolled off the bed and started to prowl the room. "Can't," he muttered. "Can't right now…"

"How much time before she calls again?"

Damon shrugged. "No telling. Five minutes. Five hours."

"Then maybe we should have that talk."

He stilled. It was an eerie, peculiar stillness. Light reflected off his eyes as he stared at me. "Kit—"

Closing my eyes, I leaned back against the wooden headboard. It was old—reclaimed wood, made from what looked like old doors and painted white. Set against the dark, burnished red woods, it shouldn't have looked so charming, but it did. The wood felt scratchy against my back and I focused on it to give my mind something else to think about as I puzzled through the mess in my head.

"We either have this talk now or we're not doing it," I finally said. "You have this idea in your head that I'm incapable of handling shit and I'm fed up."

"It's not that I think you're incapable," he muttered. "You're too fucking capable, even as you take on shit that I know should break you, that I know you should run screaming from, but you do it anyway. You do it, you handle it, and even when I think you're crazy, when almost anybody *else* in your shoes would find a way out, you just soldier on."

"So am I capable or am I a silly little fool?" I demanded.

"Both!" he snapped. "I've got messes of my own that I have to deal with, and the last thing I needed was a cocky little half-human throwing herself in my way. I don't want to do this and watch myself get tangled up with you and then see you plunge into some disaster you can't get out of."

Blowing out a breath, I said quietly, "That's a little deep, isn't it? I mean, we've known each other…what…a week?"

Gray eyes stared at me. "You want to know what rut is, Kit? Really know?"

My heart banged against my ribs. The intensity in his voice, the deep growl of it danced across my skin and I could hardly breathe. The air in the room was charged, so tight and hot.

He came to me, all hard muscle and grace and feline beauty and I couldn't think for wanting him. He knelt on the bed and braced one hand on the headboard by my head. "Do you, Kit?" he asked again, his breath drifting across my lips.

When in doubt—or terror—reach for the sarcasm. Curling my lip at him, I said, "Are you going to tell me it's some mystical fated mates shit? Sorry. I won't buy that. It doesn't work that way."

His hand curled around my neck, his thumb resting in the hollow of my neck. "No. Absolutely it doesn't. This is all on my part, and whether or not you'll ever feel a damn thing for me is up to you...but you already feel something. Even if I hadn't already figured that out, I would have gotten a clue when you came muttering my name and clutching at me during the night, baby girl." The pad of his thumb stroked over me. "No. It's more complicated...better. Easier. Worse. Harder. It started when you pulled that fucking sword on me in your office. I wanted you then, but wanting is easy. Almost any woman can satisfy a guy when he just needs to get laid."

"Nice to know this isn't just about you being horny." *Look away*, I told myself. Needed to do that because the raw intensity in his eyes was killing me. Killing me—

But that was one thing I just couldn't do. Couldn't. At all.

"Your mouth was another problem for me," he muttered, leaning in and licking my lower lip. "You fucking smart ass. Mouthing off from the get-go. I've never found a smart ass so appealing until I met you."

"Uh-huh. You're still not explaining much here."

A slow smile curled his lips. The hand he had on my neck stroked down. I had the blanket tucked under my arms, but it caught under his palm and went down under the path of his hand, stopping when he paused, just over my heart.

"Sex is easy. Rut is anything but—it's physical, emotional, mental. We focus on one woman and I started focusing on you from day one. It got worse every damn time I did something that I knew scared you...but you just snarled back at me. I knew you were smart and quick, and all I needed was your brain and your connections—I didn't want your mouth or anything else."

His thumb stroked over the inner curve of my breast as he continued. "But you didn't just give me your mouth. If you'd just been mouthy, or if you hadn't tried... but hell, you gave me everything. Five minutes after I all but brutalized you, we walked into a hall full of shifters and one of them dared to touch you and instead of showing fear, you busted his nose—you had no weapons and still you fought."

His mouth brushed over mine as he whispered, "You stood by the body of a dead kid, a wolf you didn't know and I saw the grief in your eyes and it gutted me. You had no reason to care, but you did. I knew, then, even if the Alpha *wasn't* issuing threats you would have done everything you had to do to find Doyle...that was when I really started to slip. But I'd already done the damage and I couldn't undo it, could I?"

Reaching up, I laid my hand over his. "If you couldn't undo the damage, pal, you wouldn't be in bed with me."

A smile tugged at his lips. "Well, there is that, I guess."

He shifted his hand around and caught mine, lifting my wrist to his mouth. It was the one Jude had bitten. Even that single thought was enough to send a cold sliver of fear lancing through my mind.

Damon, the bastard, sensed it and a storm danced in his eyes. "Then the vampire showed up—I wanted to tell you then that I'd keep you safe, but how could I make you believe it when you were already scared of me? When you had every right to be afraid of the Alpha?"

Something tickled the back of my mind. *The Alpha*—

But before I could latch onto it, he continued. "And he bit you. I knew he had, knew there would be troubles. There will *still* be troubles. As soon as you leave this house—" A muscle pulsed in his jaw, a growl vibrating deep in his chest. "That's why I don't want you going out there to work this until I can get back to you."

"She's not likely to turn her favorite killer out just to help round up a couple of people who like to hunt stray shifters and witches," I told him, resting my hand on his thigh. "So far, the only one who had any affiliation was Doyle. And that was a fuck-up of epic proportions, but still. I can't wait idly by for you to come back. What if they go into hiding and we don't find them?"

"And what if he sends his fucking servants after you? In *here*, you are safe, but out there? Or if you get hurt, caught by some of those fuckers? Just a few seconds after he wakes for the day and you're his, Kit."

I swallowed. "Not if his bond is broken."

Damon tensed, his grip on my wrist tightening. "Be careful where you go from here, Kit. *His* hold on you is temporary...*mine* won't be. Don't go rushing into this just because you're afraid of him. Because I'll do it. I want you that much and I won't care if you change your mind...I won't let you go."

"Who says I'm doing it because I'm afraid?" Wiggling out from under him, I moved onto my knees and stared into his eyes. "We've already established I do stupid things that I shouldn't do, right? I'll deal with Jude—no matter what happens, I'm going to find a way to deal with the shit he tried to pull. It doesn't *matter* if we snap his hold or not, the son-of-a-bitch is going to pay for the number he pulled last night."

The storm clouds in his eyes deepened and he gripped me around the waist. "You are not going after him alone, Kit. You understand me?"

"I'm starting to think *you* are the silly little fool." Then I frowned. "Well, not little. But still. And this isn't the topic we're discussing. I'll deal with Jude. I'm not doing it *now* because he'll expect it and I have to figure out the right way. I'm not stupid and I don't rush into things, nor do I think I can take him down solo. But *he* isn't what we needed to talk about."

I laid a hand on his chest, splayed my fingers wide over the black ink of his tattoo. "We're talking you and me. There *is* a you and me....right?"

"Yes." It was a low, harsh growl.

"And what will your dearest *My Lady* think?"

"She can fuck herself."

I blinked. "Ah...well, then." My mouth had somehow managed to go dry. Very dry. "What…what happens, then?"

"You better be sure," he rasped. "Remember what I said. It's permanent. I don't give up what's mine."

Mine…

It made something warm and sweet bloom inside me. Smiling at him, I tugged my wrist from his grasp and reached up, cupping his face in my hands. "I kind of like the idea of it, really. And you're mine, then, right?"

"Yes." He caught my wrist once more, lifted it to his mouth for a quick kiss. "I'll bite you. It will hurt and it will scar." His brooding gaze held mine as he pressed his lips to the sensitive skin along my wrist. "I could bite your shoulder, but I'd rather do it here…he'll see it. He'll know. He's smart so he'll get the idea that he needs to leave you the fuck alone."

Reflexively, I clenched my hand. "Ah…I guess Es has something that can speed up the healing."

"Probably." He continued to watch me.

Leaning in, I kissed him and then I sat down. It was weird that I felt nervous now. Why did I feel nervous now…?

Even as he moved around and pulled me into his lap, settling me close, so close that I could feel some very interesting portions of his anatomy pressing against my hip, I was still battling nerves. He lifted my wrist again, his eyes intense as they rested on my face, burning. Hot. Hungry.

My throat constricted until I couldn't breathe. Didn't seem like I could breathe at *all*.

His mouth opened and I twitched as I saw his teeth—they weren't completely human now. Longer. And sharper. So much sharper. As they pierced my wrist, I bit my lip to keep from screaming.

I'd asked for this—

I wanted this.

The pain was deep and piercing and it didn't end when he lifted his head. His tongue rasped around my flesh, lapping at the blood for a moment before he sighed against my flesh. "You could have made a sound, baby girl."

Jerkily, I shook my head. Making a sound when you hurt—

Shoving that thought back inside its closet, I glanced around. "I need to wrap this, huh?"

He continued to lick me. "Probably." He groaned a little. "You taste amazing, though."

"Stop it," I muttered, shoving at his head and easing off his lap. I was on my feet and looking around for something to wrap around my wrist when he emerged from the bathroom, holding a hand towel.

"We'll use this," he said quietly. "Get dressed. We'll find Es." A grim look settled in his eyes.

"What's wrong?"

As he wrapped my wrist, I noticed the odd tension in him. It called to the instincts buried in the back of my mind and I could feel myself getting edgy. My right hand heated. Readied itself. "Nothing," he murmured. "It's just…" He shot a look at the phone lying by the bed. "She'll be calling again soon. I can feel it."

"Is that a gut instinct or more?"

He stared at me. "More."

Chapter Twenty Two

Kori led us to the healing hall without speaking. There was an odd look in her eyes when she first looked at Damon, but she said absolutely nothing, which was weird, I thought.

Es was in the hall with the two girls and when she saw me, that gentle smile curved her lips. "You slept."

"Yes." I didn't mention the odd dreams or anything else. As I tried to figure out how to explain what I needed, she rose from the chair where she'd been seated and came to me.

"Ahhh..." She unwrapped my wrist and studied the punctures. They still bled. "You realize, of course, there are several ways to heal this."

Damon's hand curved over the back of my neck.

I stared at her pale eyes and waited.

"A full healing would remove any scarring but it's more invasive and you'd need rest. A day, possibly more, since your body has already been rather taxed."

As one, Damon and I said, "No."

She flicked a look at Damon. "Cat, I understand the significance, but I need her answer...hers alone."

Rolling my eyes, I said, "You heard my answer. I know what the damn thing means and I want it there. No full healing."

"Because you can't take the down time?"

"No." I narrowed my eyes at her. "Because I asked him to put it there in the first place. Why ask him to do it if I'm just going to have you remove it?"

Now she smiled again, and the look on her face was oddly pleased. "Wonderful. A minor healing spell, then. You're probably familiar with it. I can accelerate the healing—it will be like it's months old, instead of minutes."

"Ah...months?"

Any time Colleen had done such a spell, she'd just been able to ramp it up for a few days, a few weeks at best.

Es smiled at me. "I'm the mother of this house, Kitasa. I have a bit more skill, a bit more power at my disposal than some of the witches you've known. And you'll need all your strength for when you go back out."

I felt the hot power of Damon's energy slam in me, the burst of his anger flaring. *Yeah, pal. I know you don't want me going back out.*

But I couldn't wait quietly, either.

Es had her hands on my wrist and the wonderful, warm crawl of her magic was spreading through me when Damon's phone rang.

I tensed.

It was her.

Annette. The Queen Bitch. The Alpha Cat. And Damon's *Lady*.

Bile knocked at the back of my throat but I swallowed it down as I turned my head and stared at his wide shoulders. He held his phone for a moment, staring at it before he lifted his head to meet my gaze.

Then he answered it, his voice falling into that flat, familiar tone. Even just two days ago, I'd thought that tone signified reverence. It didn't. It was just... emotionless.

What had Es said—

...notices everything and she'll notice more about you than you could possibly imagine, including what you had for breakfast, the fact that you're in rut, and the fact that you hate your Alpha...

I studied him closer.

Did he hate her?

"He does," Es murmured, her voice low, very low.

I jerked my gaze to her, my mouth opening. She shook her head and mouthed, "Later."

Then she let go of my hand. I looked down. The pain was gone. She wiped away the blood and I stared at the pale, scarred skin of my left wrist. Bite marks. Very, very clearly bite marks.

A bronzed hand closed around my wrist. I looked up into Damon's eyes.

But he was too busy staring at my wrist and the look in his eyes was hot. Burning hot.

"Yes, Lady," Damon said, in that neutral voice that belied the heat in his gaze. "We found him late last night but under unpleasant circumstances. I was unable to call you at the time, because of those circumstances and I deeply regret the oversight. I'll make amends upon returning to the lair."

I heard her voice. "*You* will make amends? The investigator should also make amends, Damon. She was the one hired, the one I am paying. Bring her with you."

His hand tightened. "With all due respect, Lady, I cannot. She has seen her part in this job completed and is unable to travel back to Orlando. She's requested that her payment be deposited into her account for completion of the job."

"And *why* is she unable to travel, my dearest Damon?" Annette asked, her voice silky and smooth.

The mother looked at me and tapped her finger on something in front of me. I hadn't even noticed it.

"This is the contract we discussed, Ms. Colbana. As you've completed your assignment for the Cat clan, I'm anxious for you to get to work on this promptly. We need to know who is behind this."

Damon's shoulders tensed. He stared at Es, an unreadable look in his eyes.

Es simply watched me with a smile.

I swallowed as I heard Annette's voice drop into a growl over the phone. "Who do I hear speaking, Damon?"

"It's a Green Road witch, Lady."

"A witch…"

Pretending oblivion seemed best. Bending over the table, I studied the contract. "And the terms are as we discussed?" It looked fair. Legit. And real as all get out.

"Of course. We can only pay five thousand, I'm afraid. We aren't a rich house, but I believe you understand the importance of seeing this through—whoever has been preying on the NH children needs to be caught. You already have information in your hands so you are far more suited than anybody else," Es said quietly. Then she leaned forward, a smile in her eyes even though her face was solemn. "And I offer something that has more value than money. You already have a few friends among our house, but I offer kinship. While you do this job, you'll have whatever protection our house can offer and if you find us answers, I'll apply to the Order of Witches to have you honored with the designation of kinship. It's not often granted to those outside our order. We'll offer you aid just as we'd offer it to any of our house. When you have need of us, we'll be there."

I stared at her. Was she serious? Allies. Real, *true* allies, I realized. But was she *serious*?

Es smiled serenely. "It's all in the contract, Kit. The very valid, very legal contract. One of my granddaughters is human—not a drop of magical blood and she went into law, specializes in NH rights. She did the contract for me last night and delivered it this morning. Sign it and I can offer you a protection that you'll not find elsewhere."

I snatched the pen out of her hand so fast, she chuckled. Hell, I'd planned on seeing this through anyway.

"Put the investigator on the phone," Annette demanded. "I want to rehire her immediately, Damon. I want answers and I'll pay her one hundred thousand whether she finds the culprit or not, but she has to return to Orlando *now*."

I was already signing my name.

"Lady, I'm afraid she's already contracted elsewhere. I'm deeply regretful."

I slid him a sidelong glance. He was still staring at my wrist.

She continued to yell at him.

I listened. Drank a cup of coffee and finished half of a second cup before she finally seemed to recognize the futility of it. "You will not be bringing the investigator back when you return to East Orlando, will you, Damon?"

He sat across from me, long legs sprawled out, bracketing mine. His thumb stroked over the smooth surface of the scars. "I will not, Lady. My humble apologies," he said.

I managed to keep my snort behind my teeth, but only because I knew she'd hear it.

"Very well. You'll return with Doyle."

I scowled, thinking it was weird that she hadn't asked about him at all.

A snarl ripped through the air.

"*No.*"

I tensed. Damon's hand tightened on my hand and he looked up to see Doyle standing just inside the protective entrance to the healing hall. Doyle crouched down, his eyes bouncing between Damon and me before landing on Damon. Muscles rippled, bulged and I could see stripes ghosting on his skin before disappearing. "No," he spat again. "I won't go back."

Rathi—

My gut went cold as the sight of him and fear chittered like a caged beast in the back of my head but I slammed it down.

"Doyle," I said softly. "Your aunt was worried for you. She just wants you home safe."

He snarled and the sound of it echoed through the small room. "The fuck she does. Do you know why I ran? So I wouldn't have to go back to *her.*" He slanted a look at me, and then his head cocked, lingering on the way Damon gripped my wrist. "I won't go back—I won't—"

He lunged at me.

Damon shoved me aside.

I had my blade in the next second, rolling across the floor and coming up in crouch.

The phone lay on the floor and I could hear Annette talking, her voice calm and cool, as though Damon still held the phone instead her nephew, caught in a half-shift, pinned to the wall.

"Shut it down, kid," Damon panted. "Before I have to hurt you."

Doyle just struggled harder. I stared at his blue eyes and felt his fear dancing over my skin.

"If the boy doesn't return home, the investigator will not be paid and her life is still forfeit."

Oh, screw this. Sneering at the phone, I snatching it up. "Listen, Alpha. I can't make him come home if he doesn't want to. And if I recall shifter law correctly, once he's hit his first shift, the Assembly will see him as an independent in his own right, meaning he can make his own judgment. Now...by *our* contract, you hired me to *find* him. I have unbiased witnesses, a Green Road witch who can vouch that he *has* been found. Now whether you decide to pay or not, I did my job, but if you don't pay me, I'll make sure every fucking soul in the south knows you don't honor your fucking word."

Damon swore and I looked up. I saw the words in his eyes, but I was fed up with having that crazy woman try to terrify me into *anything*.

"Do you understand who you are talking to?" she whispered.

"Yes. A woman who is about to go back on a contract she made. The kid was found. Job completed. End of story." I hurled the phone at Damon, but he had his hands full with Doyle's struggling body and it bounced off his shoulder.

Es caught it.

I closed my eyes as she lifted it to her ear.

Shit.

I'd just drawn somebody else into the mess.

"Would this be Annette?"

"I've no business with you, witch. There is no trouble between us."

"Of course not. We've always accommodated each other, the Cat Clan and the House of Witches…have we not?" Es smiled as she moved over to study Damon and the struggling boy. "Your nephew has successfully shifted. I witnessed it myself last night. As a speaker for the Assembly, I'll be happy to register his status for you."

Doyle stopped struggling.

Damon cut a look at Es.

She turned away and continued to pace. "He's in an emotional state after his ordeal. Perhaps he just needs time to acclimate. However, I understand that you might be distraught at his behavior. That would certainly explain your behavior in recent moments…despite the fact that Colbana did in fact successfully complete a job. A job she'll naturally be compensated for."

Silence reigned.

It was finally broken by the sharp sound of the Alpha's voice as she said, "Naturally. I'll have the funds deposited once Damon returns. He'll see to it."

"Wonderful. I'll see you in session."

Es disconnected the call and laid the phone on the table by the contract. "Well. That was pleasant." Then she frowned and looked at Doyle. "Really, boy. Control yourself. If you can't discipline yourself better, you'll end up as crazy as your aunt."

Doyle flinched.

Es looked at me. Her eyes went cold and bright. "This isn't over between you two. She fixates and hates blindly. You just became her enemy."

"I think that happened the minute I was hired for this job. No matter what the outcome."

"Entirely possible."

"You…you're leaving me?"

I stood in the hallway, very much out of Doyle's line of sight, although I knew that wouldn't make much difference.

He could scent me, hear me.

Although at the moment, he was focused on nothing but Damon.

Damon, I could see. He stood at edge of the hall, right where it bended out of sight, his head angled down as he looked at the kid. "I've been called back. You might have decided to fly solo, man, but I'm still part of the clan and unless I cut ties, I have to answer to the Alpha. You know what happens if I don't."

"How can you go *back* to her?"

I closed my eyes at the sound of his voice. He sounded like what he was, really. A scared kid. A lonely one. Even if he did grow three inch fangs when he was pissed. Tiger, I was thinking. He shifted into some kind of tiger. I'd seen stripes trying to come through on his skin.

I figured that meant the Queen Bitch was a tiger, too.

Queen of the Jungle. She probably liked that.

Enemy…my hand tingled.

Now I had two of them to deal with. And those were just the local ones. Heaven help me if my grandmother ever decided to acknowledge my existence again.

But those were problems for another day.

"If I don't go back, you know what happens. I'm rogue and they send everybody after me," Damon said, his voice hard and flat.

"Then just take her out!" Doyle half-shouted.

"And step into her shoes? Shit. Grow up, kid. It's not as simple as that."

Damon's eyes cut my way and then he looked back at the boy. "Stay here. Out of trouble...the witches here can help if you start feeling shaky. They've done it before and Es is decent people. And..." his voice dropped to a threatening growl. "Keep your eyes, your paws, your thoughts off what's mine. Because I *will* be back...and as much as I love you, Doyle, you won't stand a chance if you hurt what's mine."

Doyle muttered under his breath and swore. He walked away; although I couldn't see it, I knew he was gone. The intensity in the air faded and instead of two angry shifters hovering nearby, there was only one.

My one.

He looked at me and then jerked his head as he headed outside.

There was a car waiting.

Es had said it was on loan.

It was long, lean and black, a throwback from the days of those old muscle cars and it looked like it might have been made just for him. As he leaned back against it, he stared at me with fury dancing in his eyes. "You had to do it, didn't you?"

"Yeah." I thought it all through one more time. Then I nodded. There wasn't anything I would have taken back or changed. "Yeah, pretty much."

"Fuck." He bit it off and turned away, hands braced on the hood of the car.

"Can you take her?"

He tensed. "Don't start on me. I hear it from Doyle all the time; I don't need it from you."

"That's not an answer."

His snarl seemed to echo for miles. "Yes!" He whirled around and stormed up to me, closing a hand over the front of my vest as he hauled me onto my toes. "I can. But it doesn't mean I will. I don't want to lead her fucked-up clan of maniacs and that's what I'd have to do if I killed her."

"She doesn't lead. She terrifies and abuses." I lifted a hand to his cheek. "I know what your Alpha is like."

"No," he said, his teeth clenched. "You don't. You don't have a fucking *clue*."

"I think I do." Studying his unyielding face, I brushed my thumb over his lip. "She's like my grandmother."

His lids flickered.

"You want to know why I don't flee when I'm afraid?" I said softly.

The hand clutching my vest let go and he spun away from me.

"You asked about my back. Aneira children are placed on the training field when we are strong enough to lift a training sword. I wasn't strong enough until I was six. I was slower. Weaker. I had the shit beaten out of me by cousins who were better than me, more skilled.

"The teachers pushed me hard, but they weren't cruel. Then my grandmother started coming to practices and…" I shrugged. "I was eight the first time she took a whip to me. I wasn't fast enough during one of the exams for the year-training. I failed. So I was whipped…in front of the rest of the students, in front of the teachers, in front of my cousins."

I gave him a faint smile as he stared at me, his eyes so dark they were nearly black. "You probably figured out we weren't exactly attending public schools or anything. This was at Aneris Hall—my family home, and there, my grandmother's word was law. My blood is too weak to be a real warrior in her eyes, but she'd beat as much human weakness out of me as she could. I passed the exams when I was nine, but I stumbled at the end and they took off points, so she beat me again. After that, it was like she found reasons to do it often. Sometimes it was a monthly event. It got to be where everybody knew I'd be whipped when the school session closed. A few parents could make up reasons to not attend, but a lot of them would just sit there…and watch while she whipped me."

"Enough," he said.

"No." I caught his shoulder, shoved my right arm in front of him. There were no scars—the healers of Aneris Hall were skilled and while they'd hurt me like hell, they did it without leaving a mark. "Remember when you told me I couldn't hold my blade forever and I told you otherwise? It's a skill I learned young—after my grandmother broke my arm when I was eight, and again when I was fourteen. All because I lowered my guard. I was *eight years old* the first time and I lowered my blade, Damon. I'd been practicing for four hours and I was tired. I lowered it and she broke my arm. The next time, I was a skinny, underweight teenager. I weighed eighty pounds and my weapon was a two-handed battle axe designed for a man more than twice my size. I dropped my guard in practice and while my aunts watched— *my mother's sisters*—that evil bitch broke my arm and busted my collarbone."

"Stop it," he snarled. He gripped my head between his hands, pressing his brow to mine, eyes squeezed shut. "Just…stop." A shudder wracked him. "Why tell me this now?"

"They could have stopped it. My aunt Rana would sometimes look at me with pity in her eyes. There were times she'd slip me food, or when my clothes were falling apart, she'd make sure I had something else so I wasn't walking around naked. Others would look away from me because they couldn't stand the shame they felt—I *saw* that on them. Some of them pitied me, but they were terrified of her. And if enough of them had said something, or if they'd all stood together, they could have stopped her. And Rana was strong enough to stand up to her, but she never did. So I suffered for it. Right now, the entire clan suffers because of one crazy bitch. And you're strong enough to take her out?"

His hand shot out and fisted in my hair. "You know what's going to happen if I do it? It makes me the Alpha. I'm not a fucking leader."

"Like hell." I curled my lip at him.

"I'm not. Not to mention that if I *did*, it would put you up as a target, baby girl." Curling one hand around my wrist, he pressed his fingers on the scars. "I marked you. Right now, I'm just a grunt—a strong one, but I have no real position in the pack because I won't *take* one. If I take her out, everybody around me, everybody who matters becomes a target. It's not an issue with her because nobody matters *to* her and it's not a secret. The main reason Doyle was safe was because he was a child and attacks on children are *not* accepted. Whether or not he's safe now will depend on whether or not he makes himself independent of the clan. But if I take her out, people will see you as a target—a way to get to me. Fucking *no*."

"I'm not that easy of a target," I said quietly.

"No." It was a hot growl against my lips but I turned away.

Pressing against his chest, I stared at him. "You do what you have to, Damon. But if you keep letting her brutalize and terrify people when you can do better…"

Something cold settled in me.

"I told you it was permanent, baby girl," he said quietly. "I meant it."

I arched a brow at him. "Then we better find a way to work through this because I can't live knowing you look past the kind of cruelty that I had to live with, Damon. I can't."

The silence that fell between us was heavy and cold.

He went to get into the car, but before he could, I crossed to him. I leaned in and pressed my mouth to his. "Be safe," I said quietly.

"There's no chance of that." A humorless smile twisted his lips. "Making amends to the Alpha comes with blood and pain, baby girl. But I'll survive it."

My gut twisted as I leaned back, staring at him. "What?"

Damon just shook his head. "Will you wait for me?"

"You know I can't."

A hooded look came across his face and he tangled his hand in my hair. "Then I guess I'll just have to move up my timetable," he muttered, tugging my head back. I groaned as he pressed a hot kiss to my neck. "*You* stay safe. And don't go out alone."

Our first stop was the bait store where Damon had bought me the bows.

It was a bust.

As in completely.

"It's closed up," I said quietly, staring at the vacant place.

There wasn't even any merchandise in the store.

No sign in the window or anything.

"You were just here, right?" Kori said, a frown on her weathered face. The mother had insisted I take the other witch. She'd promised protection and Kori was one of her strongest hands.

So Kori had my back for the gamut of this, it seemed.

I had to admit, I was pretty okay with it.

"Yeah." We circled the building, but it was an exercise in futility. There was nothing. No cars. No notes about what had happened. Nothing. "He knew something, that son-of-a-bitch. And when we got the kids out last night, he had a warning, somehow, and cleared out."

"Damon said there were cameras. Maybe this dude was one of the ones in on it," Kori offered. She glanced down the road and then circled back around, motioning for me to follow.

I sighed and did, rubbing my itching palm while I did so. "There's nothing here to see, Kori. Can we head on to the park? It's a day long thing—*several* days—just on its own."

"In a minute, in a minute." She crouched on the back step, studying it. "Hmm. Perfect." Dragging a finger through the dirt, she whispered under her breath.

I shivered as I felt the magic dance in the air.

I couldn't define it, couldn't understand. But I could damn well *feel* the magic and hers was strong.

"Ah, yes…there we go. Dude was scared when he packed out. Big time scared. Running for his life kind of scared."

Staring at her bowed head, I asked, "How can you tell?"

"It's in the earth. Earth has lots of secrets and she whispers it to those who can hear." With a sly little smile on her face, she shrugged. "Like me."

She muttered a little more under her breath and I felt the rise and fall of her magic. Finally, she sighed. "There's more to follow but I can't do that and help you. Let me call Es and she can decide what to do. We can do that on the road, though."

"Can you call another weapon besides the sword?"

I closed my eyes.

I really didn't want to waste my breath talking to Kori. Kori, however, *liked* talking. A lot.

Swiping the sweat out of my eyes with my forearm, I stared at the back of her rainbow-hued head. She was red and orange today. Like a damn phoenix. "What?"

"The sword. I saw what you did the other night. And the sword is amazing—I tried to touch it, you know—"

I stopped in my tracks, glaring. "You *what?*"

"Heh." She turned around, a cheeky grin on her face. "Guess that's off-limits. Same as your sexy cat? Don't worry, I only like the male species as a once-in-a-while thing. The sword is way cooler than the cat anyway."

Mine. Both of them. Possessiveness prickled inside me as I stared at her. "When did you mess with my blade?"

"Oh, I didn't. I tried." She shrugged. "I saw it on the floor while Damon was pumping the water out of you and I was just going to put it up out of the way. But when I went to touch it, it was like it…" She paused and rubbed her hands. "It doesn't want me."

"She hates anybody but me touching her."

Kori nodded. "Yes. I felt that. Her, huh?"

I just stared at her.

She grinned back at me. "So, can you call anything else?"

"No."

Black brows arched over her eyes and she cocked her head, studying me. "Ever tried?"

I jerked a shoulder. "She's the only one I feel that connection to."

"Hmmm." She shrugged and turned back around. "Might be useful to try and learn it. The sword is a cool bitch, but sometimes, you need a different kind of tool. My best magic is of the earth." She pointed off the path, waving her hand at the field of grass undulating between us and the water. "I can make that open up and swallow anything that walks over it. But sometimes I need fire and if I have to, I can throw it around almost as good as Tate does. Not for as long, of course, and it won't burn as hot, but I can do it. Now, Tate…she's short-sighted. She's got a touch of earth inside her, but she won't mess with it. It could come in handy if she'd learn how to work it, but she won't." Kori glanced at me over her shoulder. "Know what separates the superior warrior from the middle-class one, Kit? It's learning how to use every weapon, every tool at your disposal."

"Wow. You sure use a lot of words to say that very profound sentence," I drawled. Disturbingly profound. I looked at the compound bow I carried, thought of the sleek, lovely bow back in my car. And even that was enough to stir her song…I could hear her now. Whispering in my mind, the beat of her drums, thudding in time with my heart.

Well, shit.

"Work on it," Kori said cheerfully. "You never know."

Kori's ability to hear the earth *whispering* came in handy.

By halfway through the afternoon, we'd managed to find two pits.

Nobody alive, but one of them held a corpse. Kori stared at it hard for a minute and then said, "Not a witch. Shifter of some sort."

I looked at the corpse and tried to get a feel, but the life had been gone too long. I could read a person's energy, but it was tied into the soul and the soul had been gone quite a while.

"Probably another stray cat or wolf," I said tiredly, rubbing the back of my neck, thinking of my own cat.

He'd left early. It had been barely seven when he'd pulled out in that long black car and it was a bit of a drive to Orlando—two to three hours if traffic wasn't bad. He would have been there by ten. It was crawling up on three now, meaning she'd had him for hours.

A hand touched my shoulder. "Stop it, kid. He knew what he was going back to."

"Did he have a choice?"

"He's the one who chooses to stay with an Alpha half the Assembly sees as bat-shit crazy." Kori shrugged and turned away.

"If she's that bad, why doesn't the Assembly handle it?"

"Because she keeps her clan in line and doesn't let her crazy outside of it," Kori said, shrugging. "If she was like the rat you tangled with a few years ago, they'd intervene. Hell, sometimes I think people *wait* for that...and shit, if she'd come gunning for you? The Assembly could shut her down. Maybe that's why Es did what she did, offering you the protection of the house, even as she jabbed at the bitch. She'll snap sooner or later, and once she does, the laws will fall into place and she can be dealt with. She's getting worse, I've heard."

"She's bad enough already," I muttered, scratching at my arm.

"Yeah. But you can't force your boy to do anything." She sighed and settled into silence, her eyes taking on a flat look. I could feel her magic tingling my skin again.

Searching the earth, I suspected.

Something rustled in the grass and I grimaced as I caught the long body of a gator coming out of the water. Its black eyes stared at me and then moved away, headed off in another direction. Good gator. No food here. None at all.

Something whistled through the air. Familiar—

"I..."

Kori's voice stopped.

I looked over at her.

For a minute, the red stain on her shirt made no sense.

But the glint of bloody iron protruding from her shirt made sense. A lot.

She toppled forward. I tried to catch her before she tumbled into the pit, but I couldn't.

With a scream, I called my sword even as I flung myself to the ground.

The volley of arrows that came flying at me didn't let up for a long, long time.

Chapter Twenty Three

It could have been an hour.

It could have been minutes.

I didn't know how much time passed before there was a pause in the arrows coming my way. I couldn't just fade away because they'd see me and I wasn't going to reveal that secret in front of them, unless I had no other choice.

Arrows—why were they using arrows? I wondered. Stupid. Just stupid, although it gave me a leg up once I'd managed to crawl my way over to a tree and get behind it. I had a feeling there were four different archers. Wasn't positive, but I thought. Judging by the various angles they were coming from and the different kinds of bolts and arrows, there were definitely at least four, but somehow I didn't think they had a couple of people lying in wait, just to throw me off.

Regular fiberglass arrows, as well as bolts, the kind somebody would fire from some of the crossbows out there.

I'd grabbed one of the arrows closest, checked it, smelling it for some sign of poison or anything else and there wasn't anything.

Why arrows and no guns?

Didn't make any sense. Peering around the tree, I caught sight of a scrap of white. Another arrow whizzed by, but that was fine. I had a location now. Smiling, I reached for one of my arrows.

My aim is true—

Unlike theirs.

I heard the strangled scream and a furious swear bounce through the trees second later.

One down.

Another volley of arrows came raining around me. Sighing, I leaned against the tree. My eyes drifted to the pit. Was Kori alive—?

Couldn't think about that. Just couldn't.

After another twenty minutes, I found another target. The sound of his scream was like music.

Within an hour, it was down to just one.

And I was confused as hell. They were wasting all of this time, the ammo—*why*?

By the time I figured it out, it was almost too late. I heard them drawing near, another group coming to catch me in a pincer move. I didn't have time to find another place to hide myself and I couldn't leave Kori.

Damn it—

Fade—no choice now, not if they were doing what I thought.

I faded and took out the last target and then moved over to peer down into the hole at Kori.

The site of her locked, open gaze hit me like a fist to the chest. The arrow had pierced her heart, and I knew iron when I saw it. It would have killed her instantly. They'd been using fiberglass to pin me in place, but they'd specifically chosen to shoot her with iron...they'd wanted her dead. Witches were stronger than humans and able to heal, but iron weakened them. She could have healed if it hadn't pierced her heart, but it had.

Slanting a look across the water where the archers had hidden, I narrowed my eyes.

If I hadn't killed all of them, I would.

She was gone, so there was no reason to linger here.

Carefully, watching every step I took, I started to move. The path was littered with arrows and bolts and branches and I had to be careful not to touch them. I could hear them coming closer and closer now and they were quiet. Hunters, all of them, humans who liked to spend their days prowling through the wild in search of prey. Made a study of it.

Today they wanted *me* to be the prey.

No.

Absolutely no.

Once, I caught a glimpse of them from the corner of my eye and I could hear them as I made my way around the bend to where the archers had lain in wait. Four of them, just as I thought. Although one of them wasn't dead. The arrow had gone through his lung just below the heart.

Damn. My aim wasn't as true as I'd like.

I searched the rest of the area before I went to his side. As I knelt beside him, I heard the crackle of a radio.

"Where's the target, Hooper?"

The man just inches away panted, scrambling for the radio a few feet from his hand. I rose away and let him roll over, grunting, whining with pain. "She's...over. There. Saw her. Fucking bitch. Gut the bitch. Need help. Hurry."

"She's not here, Hoop," a voice said. "We're heading out. Got to find her before he gets here."

He fell back on his back and started to cry, clutching at the arrow going through him.

He...?

I knelt down beside him and faded back into sight, smiling as I covered his mouth with my hand.

"Hello, Hooper."

Grabbed my arrow, I jerked on it and laughed softly as he screamed against my muffling palm. "We should chat. Who is *he* and why is coming after me?"

It was six minutes I'd never get back.

Hooper had nothing to tell me and I ended up killing him with my knife across his throat.

It was quick, painless and easy—far easier than I'd rather give him, but I didn't believe in torture.

As I cleaned the blood off my blade, I heard a dreaded slithering sound and I swallowed the bitter, noxious taste of fear cloying in the back of my throat. Tracking the noise, I found the snake coming through the grass. Another big-ass snake, too.

Man, I think I could really start to hate those things. With a passion.

But it didn't come for me. Okay. This was looking up. It was checking out one of the dead bodies.

"Have at it," I said.

Its tongue came out, tasting the air.

Those freaky eyes watched me as I circled around, keeping a very, very wide berth. I had men to kill and no damn snake was stopping me. I just needed one thing —Hooper's radio.

It had a rugged little wrist strap which I caught with the tip of my blade, still watching the snake, keeping my ears out for the sound of any more. Did they like dead bodies? Didn't know. Didn't care. So long as they stayed away from my live one.

The radio in my hand crackled, loud. Too loud. As the snake started to coil around the body, I fumbled with the volume. "Where in the hell is she, Hooper? We've only got until sunset…"

Sunset.

My blood went cold.

I peered up at the tree, then at the bodies across the lake. I could still see most of them but I didn't know how many were there…

I had a couple of hours. Getting out of here would take every single minute of them. But if I ran into more men…Between the pack I was hauling, my weapons and the fact that I'd have to fade out and be quiet, it was going to be hell. I'd paid closer attention this time and I knew the way back, but still.

I had to get out of here.

I didn't have the missile I'd need for this fight, although why in the hell he wanted me *now* I didn't know.

Evangeline's voice echoed through my memory.

He'll be in contact soon, Colbana. You don't want to keep ignoring him. It won't go well for you.

My breathing hitched as I remembered the dream.

You…the energy in you is pleasant. I feel it without even feeding from you, but ever since I've fed…It's a pleasure like no other, Kit, and I can't wait to have it again. It's unparalleled.

It didn't make sense that he'd set this up just to try and grab me. Didn't make sense that this had been constructed for my benefit. But if Jude had been behind it all along—for fun, money, or whatever his fucked-up reasons and I got in the way…? Had he just decided to go ahead and grab me because it was convenient and he'd wanted me all along anyway?

It would make sense…if that was what Jude wanted to do.

He'd asked me if I was going back home. The boy had been found, after all.

Why not go back home?

Because it just wasn't in me, but Jude wouldn't understand that sort of thing, would he?

He would understand one thing, though—Damon had called me persistent. Maybe Jude had realized that if I didn't go home, I'd tie this to him. And he'd go down.

Was *that* it?

Strange, wet cracking sounds came to my ears. I looked up and immediately wished I hadn't. The snake was coiling around the body. Constricting. *Shit.* That was nasty, but it served as a reminder. I didn't have time to worry about *why* Jude was coming for me.

He was coming for me and that was a problem. Dumping my pack on the ground, I went through and removed what wasn't vital. The food was the first thing. I dumped everything but three bottles of water and two protein shakes. If I didn't make it out of here before I went through those, it wouldn't matter.

Jude would have found me by then and then…

I stroked my thumb over my wrist.

Then Damon would be after us both. *Nothing hurts you…*

I wasn't going to rely on Damon to save me, though. I was alive and sane because I'd saved myself, and damned if I'd stop trying to do that now. I wasn't a quitter, and despite what my grandmother thought, I wasn't weak.

I'd hold on to that.

Hold on to that, and my sword.

Hefting my lightened pack onto my back, I faded out and started to move, following a line that took me away from the hunters and straight to my car. I'd come back for them. All of them. If Kori could taste fear in the dirt, then surely Es had another witch who could do the same.

My legs burned.

I knew how to run and I could do it for a long time, but not like this.

Still, I kept moving.

Those idiots were still using their radios and it was a blessing, because a few times, I caught that warning crackle just in time to freeze.

One time was bad. They had dogs. I heard them baying after me and the excitement of the men.

I laid it on harder, until I thought my lungs might burst.

Finally, the sounds grew distant and I let myself slow. Thirty minutes, I thought…Maybe thirty minutes to the car, and almost to one of the more populated areas.

My head was pounding. The burden of keeping myself unseen was getting to me but I couldn't drop it now.

I heard a laugh—young and girlish, followed by a deeper one. Male. Young. Shit. Getting close to people.

Was that a good thing or bad?

The radio I'd hung at my waist crackled.

"Girl."

I stopped.

"Come on, girl. I know you took Hooper's radio. We doubled back and counted, saw your shit, saw the snake eating him—we won't hold that against you, since that's the way things sometimes play out when you play a real hunting game. The snake won that round. So did you. But it's time to listen to the rules of the game."

Rules of the game...you son of a bitch. I took the radio off my belt, still listening to those voices. They were still a few hundred yards away and my gut whispered, *Human.* Kids out for a hike or what?

"What do you want?" I said.

"You." The man's voice was blunt and honest. "What do you think?"

"Fuck yourself. Sideways."

He chuckled. "Now, now...here's where we have a problem. You weren't ever supposed to be a target. You're human and we don't like hunting our own."

My skin prickled and crawled.

"But we've got somebody interested in you and if we don't give you to him? He'll take it out of our throats."

"That's what happens when you fuck with vampires," I said.

There was a pause and then a laugh as he said, "Nobody said nothing about vampires, kid."

It was a lie—I heard the strain in his voice.

"I did."

More silence. "You aren't going to get out of here, girl. If you try, we'll come after your ass. We'll hunt everything, everybody you love. We'll kill anybody that gets in the way, starting with the kids who are between you and the exit of the park...are you there yet?"

Another whoop came from up ahead. He couldn't have heard them. I wasn't talking when they'd been laughing and I didn't have the button down now.

So he had people up there. Around here.

Close.

"And why should that matter to me?"

"Because you lingered long enough to make sure your friend was dead before you left her...we were watching. Because you hung around even after we let you find the kid you were hired to find, the girl witch, and the wolf. We didn't think you would come back, but you did. Since you're still here, I'm going to assume it's for a reason. You're soft. You're okay. It's okay. The world needs people like you. We don't need to waste time and play games. You don't want me killing those kids, do you? Nice girl like you, you don't like waste, but either you come to us, or there is going to be all sorts of waste."

I listened to the laughter, waited for it to fade. "You want me, you fucker, you'll have to find me. I won't leave the park, but you want a hunting game? Hunt me. And I assure you...there's going to be a lot of waste. I'm having fun with all of these gators out here anyway." I smiled as I said it. Most of the gators were back by the water and I'd left that behind a good thirty minutes ago.

He wanted to play a hunting game? The son-of-a-bitch had no idea who...or *what*...he was messing with. Bow ready, I started for the kids.

First thing to do? Get rid of the possible hostages.

I bypassed four of the hunters in silence.

I think one of them sensed me, turning his head my way. I was tempted to bury the length of my blade in him—via his throat. Instead, I ghosted past him, pausing long enough to learn his face. I was aneira—watered down version or not, I was still a fucking assassin and I'd find my target.

Thirty feet from the kids, close enough that I could intervene when the men came running, I picked my place. There weren't any others between me and them.

And fate smiled on me. One of the park rangers came driving up the rutted path. Smiling, I took aim.

My aim is true—

It landed two feet from the girl nearest to me.

She screamed and started to run.

I shot another. The boy had just thrown a football and I watched as my arrow went through it.

All five kids were screaming and running now and I heard the park ranger bellowing for them to get to his jeep even as he whipped out his radio. They didn't waste time.

Behind me, I heard cussing, swearing.

Spinning, I took aim. I faded into view—smiled at the man who'd heard me. "Gotcha," I whispered as he fumbled with his bow. I loosed the arrow, faded before he'd even hit the ground.

Night was coming.

The park was now crawling with cops, too.

It didn't matter.

I felt the ominous thud of something slam against my brain and I still hadn't managed to get to my fucking car.

It was close, but every time I almost made it, one of the hunters got in the way. I needed to avoid killing any more of them—really. Despite what they thought, I *wasn't* human and unless they attacked, if I killed them without proof, I was fucked.

And Jude wasn't going to leave a trail, I knew that.

Earlier, at least, I had them attacking me. It would go before a Banner court and one of the Banner-retained witches would question me, so I would be okay, I thought.

But if I killed one just because he got in my way, I was fucked.

So I had to dance around. Dodge.

And then I just ran out of time.

The sun wasn't kissing the horizon, but it didn't matter. I felt the chill dance through the air and I knew what it meant.

He was there. Jude was in the fucking park, looking for me.

How in the fuck had it come to this?

Six years ago, he'd saved my ass and now he was hunting it. I'd killed some of the men he'd set on my tail and I didn't even know *why*.

Somebody screamed.

I didn't know where it came from it—the sound bounced and danced through the air, echoing from all around me and ending far too soon. My gut went tight as I wondered just what had happened.

Jude wasn't a fool. He wouldn't leave a body where it could be found.

But then again, there was no shortage of hiding places here. None. At all.

All he had to do was find a fucking gator. Or a snake.

My gut clenched as I continued to run. It was futile at that point, but it wouldn't stop me. I'd keep going until—

He stepped out from behind a tree.

Elegance and beauty, a face just barely saved from being too pretty. The snapping intelligence of his eyes helped, the carved line of his jaw. Jude was a handsome bastard, I'd give him that. His hair was a darker blond than mine, pulled back from the strong, clean lines of his face and his eyes were pale green.

Other than those few minutes at my office, I hadn't seen him in the flesh for months and I really hadn't wanted to see him again until I had a rocket launcher. Or at least something other than just my sword. The silver in her would hurt him, but he was too fast for me and if I got close enough to cut him, he'd also be close enough to hurt me.

Can you call another weapon…?

My hand itched. The sword was in my hand, though.

In the back of my mind, I heard a song. Her tribal rhythm. Whispering in my mind, the beat of her drums, thudding in time with my heart. "Hello, Jude."

"Darling Kit," he murmured, the raw silk of his voice wrapping around me.

"Stop."

Cocking his head, he smiled. "Stop what?"

"Don't *darling Kit* me, don't look at me like we're some sort of friendly types. Just stay the fuck away." The itching got worse.

Call me…I'm here, I'm here—

The bow.

Shit.

I couldn't call her.

But the image of her lurked in my mind as I stared at him.

Could I?

I'd been struggling with the guard the first time my mother's sword had come to me. I hadn't even known I *could* call her, hadn't even known she existed—

Flexing my hand, I rotated the blade, watched as his eyes dropped to it. A smile curved his lips. "Why the sword, pretty little Kit? I'm just here to offer aid, as promised."

"Yeah. You should have tried that line before you set a bunch of bloodthirsty humans on my ass."

"I don't know what you mean." But there was a smile in his eyes.

"I've been dodging arrows all afternoon and a woman I liked is dead because of you, Jude. Stop the bullshit."

He sighed and shook his head. "Kit, all you had to do was come to me and all of this could have been avoided."

"You can't expect me to believe you set all of this up just to get to me?"

He laughed. "Of course not. This..." He shrugged and glanced around. "It's a game. A pastime. Those fools weren't supposed to take the Alpha's boy, but they did. I would have handled it myself, made sure he was returned, had I known. Then you barreled in and..." He shrugged once more. "Why didn't you just leave, Kit? You had what you needed. Nothing more to worry about."

"The Assembly will take you out for this."

"No." He smiled. "The games will end and nothing can be traced back to me." His fangs flashed as he murmured, "And for that matter, for all you know, I'm fucking with your head—you bitch so often about how I like to do it. Maybe this is just another headfuck, Kit. You don't know, do you?"

"Yes, I do."

He took a step, liquid and gliding. Raising my sword, I said, "Stop."

His laugh was warm and sweet, wrapping around me and if I hadn't already experienced his poison, I might have been tempted.

"You know that thing won't stop me," he murmured. His eyes started to glow. "Although it's possible you could just tease the hunger if you cut me. Then again, it might anger me. It's a risk either way."

I stared at him.

Cracking my left wrist, I listened to the song in my head. Louder, louder—

Call me—

I banished the sword and hoped.

Only a heartbeat later, the bow was in my right hand, an arrow in my left. I took aim and watched it fly.

Jude was still laughing.

He saw it coming, though, and moved—I'd been counting on that and shot off center. "Stupid, Kit," he whispered, flinging the arrow down. "And bad aim—"

The next one was in his chest.

"I don't miss, Jude."

I said it on the fly, speeding down the path and praying hard.

The arrows weren't silver tipped.

But they *were* wooden. It had gone through his heart. He was old enough that it wouldn't kill him, but I had a few minutes. He'd have to be careful pulling it out or he'd damage himself and that would take him longer to heal. It had bought me a few minutes, far more than a fiberglass weapon could

It wasn't much. But a few minutes was still a few minutes and the car was close.

The second I saw the car, I sent the bow to her place in the trunk and pulled my keys out. There was no time to fight with my pack so I just shrugged it off as I ran and let it fall.

I dove behind the wheel just as I heard a furious wail and felt the blanket of cold as it struck the air.

He'd gotten it out.

I punched the car into reverse and sped out.

There were cop cars everywhere, but I was just going to have to hope and pray I could get away from them and get to the witches' house. My cell phone sat in the cup holder and I fumbled for it.

I saw something in the rearview mirror. A pale form. Cutting through the sky.

Older vampires were a bitch. They could fly.

Scrambling for the phone, I saw I'd had calls. A lot of them. I hit the recent ones I'd made, calling Es. An unfamiliar witch answered, but at the sound of my voice, she immediately came on the phone.

"Kit, thank goodness. We have problems—"

"Listen to me. It's Jude and there are cops *everywhere*. If you have any contacts, please tell them not to pull me over—we'll both be dead if they try."

She barked out an order. "I'll send word, but I can't promise. Kit, Damon is on his way."

"He won't make it in time." I glanced at the mirror, saw the form swooping closer. I'd survived pain before. I could do it again. "I can get through this as long as Jude doesn't kill me. Maybe I shouldn't have shot—"

My car went airborne.

I swore and opened the door. It went flying in one direction even as I lunged out, but I never hit the ground.

Steel arms came around me.

"That was very, very foolish, Kit. I never wanted to hurt you until now," Jude rasped as we hurtled toward the ground.

"Funny, you trying to drown me in my dreams wasn't a good sign of that." I spat in his face.

He squeezed so hard I felt my ribs crack. He sat me down and I stumbled away from him, popping my wrist. Nope, I decided as my hand heated. I didn't regret shooting him. I was going to do it again, the second I had a chance. Enough wood in his heart might destroy him.

He swung out a hand and I ducked. Not in time, though. I was fast, but the broken ribs slowed me and vampires were faster than I was on my best day. This definitely wasn't it.

As I went rolling through the dirt, I called my blade. When he came at me, I shoved it into his gut. He howled and I bit back a shriek as the bones in my arm snapped. *Not again—*

He flung the sword away and hauled me upright. "I'll melt that thing down and make you a collar from it, you stupid bitch."

"Try it."

He let go and I swayed on my feet, gasping around the pain in my ribs, the pain in my arm. *Survive.* That's what I had to do. But my stupid mouth was going to be a problem.

"You need to be silent," Jude said quietly. "I never intended to harm you but when you attack, it enrages me."

"Gee, I never noticed. You have control issues—too bad you're a vamp. Docs have drugs for humans, but you're just out of luck."

He caught my face in one hand, cruel fingers digging into my flesh. "Little Kit...don't you understand? You're caught. Well and truly. It's time for you to shut up and accept it."

I closed my hand around his wrist and tried to shove him away.

The pale green of his eyes started to glow. Bleeding away until just a red fire gleamed. *Red hellfire*, I thought...

He grasped my wrist, jerking it up and staring.

Damon's bite—

"What the fuck is this—?"

I smiled at him. "It's pretty much exactly what it looks like, Jude."

Any answer he might have made was lost as a growl split the air. Jude shoved me backward as a giant beast, caught between man and cat, came leaping out of the night. I tried not to scream, but I couldn't stop it. Black and red dots danced in front of me and then I was gone.

"...hold her steady—have to make this fast—"

I came to with a cry as something snapped in my arm.

"There, there..."

Es. Her voice. I knew that sound.

Other sounds, I struggled to place.

Voices. Snarling. Growling. Cursing.

Through a wash of pain, I stared up at her.

"What...?"

She touched my brow. "Just wait, get your breath. They'll likely be done soon. They're too evenly matched, considering they're both wounded."

"Who...?"

"I should have gutted you the first time I saw you. I'll skin you, cat, when I'm done. Your pelt will grace the floors of my home." That voice...Jude.

"You're losing blood, leech. How much more can you lose?" Damon.

With a groan, I sat up, shuddering as the pain ripped through me.

Es sighed and stroked my head. "Stubborn girl. Be careful—I haven't worked on your ribs yet."

In the dim light, I could see them fighting. They'd go forever, I thought, if something didn't stop them. It didn't matter what Es said.

Something came in the form of the flashing silver lights of the Banner unit.

Disembodied voices washed over us, broadcast by a loud-speaker.

I also felt the ripple of protective magics settle in place, around me, the Banner cops and the witches around me. Es sniffed. "Really, as if I can't care for myself," she muttered. Then she lapsed into silence as a Banner cop started to speak.

"Jude Whittier. Alpha Damon Lee. Members of the Assembly, you are hereby under orders to cease and desist at once or face immediate action—sanctioned by the Assembly under Article Thirty-two A regarding Non-Human entities in a populated area, under emergency circumstances."

I gulped.

Article 32A gave the Banner cops the right to blow them to high hell.

"Damon," I whispered.

I don't know if he heard me or if the Banner directive got through, but he shoved off Jude and stood.

Bleeding from more wounds than I could count, he shifted from one step to another and was human as he started towards us. "Desisting," he barked out. Then he looked back at Jude. "Keep the fuck away from what's mine, leech."

Jude flowed up from the ground, paler than normal, his eyes still glittering and red. "Mine first, cat. I'll challenge that with your Alpha...and she'll acknowledge it. She won't risk my wrath over a paltry little half-human."

"Hey," I snapped. "I don't belong to you, jackass."

Jude ignored me.

Damon didn't, though. An odd little smile curved his lips as he paused, staring at me. Then he stopped and turned. "You didn't hear them as they were talking, did you, leech? They said *Alpha*. Annette died today. You want to challenge my right? Take it up to the Assembly...and they've got different ideas on that antiquated idea. Ask Es here, but I suspect they'll tell you to get fucked."

"Oh, yes." Es smiled. "We will. Vampires can no longer claim ownership just because they laid a bite on somebody...especially when you didn't explain all it entailed, Jude. Naughty, naughty, that. But I can always address it when I go to session next week."

I barely heard her.

I was too busy staring at Damon.

The cool weight of Jude's fury struck us, but seconds later, he was gone, launching himself into the air. The air lashed us with the speed of his departure and I batted at my hair as it flung itself into my eyes.

"Damon?"

I think I saw him smile at me. But then the pain in my lungs ripped through me again as I took a deep breath. Darkness rushed up at me.

Chapter Twenty Four

"It's getting to be a pattern, healing you."

I woke up in the healing hall. And once more, Es was by the bed. Damon was close by, although I couldn't see him.

Closing my eyes, I took a deep breath. No pain. Heaving out a sigh of relief, I murmured, "Oh, that's lovely."

"He shattered four of your ribs, child. And I do mean shattered. I had to work bone fragment from your lung tissue. If you'd been human, you might have died, silly girl. Whatever did you do to anger him so?"

Silly girl. Another person calling me silly. Although in this case....I popped one eye open and stared at Es. "I might have shot him through the heart with a wooden arrow."

"Oh. That would do it, yes." Her brow puckered and she looked around.

I followed the line of her gaze and saw Damon standing at the far end of the room, head bowed, arms crossed over his chest. He almost looked asleep, but I knew better.

"And here I thought you might have smoother sailing since Annette was dispatched. Jude will make just as bad an enemy, I fear," she said quietly. Then she patted my arm. "You don't do easy, do you?"

"Wouldn't know it if it bit me on the ass."

"Hmm." She checked my arm one more time and then nodded to the table. "Drink the teas. I had to do a full healing whether you liked it or not. Between the damage on your lungs, your arm, your body was just too taxed for anything else. I'll be off, but you call if you need me."

I didn't watch as she slipped away.

I couldn't look at Damon, though, either.

"You killed Annette."

His quiet sigh drifted through the room.

When he didn't say anything, though, I looked up at him. "Why?"

"Not much choice."

He blew out a breath and came my way, all caged, easy grace. Looking at him, I couldn't even tell he'd been hurt. Faded denim clung to his legs and a black shirt stretched over his chest and arms, the sleeves rolled halfway up his arms. "I was heading into her chambers when Es sent me a text—something about some magic Kori had worked. She'd had one of her witches out there all morning and kept updating me, but the last message..." He paused and then looked at me. "One of the spells caught something from the guy we bought the bow from. There was vampire magic on him. And he was running scared. The vampires around her land aren't going to be involved in what he was doing. I thought it was a stretch, but Jude seemed pretty damned determined to pull you off this job. Didn't make sense—other people can do whatever he was wanting done, although I know you've got a rep for being a bulldog. I thought maybe that was the problem. You don't let go. Plus…well, the reason I wanted to have you with me for Doyle was because you've got this uncanny way of figuring things out…"

He stopped, flexed his hands. "My gut told me I had to get back there. I walked into the lair and the first thing Annette did was attack. I was fine with that, expected it. Let her go for a few minutes and then begged leave. She wouldn't. She went at me again, and again. I went to walk out and she called her seconds." His hands flexed once more and a snarl rippled out of him. "Even if I wasn't coming after you, I don't like being a punching bag, although I take it when I need to. I heal and I can handle pain. But if I'd taken it yesterday, I wouldn't have healed in time to get to you."

I shuddered as I pictured that—I'd seen those kinds of beatings and felt furious as I imagined him just *taking* it. "And you call *me* a silly fool," I muttered.

"Yeah." A faint grin crooked his lips. "But I had reasons. Anyway…" He stared at me. "I almost didn't make it anyway. The seconds were coming in and I told her I wasn't doing this. She could either have her revenge on another day or she'd wished she'd let me walk." His voice went flat, still and smooth as the surface of a mirror. "She laughed. The crazy bitch laughed. So I challenged her."

Storms gathered in his eyes as he stared at me. "And now you don't need to look at me and wonder if I'm one of those who stand by while somebody is tortured. It's done, Kit."

I felt those words in the very heart of me. I wasn't sure if anything had ever hit me more deeply than that.

"Done." He blew out a breath and shook his head. "The clan is a fucking mess and I have to go back by the end of the day to start cleaning out."

He reached over and caught my wrist, stroked his thumb over it. "*Everything* is a mess and I've got a lot of unfinished business, baby girl." Then he looked up at me through the fringe of his lashes. "But remember…this is permanent. You got me?"

I tugged on my wrist. As I expected, he didn't let go. He came closer and I leaned in, pressing my lips to his. "Yeah. I got you."

"Good." He lingered there a minute and I wrapped an arm around his shoulders, pressing my face against his neck. "I have to go back. It's going to be…rough for a while. You know that?"

"Didn't you hear what I told Es? I wouldn't know easy if it bit me on the ass."

He laughed quietly. "You should try easier, at least."

"Mmm. Might be nice."

His hand smoothed over my hair and I snuggled closer. "I'm not done here yet. I'll find the guys involved before I leave."

"I figured you'd say that. Es is backing you up. She already agreed."

I nodded. "Kori…" I swallowed. "Kori is dead. Somebody shot her through the heart."

"I heard." He pressed a kiss to my temple. "The humans will be running scared now. They're easy to track like that. It won't take you long. Still…you better stay safe."

"Yeah, yeah. You do the same while you're setting up housekeeping…Alpha." I smirked at him.

He pressed a kiss to my smiling lips and then he pulled away. The storm clouds in his eyes were heavy and dark as he stood up.

It didn't bother me too much.

"I mean it…you stay safe," he said quietly. "Nothing hurts you. You stay safe."

"I will." His words echoed inside me as I held his gaze. I still had a job here to do and the protection of the Green Road while I did it.

As he walked away, I drew my knees to my chest and rubbed my thumb over the scars he'd given me.

It was odd, I decided. I had plenty of scars. Most of them unseen, though; scars on my heart that I'd carried for half my life or longer.

But these I didn't mind having. Not one bit.

About J.C. Daniels

J.C. Daniels exploded in being in May of 2012. She's the pen name of author Shiloh Walker and was created basically because Shiloh writes like a hyperactive bunny and an intervention was necessary.

J.C. is the intervention.

Shiloh/J.C has been writing since she was a kid. She fell in love with vampires with the book Bunnicula and has worked her way up to the more…ah…serious works of fiction. She loves reading and writing just about every kind of romance. Once upon a time she worked as a nurse, but now she writes full time and lives with her family in the Midwest. She writes romantic suspense and paranormal romance, among other things.

Read more about Shiloh's work http://shilohwalker.com
Read more about J.C.'s work http://jcdanielsblog.com/

Enjoy this excerpt of NIGHT BLADE, Book Two in the Colbana Files:

Night Blade

"Since when does a shifter bar serve meat…you're supposed to be on the menu," the skinny one said. "Not having food served to you."

"Oh, trust me. Nobody here wants to take a bite out of me." I tapped my nails on the table, keeping my hand away from my blade. "I'm too stringy."

"You'll do." He bent down and peered at me. "Get up. Get out. You're in shifter territory which means if you get fucked over, it's your own damned fault."

When I didn't move, he did. I don't know if he was going to grab me or hit me nor did I really care.

Shoving the booth back from the table, I jumped into a crouch, hand gripping my sword. Three men had eased forward, surrounding him. The man seemed to think they wanted to play. "There's not enough for everybody, boys," he said, laughing.

"Chang?" one of them said.

"She can have him if she wants him."

One gaped at him.

Another just shoved him at me.

Others took the big bastard with him down.

I wasn't paying too much attention, though, because the fucker coming at me had decided to change his skin and there was nothing less attractive than a wererat in the nude.

Muscles bulged in places they shouldn't and his legs were all out of proportion. He shouldn't be able to move well, if life and science were fair, but he could. As he came at me with a screaming sort of hiss, I held steady until the very last second and then moved, burying my sword deep, deep in the cavity of his chest.

I shoved forward with all the strength I had in me as I did so, riding him down.

He wasn't strong and his body had frozen as he took the silver of my blade. Now I was crouched on top of that misshapen body, smelling the way the silver burnt him, the stink of it in my nostrils while his body trembled and writhed under mine.

"Now. Who were you calling meat?"

The other one was roaring pitifully. From the corner of my eye, I saw him, struggling under the weight of four bodies and staring at us.

"Get the fuck off of me!" he shrieked.

I was pondering just how to answer that when the door opened and I felt the blast of heat rolling over me.

"You know, here's the problem," I said, leaning on my blade and staring down into his eyes. "One…you're on neutral ground. Drake's is very, very neutral and you attacked me for no reason. Two…I'm not human."

I smiled at him. "My dad was…but my mother wasn't."

I could feel that heat spreading over me now and despite the insanity of the situation, my body was ready to jump up and down, all but giddy with pleasure. Damon was just a few feet away. I couldn't hear him, I hadn't seen him, but I could feel him.

"Since my mom wasn't human, that means under the ANH charter, I'm not recognized as such." I continued to watch the nerves bleeding into the man's eyes. "Never mind the fact that if you hunt humans on neutral ground in East Orlando, you're fucked. We hunt your kind down and eat you for breakfast here."

"I want the fucking alpha," he snarled. "Where's the Lady?"

I laughed. "Oh, that's funny. You're a fucking rat and you want to throw yourself on the mercy of the cat's alpha?"

"There's no pack here! We have to align with somebody and you can't deny me that right. That's in the fucking charter," he said and then he whimpered as I twisted my blade.

"Well, that brings us to the third problem…and really, it's your biggest. If you're smart, you'll just move around until the silver in my sword shreds your heart," I said quietly.

Damon took a step closer.

"I want the fucking alpha!"

"Kit. Introduce him to the third problem," Damon said, crouching down by me.

"Sure." I twisted the blade again. "You sure you don't want to just kill yourself, rat?"

Also look for
Broken Blade

12737028R00122

Printed in Great Britain
by Amazon